**Mary wrapped her hair up after her bath,
then slipped on her chemise.**

For a moment, she thought about getting completely dressed and then decided against it as she climbed into the middle of the bed. As she rubbed her hair with the towel, she decided she was tired of fighting herself over Carter. She wanted him, if only for a day, an hour, whatever she could get.

As if she had conjured Carter up, the door opened. He stopped short when he saw her sitting in the middle of the bed. He must have taken a bath, too, because his hair was still damp, clinging to his forehead, and he was dressed in black, looking very mysterious. When Carter didn't move, Mary said, "Come in. The bath was wonderful. Thank you for arranging it for me."

Carter saw the heartrending tenderness in her gaze and felt more like a fool than ever. Her half-clothed body short-circuited his brain. There was so much to say, so much that needed to be said, but not knowing where to start, he stated the obvious. "You're beautiful."

Mary blushed.

## BOOK YOUR PLACE ON OUR WEBSITE AND MAKE THE READING CONNECTION!

We've created a customized website just for our very special readers, where you can get the inside scoop on everything that's going on with Zebra, Pinnacle and Kensington books.

When you come online, you'll have the exciting opportunity to:

• View covers of upcoming books

• Read sample chapters

• Learn about our future publishing schedule (listed by publication month *and author*)

• Find out when your favorite authors will be visiting a city near you

• Search for and order backlist books from our online catalog

• Check out author bios and background information

• Send e-mail to your favorite authors

• Meet the Kensington staff online

• Join us in weekly chats with authors, readers and other guests

• Get writing guidelines

• AND MUCH MORE!

**Visit our website at
http://www.kensingtonbooks.com**

# WHISPERS ON THE WIND

## Brenda K. Jernigan

**ZEBRA BOOKS**
KENSINGTON PUBLISHING CORP.
http://www.kensingtonbooks.com

ZEBRA BOOKS are published by

Kensington Publishing Corp.
850 Third Avenue
New York, NY 10022

All Kensington titles, imprints and distributed lines are available at special quantity discounts for bulk purchases for sales promotion, premiums, fund-raising, educational or institutional use.

Special book excerpts or customized printings can also be created to fit specific needs. For details, write or phone the office of the Kensington Special Sales Manager: Kensington Publishing Corp., 850 Third Avenue, New York, NY 10022. Attn. Special Sales Department. Phone: 1-800-221-2647.

Zebra and the Z logo Reg. U.S. Pat. & TM Off.

First Printing: May 2004
10 9 8 7 6 5 4 3 2 1

Printed in the United States of America

*This book is dedicated to my cousin, Carol Haught. When I was young I spent one Easter at Carol's house, and three boys brought her Easter baskets. I knew right then and there that I wanted to grow up to be just like Carol. Over the years, I've always looked up to Carol. She is pretty, smart and very sweet. Everybody loves Carol. But now I admire Carol for a completely different reason—it's not for her beauty or great personality—it's for her courage. You see, Carol has been battling breast cancer for the last fifteen years. And she has done it with a positive attitude and a great sense of humor. When I call her, she asks how I'm feeling. I hope one day that Carol will win her battle and be cancer free.*

*So, Carol, this book is for you.*
*And one day when I grow up,*
*I want to be just like you!*

## In Memory of

My mother, Bonnie Dittman, who died much too young of breast cancer. A portion of all the proceeds from this book will be donated to HOSPICE, so they can help those who can't help themselves.

# Prologue

Billy West and Mary Costner were thirty miles away when they caught their first glimpse of Pikes Peak. The mountain rose to a majestic height of 12,000 feet and its apex was covered with perpetual snow.

As they wound their way around the mountain through lofty pines and cedars, the air grew cooler so that they had to slip on their jackets. Billy wondered if there really was a mining town in this wilderness. They had ridden for miles without seeing anything other than antelope and a bear or two.

About the time he was ready to suggest turning back, they reached a small mining town. The rough wooden sign said they were in Gregory Gulch. In a field to the left was a herd of antelope grazing in a meadow. Everything appeared very peaceful, or was the word dead?

"This isn't much of a town," Billy said as they sat on their horses looking down a dirt street that had log cabins scattered on both sides. Each brown cabin looked alike—some didn't even have windows.

"I'm not sure what I was expecting, but it wasn't this," Mary admitted.

"Do you want to go back?"

"No. I'm determined to make this work. If a little hard work will bring me gold and independence, then I can handle this. However, I am glad we stopped and picked up supplies and heavy clothes. It is the middle of August, but it's cool up here."

"Yes, it is," Billy said. "I guess we should go to the claims office first and find out where your claim is located, and then we can see about finding you someplace to stay."

"I really do appreciate your help," Mary said.

Billy smiled at her. "That's what brothers are for."

It was easy to find the recorder's office because it was in the middle of the buildings and had a big sign hung on the side. When they dismounted they found a line of prospectors waiting to see the clerk, so they had to wait.

Finally Mary made it to the desk. She pulled out her deed and handed it to the man. It took him a few minutes to read it over. He reached under his desk and pulled out a very large book that looked like it contained a variety of maps.

After flipping several pages, he frowned and reached for a brown book on the edge of his desk. He turned back and forth between several pages until he found what he wanted. He scanned the page with his index finger. "Ah, yaw," he said, and tapped the spot with his finger before looking up at Mary. "You have a problem."

Mary gave a disgusted sigh. "What is the problem?"

"Somebody has already filed a claim on this here land."

"But this is a legal document. I've had a lawyer

look it over," Mary insisted, and then added, "What can I do?"

"I'd go see Marshal Stanley. Maybe he can straighten this out for you."

Billy stepped forward. "Where do we find the marshal?"

The clerk pointed. "Two doors down on the right."

"Do you know the name of the other owner?" Billy asked.

"Let's see," the clerk looked down. "Oh dear, it's Big Jim McCoy. He's an Irishman with a mean temper."

"Great!" Mary rolled her eyes. "Just what I need."

They took their horses and pack mules with them and tied them outside of the marshal's office.

Upon explaining to Marshal Stanley the problem and showing him the deed, he sent a deputy to get Big Jim.

Fifteen minutes later Big Jim McCoy strode into the office shouting, "Who the hell is trying to welsh my claim?"

The man made two of Billy. McCoy was broad-shouldered and wore faded overalls with a blue flannel shirt, a gun and a bowie knife tucked into his work belt. He wasn't a young man, but a weathered veteran.

As soon as he saw Mary, he removed his wide-brimmed hat, displaying his black hair streaked with gray. "Ma'am," he said with a nod.

Turning his attention back to the marshal he said, "Now who is this cussed sidewinder?"

"I am," Mary said, and stepped in front of him. "My mother sent me the deed." She handed him the papers. "As you can see, it's legal. It says nothing about me having a partner."

Big Jim snatched the deed from her.

Billy was proud of his sister for not backing down from Big Jim. As a matter of fact, she looked more like an angry cat with its fur standing straight up. Big Jim would scare most men with his thick black beard and long black hair that was tinged with gray.

Evidently not Mary.

After Jim read the legal paper, he threw it on the marshal's desk. Then he pulled his deed out from a pocket and tossed it beside hers.

"That deed used to belong to Toothless Tom. When he left, he told me I could have his part 'cause he was through with mining," Big Jim told the marshal.

"Do you have any paperwork to prove that, Big Jim?"

Big Jim frowned. "A man's word ought to be good enough."

"Not when it comes to property. As you well know, many have been killed over property disputes," Marshal Stanley told him. "The way I see it, you have a new partner."

"But she's a female." Big Jim pointed out the obvious.

"What's wrong with that?" Mary snapped.

"Plenty," Big Jim said, and looked directly at her. "Mining is damn hard work, and you're puny. 'Sides, every man would be after you once he saw you, and I don't have time for such."

"I've already thought about that," Mary informed him. "I'm going to dress as a man and keep my hair under a cap so everyone will think I'm a boy. As for work, I intend to work just as hard as you. What I lack in muscle, I'll make up with brains."

"I doubt that," Jim shot back.

Mary stepped closer to the man. "Well, Big Jim, you don't have a choice."

He glared at her. "You're a mouthy little thing."

"So I've been told," Mary said.

With that comment, Big Jim started laughing and all the tension in the room eased. "All right. I give you two months before you're running back home." He looked at Billy. "Who's he?"

Billy pushed away from the wall where he had thoroughly enjoyed the exchange between these two. It seemed Big Jim had a wildcat by the tail and didn't know quite how to handle her.

"I'm her brother, Billy West."

"Good. You can help her."

"I'm not staying," Billy told him.

The Irishman appeared as if his patience was all but gone. "Is she plumb loco? Life ain't easy up here."

"So I've tried to tell her," Billy said. "But as you can see, she has a mind of her own."

"I can also speak for myself," Mary informed both of them.

"See," Billy said with a shrug.

The marshal cleared his throat. "Then it's settled. You both have equal ownership in the mine. If one of you dies, then the other inherits full ownership. Is that agreeable?"

They both nodded their heads.

"Good," Marshal Stanley said. Then he scribbled the agreement on both deeds. "Sign here that you agree. Myself and Mr. West will witness the signatures." When the signatures were obtained, the marshal said, "Good. Now get out of my office. I have work to do."

Once they were outside, Big Jim asked, "Where are you staying?"

"I don't have a place yet," Mary said.

"Well, there ain't no empty cabins around here."

"Oh," Mary said as she stopped by the three pack mules full of supplies.

"These yours?" Big Jim asked.

Mary nodded.

"How about if I make you a deal?" Jim said with a smile. "Seeing as I can't get rid of you, why don't you throw your supplies in with mine, and you can stay with me."

"I'm not so sure about that," Billy said.

"Don't go getting your dander up. I have the biggest cabin up here with two bedrooms. It's a little ways up the hill. She'd have her own sleeping quarters. 'Sides which, I'm old enough to be your da. I have a daughter your age back home."

So an agreement was made.

Billy stayed another month to make sure that Mary was settled in and could handle everything. Then he decided he needed to worry more about Big Jim than Mary. She already had the man eating out of her hand.

When it was time to go, Billy did have a talk with Jim and told him if he ever made the mistake of hurting his sister that Billy would return with a vengeance.

Big Jim nodded.

Billy gave Mary a hug. "You take care of yourself."

"I will," she said in a soft voice. "You take care of yourself and my future sister-in-law."

Billy smiled. "I will."

He rode off with a peaceful mind about Mary. She was going to make it on her own. As he started down the mountain heading for home, he realized that he'd been gone much longer than he'd expected. He wasn't sure of the day but it had to be two months since he'd left. Billy did know that Mary was getting ready to start her own adventure ... one that would be harder than anything that she had ever faced.

But Mary had more gumption than anyone in the family, and it would take every belligerent bone in her body to survive mining for gold.

God help those poor men.

# Chapter 1

*Two years later—1872*
*Pikes Peak, Colorado Territory*

Mary Costner bolted straight up in bed.

She felt disoriented.

Why was her head so swimmy? And her skin clammy?

Blinking with difficulty, it took her several moments before she realized she was in her own bedroom, even though she couldn't remember actually going to bed.

She couldn't remember anything!

Panic set in. It was almost as if she were waking up in a dream. Nothing was real. There had to be a reason for her confusion.

Her breath came in short pants. And her head was killing her. She reached up to touch her forehead, and that's when she realized she had something tightly clutched in her right hand.

It was a knife . . . a bloody bowie knife.

She glanced at her hands as if they didn't belong to her. They were covered in blood. But whose blood? Hers?

"Jim!" Mary screamed.

She threw the knife away from her as if it were a poisonous snake. Glancing down, she saw blood on her clothes and all over the sheets. She checked herself and found a small cut on her arm, but other than that she seemed to be all right. She had to be alive because the pounding in her head wouldn't hurt so bad if she were dead.

The blood was sticky, and the smell . . . oh God, the smell. She was going to be sick.

She ran for the slop jar and emptied the contents of her stomach, then rested back on her heels. Feeling that she'd been plunged into a black, cold hole and was having trouble reaching the top, she grabbed her middle and forced herself to take deep breaths.

What was wrong?

Where was Jim? And why hadn't he come when she called?

Slowly she turned toward the door. There was still a light flickering in the main room, so the fire hadn't gone completely out. She tiptoed across the floor, the wood feeling cold on her bare feet. "Jim?" she called again to her partner.

They had worked the Lazy Dollar Mine for two years and had hit their third strike yesterday—a rich vein of gold. She could remember that part of yesterday, but after returning to the cabin she couldn't recall anything else. It was as if someone had erased her memory.

"Jim?" Mary whispered as she entered the main room. There lying in front of the fireplace was Big Jim. Maybe he was just sleeping. "Jim." He didn't respond.

She ran to him and knelt down. "Wake up, Jim. Tell me what happened," Mary pleaded, but she didn't receive a response. Jim normally didn't drink, and the one time he had gotten rip-roaring drunk, he hadn't been pleasant. That had been a year ago, and he'd sworn he would never get drunk again.

However, he reeked of alcohol. She rolled him over.

His eyes were wide open in a death stare and his throat had been cut—in a nasty bloody hole.

Mary started screaming and crying all at the same time as she jerked her hands back. Her heart slammed against her chest. Finally, she lost her voice as she rocked back and forth, staring at the man she'd come to love as a father. "Who did this?" she sobbed, "and why didn't they kill me, too?"

She stood up, but her legs were so wobbly, she fell back down. Now wasn't the time to fall apart. She must pull herself together. So with as much determination as she could muster, she rose again. This time her knees held, but she was still shaking all over as she made her way to the bedroom to get a sheet.

She jerked a sheet off the bed and covered Jim. *What happened last night?* Her mind screamed the question over and over. She couldn't remember anything from the minute she walked through the cabin door.

Glancing out the window, she realized it would be daylight in a few hours, and then she could go for the marshal.

Mary turned from the window and glanced at her clothes. No. She couldn't go to the marshal. Look at her, she was covered in blood, and she'd had the knife in her hand. In the eyes of the law, she'd look guilty as sin.

"Hell," she swore, having picked up some colorful language from the miners. With the evidence all around her, even she would think she'd killed Jim. But something deep within Mary told her that she hadn't. He'd even helped her hide her identity. She'd been careful to conceal the fact that she was a woman. One woman in a mining camp with thirty men would cause a distraction.

So if she didn't kill Jim, then somebody else did and wanted her to take the blame. Or maybe they were waiting to come after her again. She must do something. But what?

As soon as daybreak arrived, somebody would come by to check on Jim, and see if he was ready to head to the mine.

She began to pace. A sob escaped her throat.

"Think, Mary! Now is no time to fall apart," she said to herself. She looked back at Jim. She didn't want to leave him like this. She wanted to see to a proper funeral. Jim deserved that. But the authorities probably wouldn't listen to her. Not when they found out she'd been lying about her identity.

And the law would be coming. Soon.

*Run, Mary.*

Mary jerked around. Had Jim said something? No, that was impossible. But that was the answer. It was the only thing she could do. She ran to the sink and started washing the blood from her arms. Her stomach lurched, but she managed not to get sick again. However, she couldn't seem to stop trembling, whether from fear or cold she wasn't sure. The only thing she knew she was that she had to keep moving or she'd keel over.

Stripping off her jeans and letting her clothes fall where they landed, she stumbled to her bedroom.

*Keep moving, Mary. You're in danger.*

Why did she feel as if Jim was here with her, warning her? And what danger? She got down on her knees and reached under the bed, her fingertips brushing the old travel bag which held the only two dresses she'd brought with her. She had almost forgotten that she was a woman after posing as a boy for so long. Everyone in the camp knew her as Mark, the boy who worked with Big Jim. She'd always kept her hair tucked under a hat and in the summer she'd actually cut it short like a man, but it had grown out again this past winter.

She stepped into the dull gray wool dress and realized that her teeth were chattering. The soft material felt good on her skin. Hopefully, it would provide some warmth and she could stop this godawful shaking. She'd never felt so cold . . . and empty.

Grabbing the valise, she stuffed everything that was feminine in the bag. At least the marshal would be looking for a boy, and it would give her a little time to get away. Her true identity was the only good thing she had going for her tonight. Just before she closed the bag, she remembered the gold, and she reached under her mattress and took the two small bags she'd kept for emergencies. She and Jim had become wealthy over the last year, and they could have stopped mining, but every time they even considered it, they would strike a new vein.

Mary was getting ready to close the bag when she spotted an odd piece of green plaid material that had evidently been torn from something or somebody. She jerked involuntarily and wondered why.

Could somebody have been in the cabin? But if they had been, she would have remembered. Wouldn't she?

Snatching up the scrap, she stuffed it into the pocket of her dress, hoping that one day she'd remember everything. Something terrible had happened tonight, and she was the only one who could figure it out.

Looking around the cabin one last time, Mary slipped on her heavy wool coat. This cabin had been home for the last two years, but as always, Mary had never had a home for long. Something always happened. The mine had been her one hope of being able to support herself, and now that she was successful she had to leave. Glancing around, she realized her dreams had come to an end.

She might be a wealthy mine owner but little good it would do her with murder hanging over her head.

"But I'm not guilty, Jim," she whispered to her silent friend. "I swear I'll remember and find out who killed you."

The snow had started falling harder as the gray morning light replaced the inky black of the night before. Mary didn't have the slightest idea where she was going. She just knew she had to get off the mountain and put some distance between herself and Gregory Gulch.

She kept her head down to keep the snow out of her eyes as she rode, lost in her thoughts. She couldn't go home to her sister's even though she had planned a trip next week. If whoever had killed Jim figured out who she was, Brandy's would be the first place they would look. She didn't want that kind of trouble for Brandy and her family. When she'd left home, Mary had said she was big enough to take care of herself and she was, even though right now she could use someone to lean on, like her brother Billy. But she hadn't seen him in two years, and the last letter she'd received from Brandy a couple of months ago had said that Billy and Claire were expecting their first baby. Mary couldn't run to Billy for help. His wife needed him.

How in the world was she going to prove herself innocent? She knew running wasn't going to help the situation, but she had to have time to remember what had happened. And still the big question hung over her head. Why? That was the one thing that puzzled her. She had no reason to kill anyone. Certainly not Jim. He'd been like the father that she'd never known.

There was no telling who her real father was. Since her mother had worked in a whorehouse, she probably had no idea who Mary's father was, either. Mary hadn't grown up like normal children. She had always had to be quiet when the men visited the house, so she'd learned to keep to herself and play with the one doll she had.

Sometimes her mother would sit down and play with her. Mary smiled. That was her fondest memory of her mother.

When the ladies of Independence, Missouri, took Mary away from her mother, her mother really didn't make much of a fuss. At first Mary thought it was because her mother didn't love her, but as she'd grown older she'd wondered if it was because her mother wanted Mary to have a better life. But going to the orphanage wasn't something that Mary had wanted to do. She had to admit that she had been a wee bit rebellious—all right, perhaps she'd been *very* rebellious, but she hadn't known how to fit in with the other children. It had taken a long time before all the misfits had become their own family. But they had survived and even made a home for themselves in Denver. And then one day a letter arrived for Mary.

The one good thing Mary's mother had done for her was to give her the deed to a gold mine, and that's where Jim had come in. He had been different.

She loved how he had treated her like a daughter, but also as an equal, particularly after she'd proven she could hold her own doing the hard mining work.

The wind whipped around Mary, dusting her with fresh snow. She shivered uncontrollably as she snuggled deeper into her wool coat. She had never had nice clothes like other women, so she had always made do. But she was fast realizing that her coat wasn't heavy enough for this kind of weather. The fluffy white flakes seemed to be clinging to the material until she looked like a snowman.

Again Mary thought of her adopted family. How she longed to go and beg them to get her out of this mess. But she was too proud for that. Plus she couldn't take the chance of putting them in danger. She'd just have to figure a way out of this mess on her own.

Unwanted tears sprang to her eyes, blinding her as she thought of Big Jim. He didn't deserve to die like that, and her tears wouldn't help him. The only thing that would help was for her to remember. Reaching up, she brushed the tears from her cheeks with fingers she realized were numb.

Mary sighed. Her breath rose into the cold air and looked like steam escaping a boiling pot. She could never remember being so cold, but she couldn't stop now; she had to keep going.

She replayed yesterday in her mind. It had been

a good day at the mine. They had hit another vein of gold, and she'd promised herself that after this vein had been mined out she would take her money and let other people work the claim. It was time for her to have a life and learn how to be a woman again.

She and Jim had been in good moods as they'd returned to the cabin at the end of the day. Jim had mentioned that they would be having a guest for dinner, so she should keep her hat on, but after that everything else was a blur. She could see herself cooking supper and then nothing.

"Oh, why can't I remember?" Mary yelled. She grabbed her head as if she could squeeze the memory back into her mind.

That was her big mistake. When she let the reins slip, the horse stepped into a hole, stumbling and pitching her forward. Mary screamed as she sailed off her horse. Her arms flailed in the air as a bank of snow loomed in front of her. The next thing she knew she was barreling headfirst into the snowdrift.

And the black hole once again swallowed her.

Carter Monroe was damn sick and tired of snow.

He felt like an animal with his bearskin coat, and he was just as grumpy. The fur was much too bulky, but it was necessary this time of year in the Rockies. He removed his Stetson as he rode and slapped it on his leg to rid it of snow, then settled it back on his head. He grunted and realized he was also beginning to sound like an animal.

He glanced sideways at his deputy, Rick McCallum. Rick had ridden with Carter for years. They were about the same size and temperament, but where Carter had dark hair and eyes, Rick had blond hair and blue eyes. Carter had to admit he liked Rick. He was a good one to put up with Carter's grouchiness. "How much longer 'til spring?"

"Hasn't changed in the last hour—still three months away," Rick said in his lazy drawl. "I think you're getting old, Monroe."

"Right about now, I'd probably agree with you. My bones are starting to ache. I should have taken another assignment."

"Texas don't sound bad," Rick suggested.

"A hell of a lot warmer, too."

Rick shifted in his saddle. "Just remember, Hank needs us until he can get on his feet again. 'Sides, it's your hometown."

"I'd like to get my hands on the bastard who shot Hank. But I'm damn glad the bullet wasn't fatal. At least it will be a chance to visit Ma again and get some good home cooking."

"That don't sound bad at all. How long since you been home?"

"Ma will tell you, too long." Carter chuckled. "It's been about two years. Maybe longer."

They had just rounded a bend when Rick hollered, "What's that?"

Carter peered ahead of them. Something black was protruding from the snow, and it didn't have fur. "Looks like a body," he said. "And I don't see a horse, so it doesn't look good."

When they reached the snowbank, they pulled their horses to a stop and Carter dismounted, tossing the reins to Rick. Carter made his way over to the drift, reached down, and grabbed a handful of wool. With one mighty jerk, he hauled the body out of the snow.

"Is he dead?"

As Carter turned the body around, the hat fell

off and blond hair tumbled out across his arms. "Try *she*," he corrected. He removed his glove and felt for a pulse on the side of her neck. "For the moment, she's alive. But barely." Carter brushed the snow from her face then sat her up. He shook the snow from her hair.

"Need some help?" Rick asked.

"No. Doesn't look like there's much to her." Carter scooped the woman up in his arms, adding, "She has one hell of a knot on her head. She was either thrown or left for dead."

"No doubt. But the question is, what is she doing way out here alone?"

"Interesting question," Carter said as he studied her face. Then he handed the girl to Rick. "I guess we'll have to wait until she wakes up to find out."

"Hell, her lips are blue." Rick cocked a brow as he frowned. "She might not wake up."

Once Carter mounted, he reached for the girl. "I'm aware of that." After several tries, he managed to unbutton her frozen coat. Then he yanked it off her and handed it to Rick. "Here, you take that frozen coat, and I'll take the girl."

"Some trade," Rick grumbled as he folded the stiff wool and tied it on the back of his horse.

Carter tucked the girl under his heavy coat, pulling her next to his body. Then he wrapped the fur back around them. A shiver shuddered through his body. Damn, the woman was cold. She was small, too, he thought.

His mind burned with the memory of another woman. She'd been small, too. He let out a long, exhausted sigh. This one was going to need luck on her side if she was going to survive.

They moved on, neither man choosing to talk. It had been a long three days.

As they rode, the wind and snow increased until visibility was almost impossible. They trudged on until they could finally see the light of the small town of Appleton.

Carter felt like a wood-burning stove by the time they came to a stop in front of the hotel. The girl's body pressed next to him made his body burn.

Rick dismounted first. "I was beginning to think my butt had grown attached to that thing." He pointed toward the saddle. "How is the girl?"

"Thawed."

Rick chuckled. "I'll take the horses to the stables. You get the rooms." He took Carter's reins, then the girl.

Carted dismounted before taking the girl back. He shifted her in his arms as he mounted the steps of the two-story, brown Stratford Hotel. For someone so little, the girl was becoming heavier by the moment. Luckily, someone was coming out and held the door open for him to enter.

"Obliged." Carter nodded. When he reached the front desk, he said firmly, "I need two rooms and a doctor."

The clerk nodded. Funny, he didn't even blink an eye at the bundle Carter carried as he said, "Sign here."

Maybe people dragged unconscious women into the hotel all the time.

"My arms are a little occupied at the moment."

"That's your problem, mister." The clerk hesitated, and Carter's patience snapped. He leaned forward and said in a deadly calm voice, "The name is Carter Monroe, U.S. Marshal. I'm tired. And I'm hungry. If you don't get the lead out, I'm going to mop up this floor with you."

The clerk's eyes grew round as saucers. "Y—yes

sir. Rooms ten and eleven are at the top of the stairs. And I'll send somebody for Doc Elliot right away."

"That's more like it." Carter took the keys, but kept his smile in check. Now why didn't he get that kind of service when he'd first walked in? "My deputy will be here as soon as he stables the horses. Send him up to room ten."

Carter started for the stairs. His arms ached from the weight of the woman who hadn't weighed that much when he'd first picked her up. Now he couldn't wait to put his burden down and get out of his damn heavy coat.

Once in the room, he placed the girl on the bed and shrugged out of the wet fur, then tossed the long coat over a heavy chair in the corner to dry. He glanced around the room and decided it wasn't bad.

It was clean. There was a small fire in the fireplace which was the first thing that needed adjustment. He tossed several logs onto the grate and stirred the coals until the flames were jumping over the logs.

"That's more like it," he said as he stood and wiped his hands. The heat felt good on his face. "We'll be warm in a minute," Carter told the unconscious girl. The color had returned to her face, but she had one hell of a knot on her forehead and dark circles under her eyes. He really couldn't say she was pretty in her abused state. Her blond hair was tangled and dirty. He reached down and picked up a strand of hair, noticing there was dried blood on the end.

Carter felt the hairs on the back on his neck stand on end. Hmm. He rubbed his chin. The blood hadn't come from the knot on her head, so where had it come from? Maybe it was some sixth sense he had developed over the years as a lawman that warned him something was wrong with this woman. He'd bet a month's pay she was running from something.

The big question was, what?

One thing was certain: he couldn't get any answers until she woke up. He shrugged. Well, there wasn't anything else he could do for the moment, so he washed up and changed into clean duds while he waited for the doctor.

Twenty minutes later, Doc Elliot arrived. He shrugged out of his coat and grumbled, "Ain't fit for man or beast out there. Surprised you made it, though." The doctor turned and looked at Carter over his spectacles. "You don't look sick."

Carter pointed toward the bed. "It's the girl."

"Your wife?"

"Nope."

"Hmm," the doctor said as he placed his bag beside the bed. "Help me get the dress off her."

Together they removed the faded gray dress, and Carter placed it on the other side of the chair. He noticed her drawers were not fancy like most women's, so she hadn't come from wealth.

The doctor began to examine her. He grunted and clicked his tongue, but no intelligent words came out of the man's mouth.

"Do you know her?" Carter asked.

"Me?" Elliot gave him a quizzical look. "I thought she was with you."

"Nope. I found her upside down in a snowbank. Figured she could be a runaway or something and thought maybe she was from Appleton."

"Don't think she's from here. I know most folks around here, and I haven't seen her before," Doc

Elliot said as he listened to her chest. "Her heart is strong and her lungs are clear, so that's a good sign. I'm a bit surprised she doesn't have consumption from being out in the cold."

"I wonder where she's from," Carter said.

"Maybe the mountain. There are lots of small mining towns up there, but I've never heard of a woman living on the mountain. Life's too hard," the doc said, and then he looked at her hands. "However, appears she has done some hard work by these hands. But no woman could hold up under mining, so I'd rule that thought out."

Someone knocked on the door.

"Come in," Carter called.

Rick entered and nodded toward the doctor. "Horses are taken care of, and I've ordered us some grub. It will be ready shortly."

Carter made the introductions before asking the doctor, "What do you think about the girl?"

Doc Elliot straightened and stretched the kinks out of his back. "She has a concussion"—he paused—"but other than that she appears healthy."

"What can we do for her?"

"Not a thing," Doc Elliot said as he placed his instruments back in his black beg. "She may wake up tomorrow or it may take several days." He picked up his bag and turned toward Carter. "Seems the body is a strange instrument. She might not be able to tell you anything when she comes to. Her memory could be gone or she could be completely normal and then all your worries will be over. If anything changes tonight, call for me."

"I'll do that. Thanks, Doc," Carter said.

After the door shut, Rick pushed away from the wall. "So what are we going to do with her?"

Carter's expression was tight with strain. "Damned if I know," he said with a sigh. "Let's get something to eat. I've suddenly developed a rip-roaring headache."

Rick chuckled. "Yep, and there it lies in bed."

# Chapter 2

Carter wasn't sure he'd enjoyed dinner as his thoughts reluctantly kept returning to the unconscious woman upstairs, but at least his stomach had quit growling. And they were inside, out of the miserable snow. Spring couldn't come soon enough for him.

Rick had grumbled all through dinner about how sorry his company was, and he was probably right. Carter had been quiet throughout the meal. Usually they'd discuss the next day, but tonight Rick had talked and Carter had barely managed to grunt his replies. He'd never admit to his sidekick that his mind was upstairs because then Rick would never let him alone about the girl.

They had left the table and were headed for the stairs when Rick asked him, "You want to bunk with me?"

"No. I'd better keep an eye out for our pris—I mean the girl, in case she wakes up. Don't want her to bolt before I have some answers," Carter said with a grin. "If I get tired, I'll sleep on top of the blanket, so she doesn't wake up crying rape."

"Yep." Rick chuckled. "I'd hate to have to arrest you."

Carter turned the doorknob and entered the room while Rick stood back leaning against the doorjamb.

Carter arched his brow. "Arrest me? That will be the day."

"You can't possibly care one thing about that little filly."

"Of course, I don't," Carter snapped, then he jerked his arm toward the girl. "Look at her. She looks like something the cats dragged in, but she's also very young and, at the moment, helpless. I know I've been accused of being a coldhearted SOB, but I do have compassion once in a while."

Rick gave him a half smile. "I'll guess somehow I missed that side of your sterling personality. I bet the outlaws you've hauled in would have a different opinion."

"A criminal doesn't deserve compassion," Carter said as he sat down on one of the chairs by the fireplace to remove his boots. "The ones I've met are guilty until proven innocent."

"That's what I like about you . . . everything is either black or white. There is no in-between."

"It's worked well for me in the past." Carter grunted as he jerked off his left boot. "So I see no reason to change."

Rick folded his arms across his chest. "I hate to bring up the subject, but what are you going to do with her"—he nodded toward the bed—"when we get ready to leave?"

Carter stared at the woman for a long moment. "If she's awake, we'll leave her in the good hands of the sheriff. If she isn't"—he paused, rubbing his chin—"I'm taking her with me."

"You're going to haul an unconscious woman all the way to Windy Bend?"

"If need be."

"I don't believe what I just heard." Rick scowled. "I must be plumb loco. But I'm going to ask anyway . . . why?"

"Since I'm a betting man"—Carter paused from staring at the girl to look at Rick—"I'd wager she's running from something or someone, and I just don't feel obliged to leave her helpless. Think about it. Doesn't she appear to be about your sister's age?" When Rick nodded, Carter asked, "Would you want somebody to leave your sister alone to fend for herself?"

Carter didn't wait for Rick to answer. Instead he said, "I just want to give her a fighting chance. What if someone is after her? We know she's safe with us, but someone else could take advantage of her."

Rick knew that Carter was probably thinking of his own sister, not Rick's. That was the one dark cloud that hung over Carter's head and the one subject that Rick steered clear of. He didn't even know the whole story, but he had a feeling Carter was seeing his sister lying asleep in that bed. "I guess you're right, but what if she's a criminal?"

Carter's gaze was steady as he said, "Then I'll arrest her, and she can stand trial like all the other crooks."

"Now you're talking like the Carter I know. What's that nickname, 'Coldhearted Monroe'?"

"Remember," Carter said, his jaw clenched, his eyes slightly narrowed, "letting emotions into our business shortens one's life considerably."

"I agree." Rick nodded. "So on that note—Cold-hearted Monroe—I bid you good night." Rick chuckled and pulled the door shut just as a brown boot bounced off the door. "I'm not sure I envy the woman when she does wake up," Rick said to himself as he walked down the hall. "It might be the worst luck the woman has ever had because Carter never shows mercy."

On the other side of the door Carter was swearing up a blue streak. He wasn't as coldhearted as Rick seemed to think. It's just that Carter had never met anyone who interested him. But he wasn't going to correct his friend, because in Carter's line of business a bad reputation was a good thing.

He smiled as he finally tore his gaze from the closed door back to the bed. The nice warm bed . . . the inviting bed.

He had intended to sleep in the chair, but as he shoved his boots under the chair, his head felt too much like a large rock perched upon his shoulders, and he knew if he was going to fight that snow tomorrow he had to get some rest. And that bed looked very inviting.

He stacked plenty of wood on the fire so they'd be warm, and then he climbed onto the bed, staying on top of the covers. He also said a small prayer that the female wouldn't wake during the night—he needed a good night's sleep.

His head had barely hit the pillow before he was sound asleep.

The next morning came much too soon, Carter thought as he stretched and yawned himself awake. He felt much better than he had the night before—until he turned to see that his female companion hadn't moved at all. She was in exactly the same position she'd been in when he went to sleep, and that concerned him. Leaning up on his elbow, he reached over and felt for a pulse. Thank God there was one. He realized he'd been holding his breath and let it go. He also admitted that he would have cared if the girl died and that thought bothered him. He didn't know anything about the woman, so why should he care?

He shouldn't, he reminded himself. There was no room in his life for emotions.

Carter slid out of bed with his disturbing thoughts and walked across the cold floor to the hearth, still warm with glowing embers. He loaded the fire down with plenty of wood. One thing he was going to do now that it was morning was to hire some women to give the girl a bath and wash her dirty hair. For that, they needed warmth.

After he dressed, he went downstairs and asked for some women to see to the girl. Maybe the water would jolt her back to life, but if nothing else happened at least she'd be clean.

Carter had breakfast with Rick and reported there was no change to the mystery woman. They decided while they waited for the girl that they would mosey over to the local sheriff's office.

The snow had stopped about an hour before, so maybe they could make some time this morning since they would not have to fight the wind and snow. With any luck, they would be home by nightfall.

As they entered the sheriff's office, a young deputy, who seemed very excited by the tone of his voice, was describing to the sheriff what he'd seen.

"It was the damnedest thing I ever saw." The boy shook his head. "Blood everywhere. The guy was

carved up pretty bad. They're looking for somebody named Mark, Big Jim's partner, but he ain't
nowhere to be found, so he's either dead or maybe
he did the killing. If'n he did, he had a lot to gain
since they'd just struck a rich vein of gold."

"Sounds like you got trouble, Sheriff Moody,"
Carter said.

Moody smiled. "Good to see you, Carter, Rick."
Moody nodded. "Just heard there was a murder up
on the mountain. Surprised there aren't more.
Greed has a funny way of turning men into animals. Marshal Forester is the law in Gregory Gulch
and he has his hands full."

"You don't have to tell me," Carter said. "I've seen
my share of scum."

"In your position, I'm sure you have." Sheriff
Moody nodded. "There are times when I think the
bad guys outnumber the good ones."

Carter sat in a chair beside the potbelly stove.
"And there are some who are a little nastier than
the rest."

"So where are you headed?"

"Back to Windy Bend."

When Carter didn't say more, Rick finished for
him. "Hank O'Toole was shot, and on top of that
he got influenza. So we're going down to help out
since it's Carter's hometown."

"Traveling will be tough," Moody said as he leaned
back in his chair. "We had one hell of a storm last
night."

"We'll make it," Carter assured him. He pushed
himself up out of his chair. "If you or Forester
need any help with the investigation, send a wire
to Windy Bend, and I'll swing back this way."

Moody nodded. "I'll do that. Have a safe trip."

First, Carter had to check out the lead on his sister's killers. He'd gotten two of them, and he had two more to go. Revenge had now become his middle name. He'd get them—he'd get them all.

When they returned to the hotel room, Rick went to get his gear and Carter went to check on the girl. If she was awake, he'd question her and leave her. He reached for the door just as it sprang open.

Two women shrieked and jumped back upon seeing him.

"Lord, you got me shakin' like a frog," the taller woman said.

Carter ignored her. "Has the girl regained consciousness?"

"No, sir. With a knot like that one, I ain't too sure she's going to make it, but we cleaned her up real nice. She's a right pretty little thing even if she is a mite thin."

"Obliged," Carter said as he handed them a few coins for their work.

Once in the room, he gathered his saddlebags and put them in the hall for Rick to pick up, and then he strolled over to the bed.

He couldn't believe the change in the girl's appearance. The women had done a good job of cleaning her up. Reaching down, he picked up a lock of golden hair. It was soft and wavy and the color of a wheat field. Her features were flawless except for the large knot on her head.

His hand drifted to her cheek, so soft and delicate, and much too inviting. Her lashes were long and black, and her cheeks had a soft rose color. Carter snatched his hand away as if he'd been burnt. And he wasn't too sure he hadn't been. What was wrong with him? She was just a woman, he reminded himself. One he knew nothing about.

He sighed. They had to get moving this morning.

He fetched her threadbare wool coat, which had dried overnight, and returned to the bed. He was going to have to get this coat on her one way or the other.

Pulling the girl up to a sitting position, Carter managed to get one of her arms into the sleeve. She smelled of flowers as he bent closer to her hair.

He grunted. He didn't need to get this close to her anymore. His response had been quick and lustful. Hell, he didn't even know who the woman was. It was just his damned horny body responding and that was one thing he could control.

Once he'd gotten both her arms in the sleeves, he let her recline so he could button the front of her coat. A slow smile spread across his lips.

Since when had he dressed a woman? Usually he was helping women unbutton their clothes, so they could slip them off, not putting their clothes on. But he was going to fasten her coat all the way up to her chin.

*Safe. That's what he liked. Safe.*

Carter straightened, having finished his task. The girl looked innocent as she slept, so he could imagine all kinds of things about her. It was when she woke up that he'd find out if she was as gentle as she appeared.

Was she an angel or the devil in disguise?

It was midmorning when they finally headed out for Windy Bend. Rick hadn't said a word when

Carter walked out carrying the girl. It was just as well, because he didn't want to hear it anyway.

At least today was a far cry better than yesterday. The sky was clear blue with a bright sun overhead. The sun made the snow sparkle like stars, and was a little blinding as they rode, but thank God the blizzard had blown over.

If they rode hard all day, they would make it home shortly after nightfall. Carter looked forward to sleeping in his old bed and getting some of his mother's home cooking, but it would be a while. First, they would have to traverse the mounds of snow that lay in front of them. At least Blue, his black stallion, was sure-footed and dependable in the white fluff. Blue would get them home.

Carter repositioned the woman in his arms. Now that it was quiet, he'd had time to think and question the logic of dragging an unconscious woman with them.

Stupid was the first answer he came up with.

And then he figured there must be another reason. He didn't normally make spontaneous decisions, and he wondered why he'd picked today to start acting irrationally. Maybe it was because of this damnable weather, and the girl had appeared so cold and helpless.

Perhaps once she'd recovered, he could make arrangements for someone else to escort her home—wherever that was. And then he could go back to what he always did, keeping the law. And looking for his sister's killers. Always. It was the one thing that drove him. The Carlson gang had slipped his grasp several times, but one day he'd be ahead of them and they would be his. And they would pay for what they'd done to his sister.

Yep, they'd pay.

* * *

Slowly, Mary opened her eyes.

And for the second time, she had no idea where she was, but this time, she felt movement.

Moving?

It was dark. She couldn't see anything. And there was intense heat on her right side. She tried to move, but found she couldn't.

Dark. Hot. My God, she was in hell!

She had gone to hell without having a chance to clear her name. Life wasn't fair.

Panic set in, and Mary's heart began to race as she struggled. Suddenly, the darkness was shattered by a blinding light, causing her to blink several times before she could focus. And then she saw the face—the face of the devil.

"Get still!" the devil shouted.

"Go to hell," Mary yelled back, and then she remembered she was already in hell. She screamed and fought all at the same time. She wasn't going down without a fight.

Somewhere a horse whinnied, followed by the devil swearing while he tried to pin her arms down.

She struggled harder.

The next thing Mary knew, she was flying helplessly through the air until she landed in a mound of cold snow which, thank God, cushioned her fall.

As soon as Mary was able to catch her breath, she fought through the cobwebs of her confusion, then blinked with bafflement. Snow?

Still a little foggy, she thought. Hell didn't have snow.

Quickly, she looked around her. Even that small movement sent sharp pains screaming though her head.

A voice came from behind her. "Of all the confounded stupid things."

This time she slowly turned, and he continued, "I should have left you where I found you," he snapped, and glared at her with eyes as black as coal.

Someone was laughing.

That's when Mary noticed a second man sitting on his horse, Stetson pushed back on his head, as he leaned on his pommel and stared down at both of them. Laughing, he looked much more friendly than the man beside her. "I must admit, Carter, I've never seen you dismount quite like that before."

"Go to hell, McCallum."

"I thought we were in hell," Mary said.

Carter's lip curled. "Not yet, darling."

She warily watched the devil, or whoever he was, as he rose and brushed off his breeches and coat. He reminded her of a bear with his huge heavy fur coat. He looked like someone who could gobble her up. But instead of shivering, she straightened her spine.

Mary Costner wasn't afraid of any man.

Of course, she'd never met a man like this one before. He was very tall, broad-shouldered, and no one she recognized, because she'd remember a face like his. It was hard, rugged, and very handsome. "Who are you?"

He didn't bother to answer. Instead, he extended his hand toward her. She hesitated, trying to comprehend what was going on. Did she really trust him?

"Grab my hand before your coat and clothes get soaked."

She watched him warily. "Who are you?"

His expression was one of pained tolerance. "I'm the poor soul who pulled you out of the snowbank where I found you. The wisdom of which, I'm now questioning. Now, grab my hand."

Finally, she took his hand. He jerked her to her feet, but her head hurt so bad that she stumbled and fell against him. He was like a rock, she thought as she grabbed her head and groaned. Why did her head hurt so bad?

"I hope you're not always this stubborn," he grumbled. "I could have taken advantage of you a long time ago if you had appealed to me."

Mary couldn't believe the arrogant jackass. "Like your friend told you, go to hell, mister."

Carter shook his head. "Such language."

"I do wish you'd quit shouting. My head is killing me," Mary grumbled as she tried to straighten and stand on her own.

"I guess it does," he told her. He took her hand and placed it on her forehead.

"Oh my," Mary gasped. "How—?" She stopped as she remembered being thrown from her horse. It had been her fault for not paying attention.

The big man found his Stetson and slapped it against his leg to dislodge the dusting of snow before mounting his horse. "I'd like to stand here and fill you in on the little bit we do know about you, but it can wait. We need to get moving," he told her, then reached down for her hand.

"Where's my horse?" Mary asked, but at the same time took his hand and swung up behind him.

The other cowboy rode up beside them and answered her. "Good question. Did you have a horse or did somebody dump you out there?"

Mary wrapped her arms around the man in front of her. His fur coat felt soft and warm against her cheek. She was getting ready to answer the other cowboy when the sun caught something shiny on his chest.

Good heavens. He was a lawman. And she'd bet a dollar that the man she had her arms wrapped around was a lawman, too.

*Did bad luck have to follow her everywhere? Couldn't she get a break just once?*

She needed time to solve the murder. "Ah," she stammered.

"That's okay," the cowboy assured her. "The doc said you might not remember anything when you came to, but it will come back to you. Just give it time."

All right, she could go with that. They evidently didn't know who she was, and she wasn't about to provide the information. Just as soon as they found out that she'd woken up with a bloody knife in her hand, no memory of what had happened, and a deed that stated if anything happened to one partner then the other inherited—they'd throw her in jail. Hell, *she* even thought she looked guilty. "I'm just a bit fuzzy. Do I know you? What are your names?"

"No, ma'am. I'd remember somebody like you." He smiled before he continued. "I'm Deputy Rick McCallum and the man who looks like a bear is Marshall Carter Monroe. We're U.S. Marshals, so you're in safe hands."

*Damn! Damn! Double damn!* Of all the rotten luck! U.S. Marshals? Well, she might as well ask. "Am I under arrest?"

"Is there any reason you should be?" Carter asked.

Mary almost blurted out, *There is a murder that I'm trying to sort out,* but she caught herself. "I—I don't think so."

"You don't sound too sure. We'll talk later," Carter said in a deep voice that she found she liked, even if he did seem to be very disagreeable. "Do you remember your name?"

"Mary," she said, but quickly added, "I don't remember my last name."

"Well, Mary, you just hang on, and if we're lucky, we'll be in Windy Bend by nightfall."

"I don't know where that is."

"I should hope not," Carter said, "especially since you can't remember anything."

Mary swallowed hard. She was going to have to think before she spoke if she was to pull off her deception. And that wasn't something she usually did. However, it would have been nice if she really couldn't remember. She wanted to wipe the sight of the murder out of her mind. Swallowing quickly, she held her breath to prevent the tears that were threatening to pool in her eyes.

U.S. Marshals were not dumb. They were savvy hunters. They were also the best lawmen around, and she had the feeling that the man in front of her was one of the best, but right now she just couldn't think anymore. It made her head hurt too bad. So she closed her eyes and rested her head against Carter's strong back and let out a small sigh.

Funny, here she sat in the middle of a very dangerous situation with men who could arrest her and put her in jail, yet at the moment she felt very safe.

Trouble . . . she was in a world of trouble.

# Chapter 3

Gregory Gulch was coated with pristine white snow. The scent of green pines and evergreen filled the air.

At first glance no one would have imagined the grisly scene Marshal Forester had found yesterday. He had only been in Gregory Gulch six months, having replaced Marshal Stanley, so this disruption to the peace was new to him. So far the camp had been quite peaceful during that time—until yesterday.

Forester still wasn't sure he could believe the way Big Jim had been cut. How could the boy have done something like that, but who else could have killed Big Jim? Everybody in town liked him. But with the boy missing, he sure looked guilty, Forester thought as he watched the miners lower the pine box into the ground.

The miners had to use their picks on the frozen ground. The clicks of the mining tools echoed around them. Usually when someone died and it was this cold they would store the body until it was warmer. But not this time. The miners were determined that Big Jim would have a proper burial.

The ugly rust-colored dirt provided a harsh contrast to the pristine white snow. It was also a reminder that though this pretty country looked clean, it was also full of danger.

One of the men said a quick prayer, his breath rising into the cold air like steam escaping a locomotive. When he'd finished everyone said amen, then quickly picked up their shovels and began covering the pine box with stiff dirt that sounded more like rocks hitting the wood than snow.

That was, all but one man.

He was a stranger. Forester recognized him as the snake oil salesman who'd arrived yesterday morning. He wouldn't have to wonder long who the man was because the stranger was walking his way.

"Marshal." The man greeted him with a curt nod. "My name is John McCoy. I am Jim's half brother."

"I heard you'd arrived yesterday. Didn't have any idea that you were related to Big Jim."

"I didn't tell anybody."

Forester cleared his throat. "So you got to see your brother before . . . ?"

McCoy nodded. "Yep. I parked my wagon near his house and Jim invited me to supper."

"Walk on back to the office with me. I want to get what information you can give me," Forester said, but he didn't wait for a reply. It was too damn cold to jaw-jack in the street. And he wasn't used to getting arguments, anyway.

At the jailhouse, consisting of two small rooms, Forester shrugged out of his coat and hustled over to the potbellied stove to stoke the fire. The strong smell of coffee beckoned him. "Have a seat," he said over his shoulder. "Want some coffee?"

"I'm fine."

Forester poured himself a cup of black coffee before sitting down behind his desk. He reared back in his chair as he looked shrewdly at the man in front of him. John McCoy sure didn't look anything like Big Jim. This man was downright skinny with black hair and small, shifty black eyes. However, Big Jim had been broad-shouldered and had always worn faded overalls with a blue flannel shirt, a gun and a bowie knife tucked into his work belt. He hadn't been a young man, but a weathered veteran. Big Jim would scare most men with his thick black beard and long black hair tinged with gray.

Nope, these two were different as night and day.

But then, Forester thought, maybe he was judging the man too quickly. "So, tell me what you know about what went on yesterday." Forester steepled his hands in front of him and watched McCoy. "You were probably one of the last people to see Big Jim alive. Why did you come to Gregory Gulch, anyway?"

"There's no law against visiting my brother, is there?"

"Not until a murder takes place. Then I have to start asking questions."

"I see," McCoy said, rubbing his chin. He paused and seemed to be thinking of what he should say. "Well, I hadn't seen my brother in a few years, so I figured I'd come up and see what he had going for him. Thought I might help him work his claim for a spell. Anyway, he told me to come by his place about six, and I could have supper and meet his partner."

"And did you?"

"Yep."

"So what happened?"

"Supper started off normal, but right after that the kid and Jim got into an argument."

"I'm surprised," Forester said as he got up and poured himself another cup of coffee from the old silver pot on the stove. "Sure you don't want a cup?"

"I believe I will this time," McCoy said. Once he had his coffee in hand, he asked, "Why would you be surprised? I'm not sure I liked the boy."

"That a fact? Most people in camp liked the kid. And yesterday I heard they struck another vein of gold. They were in pretty good moods the last time I saw them."

"Their argument had something to do with the gold," McCoy said with assurance. "I didn't stay long after supper. I told Jim I'd meet him in the morning, and 'course you know what I found the next day."

"As I recall, you were the first person there," Forester said and took another sip of coffee.

"So what you going to do about it, Marshal?"

Forester leaned forward and placed his coffee mug on the desk. "MacHenry is going to sketch a picture of the boy and then I'm going to have it circulated to all the law offices in hopes that somebody finds him. I'm real interested in what the kid has to say."

"Must have been an evil kid to do something like that."

"For now, it's just suspicion of murder. We won't know the whole story until we find the boy and get some answers."

McCoy shifted in the chair. "I guess the mine belongs to me now that Jim is dead, seeing as I'm his next o' kin."

Forester stared at the man, wondering what was it about the man that struck him wrong. From his appearance, he looked like an upright citizen, but yet . . . "I'm not too sure about that, but now that you've brought up the subject, I'll walk with you to the Register of Deeds office and we'll check. I probably need to know that information myself."

They trudged through the snow to the second log cabin on the left and entered the building. "Usually there's a line. Guess we got lucky today," Forester said when they walked right up to the counter. "Jake. We need you to pull Big Jim's deed and see who he left it to."

Jake nodded and went over to a wooden file cabinet where he started rummaging through his files. "Here it is." He pulled out the deed, walked back over to the counter, and unfolded the document. "Let me see." He scanned down the document. "It says if something happens to Big Jim that his part of the mine goes to Mary Costner, but that must have been a mistake. It should have said Mark Costner, his partner."

"So he didn't leave anything to his family?" McCoy asked.

"Only in the event that his partner dies. Mark's half of the deed says the same thing."

Forester turned to McCoy. "Guess you're out of luck. What are you going to do now?"

"Don't know, Marshal. Reckon I'll have to hope they find the boy so everything can be settled," McCoy said as he walked out of the office with Forester. "I'll be seeing you. Not much use of me staying around here. Need to earn a living with my snake oil."

"Before you leave town I guess I need to ask you a few questions."

McCoy looked surprised. "Such as?"

"You said you had dinner with Big Jim. And you were the first person to find Jim?" Forester watched as McCoy nodded. "So where were you in between those times?"

"Are you accusing me, Marshal?"

"It depends on your answer." Forester gave the man a slow smile. "Everybody here is a suspect. And seeing as you could possibly gain a gold mine, some would think that you look as guilty as the boy."

"Can't help it if I'm kin," McCoy blustered, his face turning red. "You see, Marshal, I have an alibi."

Forester leaned against the post and crossed his arms. "I'm listening."

"I spent the night with the lovely Kate. She'll be glad to vouch for me."

Forester chuckled. "Didn't take you long to meet the town whore."

McCoy smiled. "Man's got urges."

"Have to agree with you there. I'll check out your story, and if it holds water then you can go. But you probably should leave some way I can contact you in case something comes up."

"How 'bout I swing back through in a month?"

"Fine," Forester said, and headed back toward his office, thinking that the man sure was quick to point out that he stood to inherit the mine. But if he had an alibi there wasn't any way he could hold him.

As McCoy watched the marshal walk off, he

turned, his face burning with anger. There was always something in his way. Just when he thought he had the perfect plan, something went haywire. He could feel the wealth at his fingertips. And he still couldn't get his hands on that gold. Such easy money for the picking—no more working his ass off for tips. Good thing he had an alibi—didn't need the marshal getting suspicious.

The only thing standing in his way was that Costner woman. It was up to him to end the problem, one way or the other. He needed to find the girl before the marshal did and figure out who she was.

By the time they stopped in Windy Bend night had fallen.

Mary had been dozing off and on as she snuggled into the fur to keep warm. She actually felt as though she'd been riding with a big bear, but since she was warm and his back soft she wasn't going to complain. Her headache had finally eased off into a dull thud, but the rest of her body was sore and cramped from the long ride.

"We're here," Carter said.

She straightened, her aching body protesting as she did, when they stopped in front of a gate. She glanced around Carter and saw two men standing with shotguns across their arms. With belligerent scowls, they blocked the way.

"That's far enough, mister. State your business and be quick about it," one of the two burly guards shouted.

"Has it been that long, Stanley?" Carter asked.

"Well, I'll be a clabber-headed idiot," Stanley

drawled. He moved over to shake Carter's hand. "Your ma will be mighty glad to see you." Stanley peered around Carter. "Is that your wife peeking out from behind you? She's a right pretty filly, the best I can see."

Mary wasn't sure she liked being compared to a horse, and she definitely wasn't anybody's wife.

"No. She isn't my wife," Carter told him as she shifted in his saddle.

Mary noticed he didn't sound too thrilled with the idea, either. Maybe they were both just alike; if so, there were bound to be fireworks ahead. Instinctively, she wanted to lash out at Carter, but wisely she kept her mouth shut. She didn't want to do anything to draw more attention to herself.

"Open the gate. We're bushed," Carter said. "I'll see you tomorrow, and we can catch up on what's been happening."

Stanley shoved the gate open. "You got it."

Mary peeked around Carter to see a very large ranch house at the end of the road, surpassing anything she could have imagined. Smoke curled out of several chimneys into the black sky. She could smell the smoke from her perch.

Snowed covered the brown cedar shingles of the ranch house and soft lights shone in the windows, providing a welcome sight. The perfect home, Mary thought. When they drew closer, she could see that a long porch ran across the front of the house. There were four rocking chairs that would be used when the weather was warm.

Carter stopped at the hitching post, and Rick dismounted and tied his horse, then came over to help Mary off. The minute her feet touched the ground, she collapsed. Rick caught her and held her up. "Whoa, little lady. I bet your legs have gone to sleep."

"I think so," Mary agreed. "They're tingling," she added as she clung to Rick's neck.

Carter was on the ground frowning at both of them, and Mary wondered why as he reached for her. "I'll take her."

"I'm perfectly capable of walking," she informed him, shaking off his arm, but as she took a step, she stumbled. Mary was determined to prove she didn't need him, but her legs gave way again and she almost fell.

"I can see that," Carter said, slipping his arm around her waist. "But since you have finally woken up, let's not take the chance of you falling and hitting your head again."

Slowly, the feeling started coming back to her legs. "My legs are much better now," she insisted. "You can let me go." When Mary was being held this close to Carter, she experienced a delicious and decidedly uncomfortable feeling that she didn't understand. Until she did, she would just as soon stay away from him.

"Humor me." There was a hard edge to his voice that warned her not to continue.

The front door of the ranch house flew open and a beautiful woman appeared. She took one look at Carter, squealed, and threw herself into his arms.

Mary stepped quickly to the side. It was a good thing she could stand, or she had the feeling she'd be on the ground, Carter had let her go so quickly. Evidently, he wasn't as concerned about her safety as he'd said.

She watched as they embraced. This had to be Carter's mother, Mary thought. Who else would be so happy to see him? After all, he hadn't been that easy to get along with up until now.

They had the same hair color, midnight black that shone as if it reflected moonbeams. And, Mary had to admit, Carter was handsome with rugged masculine strength carved into every inch of his jaw. A very stubborn jaw, she guessed, but today he was not her friend, no matter how pretty the package.

"It's about time you came home," the woman said as she stepped back and straightened her clothes. "I was beginning to worry something had happened to you." She turned and looked at the other man. "This must be Rick."

The woman moved over and hugged him. "I've heard so much about you. Welcome to Monroe Cattle Company," she said.

Mary had thought maybe the woman hadn't seen her, but suddenly she whirled and stared directly at Mary. "And who is this, Carter? You didn't say anything about bringing company with you. Could this be my future daughter-in-law?"

"Not hardly, Mother," Carter said with a wry chuckle.

Mary glared at Carter. She really didn't like the sarcastic way he'd said that. It was like she was mud on his boot. Of course, she wasn't his future anything; however, she didn't like the fact that he hadn't even considered her as marriage material. How insulting. Of course, she wouldn't marry him. She didn't even know who in the hell he really was. But she took insult at his comment, nonetheless.

Carter took Mary's elbow. "This is Mary. She's had an accident and doesn't remember anything about herself." He turned to Mary. "My mother, Judith Monroe."

"You poor dear," the woman said as she slid her arm around Mary. "How frightening it must be for you. We'll get you settled in, and you'll feel better before you know it." Judith ushered Mary into the house and straight over to a staircase on the right side of what appeared to be a huge parlor.

They started up the long staircase, leaving the men behind. Mary was so surprised by Judith's warm welcome that she had done nothing more than nod in response to everything the woman was saying. She was being treated like a guest instead of a criminal.

Once upstairs, they moved down a long hallway. When they reached the third door to the right, Judith stopped. "I think you'll like this room." She opened the door. "It's cheerful and bright. Stay right here until I light the oil lamps." When she had lit the last lamp, she gestured for Mary to enter the room.

It was the prettiest room that Mary had ever seen. It was decorated in several different shades of green. There was a dark green rug on the floor and the huge bed was covered with a light green quilt. The pillows were ruffled with white eyelets all around.

"This is so pretty," Mary said. "Am I taking somebody's room?" She knew this bedroom had to belong to a woman. Perhaps Carter's wife? No, that couldn't be it because Judith had thought Mary was his intended.

"This was my daughter's room. I think it will suit you well."

"Thank you, Mrs. Monroe. But—"

"Please call me Judith."

"Thank you, Judith, but will your daughter mind?"

The woman was quiet for a long moment. "I guess Carter didn't tell you. Of course, he didn't, he never talks about it. You see, my daughter is dead."

Mary gasped. "I'm so sorry." She could see the pain in the woman's eyes.

"It was a long time ago, but the hurt never goes away," Judith said in a quiet voice. "However, you have just arrived. I'm sure you must be very tired. We can talk later, after you have rested." She reached out and touched Mary's forehead. "My goodness, you do have a nasty lump on your head."

"It hurts—" Mary almost said like a son of a bitch, but caught herself. Her language was terrible from working around so many men for so long. "Too."

"I imagine it does. I'll bring you some ice for the swelling. Does Carter have your bags?"

"I—I don't have any. To tell you the truth, I'm not sure how I ended up in your son's company. I just know that when I came to, I was on a horse with your son."

"Sounds dreadful." Judith walked over to a wardrobe and pulled out a drawer. She removed a white flannel gown trimmed with pink lace, and a wrapper. She shook out the garments. "You are about the same size as my daughter, so you might as well use her clothes. They have just been lying there collecting dust for years."

"Oh no, ma'am, I couldn't," Mary protested, holding her hand up and shaking her head.

"Nonsense. I insist. Lisa wouldn't have minded at all. Now, you rest. In the morning everything will look much better," Judith insisted. She handed Mary the gown, and then gave her a hug. "You get a good night's sleep, and I'll see you in the morning." Judith paused at the door. "Should I have a tray of food sent up?"

"I can wait until morning," Mary replied. "Good night."

Judith didn't see the tears in Mary's eyes before she shut the door. Mary had never known anyone to treat her so nicely, and she didn't even know this woman.

She removed her clothes and wondered if tomorrow would truly be better, because right now nothing was making much sense to her. She was so weary that she stretched out on the bed and snuggled under the green quilt. She felt so very much alone. Though she had no idea what had happened to her, she knew she must be in trouble, and she had no clue what to do.

Mary needed a plan, but until she knew what had really happened, she couldn't even do that. She just hoped to God she figured something out before she was arrested and hung for something she hadn't done.

Rick turned to Carter as soon as Judith and Mary had disappeared around the corner. "I wonder if your ma realized that you came home, too?"

Carter chuckled. "I'm not too sure. But she does seem happy that I brought the girl, no matter who she is." He rested his hand on Rick's shoulder. "I don't know about you, but I'm too damned tired to think of much of anything tonight. Let's grab our gear and turn in. We can talk with Mother tomorrow. She's going to want to know everything we've been doing."

"I'm with you," Rick said. "I got a feeling your mother is going to want to know everything about the girl."

"I think you're right. But she's just going to have to get in line. I want to know many things about our Mary. The sooner her memory returns, the better."

# Chapter 4

Carter was awakened by the morning sunshine pouring in through the window, which meant if they were lucky, warmer weather was just around the corner.

He had to admit that last night had been the best sleep he'd had in a long time. He stretched. Perhaps it was due to the fact that he didn't have to worry about being shot in the middle of the night while he slept, or maybe it was because this was really home. No matter how far he roamed, a part of him would always be here at the ranch.

Time to get moving. He threw off the covers and strolled to the window to look out. The room was chilly since the fire had burned down, but the sky outside was clear. No snow today. Carter's mood improved greatly.

He dressed and went downstairs to the dining room, where he found Rick and his mother already at breakfast. Since when did Rick beat him out of bed? *I must be getting soft,* Carter thought.

Judith Monroe looked at Carter with pride. She

couldn't help admiring her son. He'd grown into a handsome man with good, strong features. She'd bet he had turned many a woman's head since he'd been away. However, knowing her son, he probably hadn't noticed. He was too focused on his job. He'd managed to build a wall around himself, which she didn't like, either, but if she said anything, he would deny the truth and withdraw more. If nothing else, Judith wanted his time at home to be pleasant.

However, if she could show him that there was more to life than work and the insistent wish for revenge that drove him, she might have a chance to turn her son into the loving man he could be.

She missed her daughter, too, and always would, but after a while the pain of her loss had finally receded to a dull ache. Now, it was time to put the past behind them.

As Carter took his seat at the table, Judith admired his stubborn chin and those wonderful black eyes. Sometimes he was too much like herself, she thought. She smiled at him with a mother's pride.

Once she'd expected him to take over the ranch. It had looked hopeful, until his sister was—well, Judith didn't want to think about that. Not this morning, when she was so happy to have her son home again where he belonged.

"The girl hasn't come down yet?" Carter asked as he served himself a large helping of scrambled eggs and sausage from the plate on the sideboard.

Judith took a sip of hot coffee, swallowed, and thought, *Could it be that he might care just a little for the girl?* Since those had been the first words out of his mouth, she wondered. "I just sent Maria up to check on her. How long are you staying?"

"Not sure." Carter reached for the yellow crock of butter. "How is Sheriff O'Tool?"

"On top of the bullet wound," his mother said, frowning that Carter hadn't answered her first question, "now he has influenza. It's hit the town pretty hard."

Rick was buttering his toast when he glanced up. "That's too bad. At least he won't have to worry about anything now that we're here."

"Very true." Judith frowned again. "But I hate to know that the town has to have a catastrophe before I can get you to come home."

Carter noticed that she was looking directly at him as he finished off his eggs. "I hear you, Mother. I have not forgotten about you. I've been busy. And I have a lead—"

He didn't finish because the girl came through the door and stopped. She looked nothing like the waif he'd rescued. Her blond hair was soft and shiny, tumbling around her shoulders. She wore one of his sister's gowns, but it had never looked like this on his sister. It was a royal blue color that complemented her complexion, and made her eyes just that much bluer.

"Have a seat, dear," Judith said, motioning to a chair next to her and directly across from Carter.

Mary felt funny walking into a room full of strangers. It was as if her life had only begun two days ago. And, in a sense, it had. She wasn't the same person she'd been before, and she definitely wasn't in the same location, but since her money had disappeared along with her horse and the life she'd once known, she didn't have much of a choice but to play along until she knew what had really happened.

Noticing that everyone was still staring at her, Mary felt as if she were walking in a cloud of uncertainty. If she took the wrong step, she'd fall through a hole, go tumbling into nowhere, and never be heard from again. How long had it been since she'd even resembled a woman?

"I'm not dressed properly?" Mary asked when they continued to stare at her.

"You are lovely, my dear." Judith smiled. "Come in. We won't bite."

Mary smiled slightly at that and stepped toward the table. A big Mexican woman swept through the door with a bowl brimming with scrambled eggs and tortillas and set it down at Mary's place.

"Oh my," Mary said as she looked at all the food in front of her. There were eggs, toast, and large slabs of ham. And in a separate bowl was a large portion of home fries waiting for her.

"I thought you might be hungry this morning," Judith said with a bright smile. "When was the last time you ate?"

Mary opened her mouth to say something, then thought for a moment. It has been at least two days ago. She could remember cooking for Big Jim and—someone else. But who? And why couldn't she remember eating?

"That must be a hard question," Judith chuckled.

Mary smiled. "I was trying to remember. It must have been before I was hurt, because I'm starving as if it's been days."

"Good. I'm glad to hear that," Judith said. "Not that you haven't eaten, but that you have an appetite. That's a sign your body is healing." She picked up a brown earthenware pitcher and poured Mary some milk. "Now that we're all here, tell me how you and my son came to be together."

"She really doesn't know much, so I'll answer," Carter said as he sat back in his chair, holding his coffee cup between his hands. "When we came across Mary, she was upside down in a snowbank. We thought she was dead. From the looks of her she'd been there several hours. She was unconscious and barely alive. As you can see by the lump on her head, she had a concussion. I'm glad to see the swelling has finally gone down some."

Judith turned to Mary. "What in the world were you doing out in that kind of weather? And all alone?"

Mary hesitated. "I don't know."

"The doctor said she might have temporary memory loss from the knock on her head," Rick supplied.

*And it's going to stay that way,* Mary thought. She did feel bad lying to this nice woman, but she also didn't want her neck stretched for something she didn't do. At least, she didn't think she'd murdered anyone.

Judith reached over and patted Mary's hand. "How scary that must have been for you."

Mary nodded, then turned her attention back to her plate. She hadn't been kidding—she was starving. And the busier she looked eating, the less likely they were to keep asking her questions that she couldn't—or wouldn't—answer.

"You are welcome to stay here until your memory returns." Judith offered. "Surely your family is very worried about you."

Mary nodded again, too overwhelmed to speak. Besides, her mouth was full with the first bite of juicy ham. Yes, her family, Brandy and Thunder, would be worried, that is, as soon as they found out. She'd promised to return home next week for a visit. When she didn't arrive, would they come looking for her?

Everybody else at the table had entered into an animated conversation, so it gave Mary time to enjoy her food without having to answer questions. It also gave her a few minutes to think about what she would say when she did finally answer.

Mary didn't have a normal family. Hers was a very unusual group made up of misfit orphans no one wanted. But together, after much struggle trying to make it on their own, they became close.

Along with Mary, there were Brandy, Billy, Scott, Ellen, the baby Amy, and her newest little brother, Willie. It was the family that Mary had joined when the women of Independence, Missouri, had placed her in the parsonage run by Father Brown, who'd died soon afterward.

At first she hadn't really gotten along with any of them—none of the kids had, and they'd all hated Brandy. She had been the oldest, the smartest, the prettiest, and Father Brown's favorite. When Father Brown died and left Brandy in charge, their safe world had fallen apart. The parsonage had run out of money and would close in a month. They would have been out in the streets if it hadn't been for Brandy's quick thinking of becoming a mail-order bride. Of course, at the time Mary thought it was the stupidest thing she'd ever heard.

Still Mary had hated Brandy. Now Mary realized she had been very jealous and perhaps a little rebellious, but she'd been young then, too.

Finding no way out of their situation, Brandy

answered an advertisement for a mail-order bride, and they soon found themselves on their way to the Wyoming territory. That's when the whole family met Thunder.

However, he didn't want any part of them.

How Brandy managed to rope Thunder into helping them with their wagon as they went west still amazed her. Somewhere along the way Brandy and Thunder had also managed to fall in love, though neither would admit it for a long time. Finally they all became a family.

Mary wished Brandy and Thunder were here now to help her. Even her brother Billy's help would be welcome. They would know what to do. But they were far away, and Mary once again found herself among people she didn't know and wasn't sure she could trust. And she really didn't want them to know anything about her until she was ready.

She'd just finished the last of her breakfast and placed her fork on the plate when an uncomfortable feeling shuddered through her. Mary looked up to see everyone watching her.

"Are you all right, dear?" Judith asked.

Mary realized she hadn't said a word since she'd started eating. "I'm fine. As you can tell, I was very hungry. I'm sorry for not joining in the conversation."

"We can get you something else if you're still hungry," Carter said.

For the first time since they'd been together, Mary looked directly at him. There was something about the man that disturbed her. He was handsome with dark, unreadable eyes. He also had an air of authority and the appearance of one who demanded instant obedience. The problem was, Mary had never been obedient in her life. And she didn't intend to start now.

The lines in his face were much softer today than yesterday. He seemed rested. Evidently, it had done him good to come home. Maybe he could be a nice person, but she wasn't going to stick around long enough to find out—Carter was the law.

And until she was certain she hadn't broken it, she was planning to give Carter Monroe a wide, wide berth for the moment. She also didn't like the way he was looking at her as if he was trying to peer into her mind.

Carter leaned back in his chair and watched Mary. "Have you remembered something?"

"I—I don't remember anything," she replied, her eyes shifting quickly away from him.

Like hell she didn't, Carter thought. Why did he feel she wasn't exactly telling him the truth? It was plain to see from her evasiveness that she was holding something back. "Perhaps in a few days you can tell us something about yourself, so we can get you back to your family."

"I hope so," she replied, meaning it sincerely. Then she changed the subject. "Is this where you live and work?"

"This is my mother's home," Carter emphasized. "Rick and I came back home on temporary assignment. The local sheriff is feeling poorly, so we'll be here until he's fit for duty."

"I see, but what should I do in the meantime?"

"You can help me around here," Judith said. "And maybe once you're rested and healed, something will help you regain your memory."

Carter shoved back from the table and so did

Rick. "Mother, we're going to ride into town," Carter said.

"You'll be home for dinner?"

"Hope so," Carter assured her, then they found their hats and sheepskin-lined coats before heading out.

Mary watched the two men leave. Again, something about Carter puzzled her. She felt different when she was around him, both giddy and scared. Could she be coming down with some ailment? It sure felt like it.

Even though she couldn't read his expression or tell what he was thinking, he seemed to be able to see into her mind even if she didn't want him to. And he kept looking at her in a strange way. It made her feel both guilty and giddy at the same time.

After the men had gone, Mary glanced at Judith. "I don't think your son likes me very much."

"He doesn't know you." The expression in Judith's eyes said something else entirely.

"I guess you're right. It's just—"

Judith placed her hand on Mary's arm. "Carter doesn't like things he can't figure out. He also has a demon driving him that I wish would go away." Judith rose from the table. "Come with me. I want to show you something."

Mary followed the woman through the sprawling house. She liked the feeling of spaciousness that surrounded her as they entered the main living area. There was a large fireplace in the center of the wall and three couches, two that faced each other and one that faced the fireplace. Above the mantel hung a large portrait of a very beautiful girl.

Mary thought she looked very much like Carter and his mother. They had the same dark hair and eyes. "This must be your daughter?"

"Yes, that's my Lisa. The portrait was painted six months before she was killed." Judith patted the seat next to her on the couch. "Come and sit beside me,"

After Mary sat down, she said, "I am so sorry. I hope they caught and punished the person who did it."

"No." Judith shook her head. "I'm afraid they didn't." Her voice was very soft, and sadness washed over her face. "This isn't a pretty tale, but one you should know if you're going to understand my son." She took a deep breath.

"Lisa and Carter had gone to town for supplies. Unknown to them, a bank robbery was taking place at the same time. Lisa had been waiting in the wagon while Carter carried their purchases. He came out of the dry goods store, his arms full of packages.

"He told me that everything else from that point on seemed to happen as if time had slowed. The wagon wasn't directly in front of the store, but several stores down. When Carter realized what was happening, he ran toward the wagon, but he wasn't fast enough.

"The robbers spotted Lisa and swept her from the wagon, then continued on out of town.

"Carter heard her screaming all the way out of town, but he could do nothing. By the time he'd dropped the packages and pulled out his gun, it was too late. And he couldn't shoot for fear of hitting his sister."

Judith's voice broke and Mary looked at the tension in Judith's usually calm face. Mary waited a minute before asking, "Did Carter go after them?"

"Carter was young then, he did the only thing he knew, he went to the local sheriff, who was slow pulling a posse together. It was five days before they found my little girl." Judith looked off into nowhere. "Or what was left of her." Judith's words hung in her throat, and it took a moment before she could continue. "They had used her badly, then beaten her until we could barely recognize her face." Judith sobbed.

By the time Judith had finished her story, Mary was crying, too. She reached over and took the woman's hand. "I'm so sorry for your loss," Mary finally managed to get out as Judith clung to her hand.

"I've never told anyone the whole story. And I don't know what made me open up just now." Judith wiped the tears from her cheeks. Talking about Lisa's death always dredged up feelings that Judith thought she had gotten over, but for some reason she'd wanted to confide in Mary. There was something about this child that reminded her of her daughter. "Carter wouldn't let me see her. That's when I knew my baby must have suffered."

"Did they ever get the men?"

"No. Perhaps if they had, Carter would be different. Instead, he took the whole thing as if he believed it were his fault."

"But it wasn't," Mary said, taking up for a man she hardly knew.

"Of course it wasn't. He could have been killed, too, and I would have lost both my children. I wouldn't have been able to bear that." Judith choked back another sob. "Sometimes I feel as if I have lost Carter anyway."

"How so?" Mary asked gently.

"Where once he'd been content to take over the ranch, now his only goal is revenge. After his sister's murder he became a lawman, determined to track down the men who killed his sister. He'd gotten a good look at the men."

"Has he caught any of them?"

"He's killed two. There are two more to go."

"Killed?"

"I would like to think that he would have brought them in for trial if he could have, but they are dangerous men."

"Carter seems like a man who takes his job very seriously." Mary shivered. "I'm sure he is very good at what he does."

Judith smiled. "Yes, he is the best. I'm very proud of him but . . . Carter needs a life, a home, and a family. He can't be driven by the past. He needs something in his future. Something to look forward to."

"Instead of the past." Mary sighed. "Maybe one day he will find that something."

Judith turned and looked at her with a sad smile. "Maybe."

Marshal Forester was hitting dead ends everywhere he turned. Nobody had seen Mark Costner, and it seemed that nobody knew much about him. So Forester looked for the address on the deed, maybe some of the boy's kin, people who could shed some light on why he would murder anyone. Forester shook his head. Something wasn't right with the whole situation, but he was going to keep digging until he found his answers. Big Jim deserved that.

So Forester left his deputy in charge of Gregory Gulch and mounted his horse. He was going to Denver to a ranch called the Wagon Wheel.

Maybe he'd get some answers there.


Brandy couldn't imagine where any of the children were as she walked through the house. Couldn't somebody besides herself answer the door? It wasn't as though they had visitors every day.

When she reached the door, she opened it to a man she didn't know, but she knew he had to be a lawman by the star on his chest. He was an older man with a leathery, wrinkled face, but his eyes were clear and sharp.

"Something's happened," Brandy blurted out, forgetting the hello-how-are-you greeting she should have politely greeted him with.

"Yes, ma'am, I'm afraid it has," Forester replied. "I need to speak with you."

Suddenly Brandy felt light-headed as she opened the screen door for the man and motioned him toward the sofa.

The back door slammed, and Brandy knew who it was before her brothers dashed into the parlor. They sounded like a herd of horses stampeding through the house.

"Who's the company?" Scott asked as he entered the doorway, followed by Willie.

"Name's Marshal Forester," the stranger said.

"These are my brothers." Brandy made the introductions before addressing Scott. "Go get Thunder. And Willie, you fetch Ellen from upstairs."

Once the boys had disappeared, she looked at the stranger. "If you will give us a moment, we do everything as a family, so I want them here before you start talking," she explained. It also put off the bad news for a few moments longer. Of course, the man hadn't said it was bad news, but she knew. The law had never brought good news to her.

Thunder strode into the room, commanding everyone's attention. Brandy felt better the moment she saw him. He'd always had that effect of her, except, of course, when she was hopping mad at him. Thunder was her tower of strength whether he wanted to be or not.

His piercing silver eyes went to her immediately. "What's wrong?"

Scott, Willie, and Ellen entered the room and sat down.

"I don't know," Brandy said, and turned her attention back to the marshal.

Forester cleared his throat. "I've come to ask you some questions about Mark."

Brandy gave him a funny look. "I don't know a Mark." She looked at Thunder. "Do you?"

"Could you have made a mistake?" Thunder asked, his deep voice filling the room.

"Don't think so." Forrester pulled out the deed. "It says right here for his address, the Wagon Wheel. That's this place, right?"

They all nodded.

"Good. It says right here, Mark Costner."

Thunder smiled. "You mean Mary Costner."

Immediately, Brandy asked, "What's happened to Mary?"

Now it was the marshal's turn to look confused. "Wait a minute. I'm looking for a young boy."

"I'm young," Willie said.

"A mite too young," Forester told him, still frowning. "I'm looking for a young boy about her age." He pointed to Ellen.

"You're from Gregory Gulch?" Thunder asked.

"Yep. But I'm telling you that for months I've been seeing a boy. Don't think my eyesight has gotten that bad. He was a boy."

Brandy laughed. "Mary was dressing as a boy. She hid her hair up under a cap so she could work her claim without the men bothering her."

Forester scratched his head. "Sure fooled me."

Brandy scooted to the edge of the couch and looked at the marshal. "How is my sister? Nothing has happened to her?"

"Don't know."

Brandy shot to her feet. "You don't know?"

"Perhaps you'd better explain," Thunder said as he reached out for his wife's arm.

"She's disappeared. Been gone a good week."

"Disappeared?" Ellen said as she moved closer to the conversation. "Someone has taken Mary?"

"I bet she's real scared," Willie added.

"Don't know." The marshal shook his head. "A week ago her partner was found dead, and there was no sign of Mark—I mean Mary. We put out wanted posters for Mark Costner, but there hasn't been one lead that has turned up."

Brandy grabbed her chest. Thunder steadied her. "You don't think she is dead, too?"

"Don't know." The marshal repeated the same answer, and Brandy realized that seemed to be the only answer the man had. "If they killed her, why didn't they leave her behind with Big Jim?"

Thunder folded his arms across his chest. "Makes sense. So you think that Mary killed Big Jim since you didn't find her there?"

"Mary wouldn't do anything like that," Scott insisted. "She threatened to kill me a bunch of times, but she was just fooling around."

Forester smiled. "I hope she didn't do it. And if she did, why? Was she threatened? But I can't find any of those answers until I find the girl. I was hoping she'd come back home."

Brandy turned to Thunder. "What are we going to do?"

His silver gaze met hers. "*We* are not going to do anything. But *I'm* going to pack my gear and return with the marshal and see what I can find out. Mary is probably very scared and not thinking straight."

"Do you want me to go with you?" Scott asked; at fifteen he was starting to get tall.

Brandy smiled at Scott. It didn't seem like he was fifteen. Every time she looked at him, she saw a seven-year-old who never stopped talking.

"No," Thunder replied. "You're the oldest man here, you need to take care of the place while I'm gone."

Scott beamed with the praise. But Willie tugged on Thunder's hand. "What about me?"

"You need to help just like you have with the cows. Scott will have his hands full while I'm gone. You're a member of our family," Thunder said.

Brandy remembered when the scared five-year-old had come to live with them. When her brother Billy told them that Willie had been living on the streets of New York City by himself, Brandy immediately adopted Willie into the family.

"We'll take care of the ranch," Brandy assured Thunder as she gave him a shove toward the bedroom.

"Yeah, we'll be fine as long as Brandy don't do no cooking," Scott said, and started giggling.

Brandy cut her eyes at him, but followed her husband into the bedroom. She was glad Thunder had been raised by the Cheyenne. If anybody could find Mary, he could.

She watched him gather a few of his things, shoving them into his saddlebags. "What do you think?"

"I think Mary is in a lot of trouble."

"I bet she's frightened," Brandy said. "And it's hard to scare Mary."

"I'm sure she is frightened, but we're talking about our Mary. She isn't the typical helpless woman—kinda like you."

Brandy laughed. "I needed that, thank you. Mary will use her head. I just hope no one hurts her before we can find out what really happened."

Thunder turned to his wife and put his hands on Brandy's arms. "Somebody killed Big Jim. Did Mary do it? I don't think so, unless she was threatened some way. But if she didn't, somebody else did, and that somebody knows Mary is a witness. Now give me a hug."

Brandy hugged her husband tight. "Find her."

"I will," he murmured into her brandy-colored hair. Then he tipped her face up so he could kiss her with all the fire and passion they'd always had.

Some things never changed.

# Chapter 5

A week had passed and Mary hadn't gotten any closer to figuring out what had happened to Big Jim. She could picture bits and pieces of that day, but nothing that made sense. She just couldn't have done such a thing, so that meant someone else had been there, and she needed to figure out who and why. Then something occurred to her. If she'd actually seen this person, then she could identify him as soon as she remembered his face. And that made her very dangerous to the mystery man.

Would he come after her?

Mary shivered. He couldn't possibly find her. Once the marshal had picked her up, that should have thrown him off the trail if he had been following her. She didn't even know exactly where she was.

My God. She'd gone from being simple Mary to being wanted by everybody. Just the thought made her short of breath. She just couldn't deal with all the possible unknowns that faced her, so she shoved them to the back of her thoughts. Later, after she was fully recovered and had her strength back, she would decide what she had to do.

In the meantime, she had settled into her temporary home. A home she felt completely safe in as long as they didn't know her true identity. She couldn't deny she liked the way Judith pampered her. In all her life, Mary had never been treated so special. She figured it wouldn't hurt to indulge herself for a little while. Plus, in a strange way Mary found that her being here at the ranch had helped Judith. Mary was glad of that. She heard Carter say that it had been a long time since his mother had smiled so much.

It was almost time to go down for dinner. Mary walked over to the wardrobe to choose a dress. She couldn't get used to changing clothes just to eat dinner. The rest of her family would laugh at her for even suggesting such a thing, but on the other hand, Judith might also laugh if she knew that Mary's previous wardrobe had consisted of three dresses.

Now, what to wear? After looking for several minutes, she chose a peacock-colored wrapper dress for dinner. Lisa had liked bright colors, Mary was finding out. It was such a shame that she'd died at such a young age. She was a very lucky young woman to have had Judith as her mother.

When Mary first caught a glimpse of Lisa's wardrobe, she was overwhelmed. Lisa loved brilliant colors and so did Mary. Her wardrobe had consisted mostly of varying shades of brown when she was growing up.

She stepped into the petticoats and eyed the bustle. She didn't know exactly how to wear one of those things, and she was too embarrassed to ask, so she tossed it to the side.

Once she had finished dressing, she brushed her hair. She wanted it to shimmer tonight, so she left it hanging down her back. She'd had to tuck it up under a cap for so long that it felt good not hiding her female traits. Not that it ever did her any good. The way she saw it, she'd failed as a woman.

Mary couldn't help wondering where she'd be if her horse hadn't thrown her. Probably some small town where she would have bought a house, but she'd still be alone and in trouble. Mary really couldn't remember when she hadn't been in some kind of trouble, but nothing like this. So in the long run, perhaps things had worked out for the best. At least she had Judith to keep her mind off the murder.

Earlier, Judith had told Mary that Carter and Rick would be having supper with them tonight. It would be the first time since she'd arrived that everyone would be present at supper. The men had spent most of the week in town, returning late at night and leaving before Mary had awakened. She often wondered if they were avoiding her, but then she realized that couldn't be possible since they hardly knew she was alive—especially Carter.

No matter, Mary found she was looking forward to seeing them; though, she wasn't sure why. She told herself it was because it would be somebody different to talk to. It had nothing to do with the fact that they were two of the best-looking men she'd ever laid eyes on.

They looked nothing like the grubby miners with their dirt-stained clothes and filthy hands. These two were men in every sense of the word, not that she'd seen all that many men. There were a few on the wagon train that she'd thought were nice looking, especially Hank. He'd given Mary her first kiss, awkward as it was, but when she left the wagon train she'd lost all contact with him.

And, of course, there was her adopted brother Billy. She had been sweet on Billy since she'd first come to the orphanage. They had done everything together, even pranks, like cutting up Brandy's clothes. But as they grew older and had more responsibilities, Mary realized that Billy had grown away from her. He started thinking of her as a sister and nothing more.

It took Mary a long time to realize that Billy was right—they would always have a special bond that no one could break, so she finally accepted him as just her brother.

But it also hurt. Billy had been Mary's first love, no matter how lopsided it had been. What would it be like to be loved and have someone love her back? *An impossible dream.* She sighed. Maybe someday . . . She could always hope.

Mary blinked. She realized she was still brushing her hair, which now glistened like golden threads. Placing her brush on the table, she pulled her hair up on both sides and secured it with gold-colored combs. She peered into the mirror again and pinched her cheeks. That was better, she thought. Satisfied with her appearance, she headed downstairs.

Upon entering the main living quarters, Mary noticed everyone waiting for her. The men stood up as she approached them. Refreshing, Mary thought. At home it would be a race to see who got to the table first.

Rick smiled at Mary. Carter nodded. Evidently he wasn't as happy to see her, or maybe the man never got excited about anything. He'd had the same expression on his sternly handsome face every time she saw him. And it wasn't an expression of pleasure. He was much too serious.

However, Rick looked very glad to see her as he stepped forward and offered his arm. "You look so much healthier since the last time we saw you."

Mary smiled at him. "Judith has taken good care of me." She placed her hand on Rick's arm. She couldn't help but like him, even if he was a lawman. He was just as big as Carter—well, maybe an inch shorter—but Rick seemed to have an open way about him, while Carter . . . well, he seemed to be Carter. She did feel that she understood Carter a little better after talking to his mother, but she still didn't know how to talk to the man.

Judith stood. "It has been a pleasure. I've enjoyed Mary's company very much. It feels good to have another woman in the house." Judith swept her hand toward the dining room. "Shall we?"

Carter had been a little startled to see Mary looking nothing like the woebegone creature he'd brought here, but he snapped out of his bumfuzzlement and escorted his mother to the dining room. He wasn't a man who could have his head turned by a lovely female. However, he couldn't help noticing how much younger his mother seemed, and he knew the reason. Mary was good for his mother, so maybe he hadn't made such a bad decision in bringing a strange woman here with them, though he still wondered why he had.

But what would happen once Mary regained her memory? He didn't want his mother slipping back into the melancholia she had been in since his sister died. It hurt him every time he saw the pain in his mother's eyes, and he felt responsible. He should have protected his sister better.

Once they reached the table, Carter paused and held the chair out for his mother, who sat at the head of the table, and then he took his chair to her right. Rick seated Mary to Judith's left and right across from Carter, and then Rick sat beside Mary.

However, Rick was sitting much too close to Mary, Carter thought. He'd been smiling and acting like a jackass ever since the woman had walked into the room. Carter would have to have a talk with him about fraternizing with the pris—Wait! Mary wasn't a prisoner. Damn if he knew what she was.

Well, no matter, it would be better for them to keep their distance until they knew who Mary really was. He frowned again. Did Rick have to laugh at everything the woman said?

Carter wouldn't deny how beautiful Mary was now that she was clean and dressed well. Her delicate face was framed by a halo of golden hair and the gown she wore brought out the blue in her eyes, making them look like rare jewels twinkling in a face so mysterious that he found himself wanting to know more about her. Not because he knew nothing about her, legally speaking, but because he *wanted* to know about her.

The kitchen staff started bringing in platters of food as if someone had rung a small bell. It had always amazed Carter when he was young just how the servants knew when to bring in the food.

The first dish, pot roast brimming with roasted potatoes, carrots, and onions covered in rich brown gravy, made his mouth water. The servants set a loaf of light bread and a pan of buttermilk biscuits on either side of the table. Bowls of corn and snap beans that his mother had probably canned last summer were the last items to be placed on the snowy white linen cloth.

Carter glanced at his mother. "Thank you."

"For what?" Mary asked before she thought. It really wasn't any of her business, but she hadn't been able to stop her curiosity. Maybe they didn't want her to know what seemed like a private joke between them because Judith was smiling from ear to ear.

"Mother had the cook make all my favorite dishes," Carter explained, and he actually smiled for the first time since Mary had known him.

Maybe it was better if Carter didn't smile, because he was a real charmer when he did, and she knew it was the reason it made her grow warm all over. Finally, she found her voice and squeaked out, "Oh. The only thing missing is apple pie."

"How did you know that was my favorite?" Carter asked.

Mary gave him a saucy smile. "I didn't. It's *my* favorite."

"Aha," Rick said from beside her. "See, you've remembered something already. And I think food is something pretty good to remember. I know it's one of my favorite things."

Mary laughed. "You sound like my little brother." She could have bitten her tongue the minute the words slipped past her lips.

Rick patted her hand. "You're doing good. Anything else you want to tell us?"

Mary's cheeks must have looked like embers in the fireplace, they felt so hot. She knew they were waiting for her to say something more. She'd already glimpsed a sharpness in Carter's eyes that suggested suspicion. He seemed to pick up on every little slip. "I don't remember anything else."

"It's a start, dear," Judith said with an encouraging smile. "And soon, little by little, you'll be able to tell us everything about yourself."

Panic welled in Mary's throat. *I doubt that.* Then she felt bad because Judith was being so nice without knowing anything about her. Mary longed to tell them everything, but she didn't think they would believe her, and she couldn't risk it.

"All right, that is enough questions for Mary," Judith scolded both men. "She'll remember in her own good time. Now, tell me, how is Hank? I haven't seen him in over two weeks with the heavy snow." She shook her head. "That was a nasty bullet hole."

Carter shifted his gaze from Mary to his mother, glad to get his attention on something else. "Hank's still in bed. It seems he was just about ready to start getting around when influenza flattened him again."

"Influenza has been terrible this year. I'm hoping the worst of the outbreak is over. I've helped all that I could. First with Donna, then Mary Sue, plus I've visited a few others with Doc Moore," Judith told them as she buttered her biscuit. She laid her knife down and said, "We've had five people die from this dreadful sickness."

"So we heard," Rick commented. "Pass the roast, please. Thanks," he said as he took the platter. "Today folks seemed to be getting out on the streets again for the first time since we've been here."

"That is good to hear, because two days from now, I'm going to play the piano at the opera house." Judith smiled at the surprised faces. "After dinner, I want you to listen to the piece I've chosen to play."

"You play the piano?" Mary asked.

"She is very good," Carter praised his mother before she could answer. "She always wanted to perform in a big city. However, we never made it any farther than Windy Bend," Carter told Mary, then he addressed his mother. "Do you think it's wise to get out among everyone before the town is fully recovered?"

"We can't stay locked up forever. Besides, I've already been exposed. As you can see, I'm fine. I think music is just what the town needs after this bout of sickness and dreadful weather."

Carter realized that he was fighting a losing battle, so he sat back and listened while they talked about the different songs they liked. It also gave him a chance to study Mary, who'd let a few things slip about herself.

Even though she was lovely all dressed up, he sensed there was more to Mary than frills and ruffles. Most women would fall over in a dead faint as soon as something happened. Somehow, he just couldn't think of Mary being that way. She had grit. He smiled as he remembered Mary had been prepared to take on the devil when she'd first regained consciousness.

She was like a puzzle to him, one he wanted to figure out even if it was piece by piece. Yep, the woman sitting across from him had backbone, and he had a feeling she gave as good as she got, which made her all the more interesting.

Just who was Mary No Name? He watched as she licked a pie crumb from her soft pink lips. He bet those lips would taste much better than the pie.

"The apple pie was wonderful," Mary complimented, and before he could blink she turned to look at him with those wonderful blue eyes of hers. *Just what would you taste like, Mary No Name?*

She must have read his thoughts because she blushed, which left him wondering if she was thinking the same thing. It might be interesting to find out.

Judith slipped her chair back from the table. "Let's retire to the parlor."

In the large living area, which was much bigger than any parlor that Mary had ever seen, everyone found a place to sit. Judith and Carter settled on one of the brown couches and Mary and Rick on another. The décor of the room was in varying shades of brown, from the darkest earth tones of the sofa to the rust-colored chairs. The entire room had a very warm and comfortable feel to it.

The big picture windows gave a good view of the trees and mountains bathed in moonlight, and reminded Mary that it was still cold outside, but beautiful.

A fire blazed in the hearth, giving a warm glow to the surroundings. It was cozy and perfect, Mary thought. Finally, she began to relax and think of the men as other than the enemy.

"When Carter and Lisa were young," Judith began, gaining everyone's attention, "we would tell stories after dinner. I thought that we might like to tell a story while our dinner settles, and then I'll perform my masterpiece."

"What story shall we tell?" Mary asked, warming to the subject. It reminded her of the wonderful stories that Mr. MacTavish told them on the wagon train every night after dinner. It was one of Mary's fondest memories. Thankfully, she kept her thoughts to herself, this time.

"We'll make it up as we go. It will be fun. You'll see." Judith's smile was infectious. "Tell you what, I'll start. Once upon a time in the vast region known as the Colorado Territory, it had been a cold winter and it was snowing so hard that nobody could see a foot in front of them. Oh, how they longed for the warmth of spring."

"Mother, you wouldn't be talking about yourself, would you?" There was a trace of laughter in Carter's voice.

Judith smiled. "Don't interrupt, son, until it's your turn. Now, as I was saying, they longed for spring but that wasn't to be." She nodded to Mary; it was her turn.

"The five children who had just lost their home didn't know which way to go. It was dangerous out there. They could freeze to death or be attacked by wild animals, but they couldn't go back even if they didn't know what lay ahead of them," Mary added and pointed to Carter. He frowned, but evidently he decided to be a good sport. She wondered if the man believed in having fun.

"The oldest, a big, strapping lad, wondered if it would ever stop snowing or if they would die out in the damned cold," Carter grumbled, clearly not into the game.

Mary laughed, and Judith frowned at her son. The man lacked imagination.

Rick was smiling as he took up the story. He had a completely different attitude. "Sounds a bit like you, Carter," he said with a chuckle before he started the story. "Now to make up for your shortcoming, Carter. Let's see . . . then out of nowhere a man on horseback appeared on the top of the next hill. He rode a big, strapping black stallion who was stomping his feet and snorting with impatience. Slowly, the rider started toward the children.

"They gasped as the stranger drew nearer. Who

was this man? Would he kill them? They huddled closer to each other in a small group, shivering and waiting." Rick paused. The two women were staring at him with anticipation. "Shall I go on?"

They nodded.

"Suddenly, the rider was on top of them. He pulled on the reins and the horse halted just before the children were trampled under the mighty beast's hooves. The cowboy shoved back his hat and looked down at the group. 'What are you children doing out here?' he asked in a very deep voice.

"The children answered, 'We're lost.' Slowly the man pulled back his coat. He was going for his gun. 'No!' the children screamed.

"But he hadn't gone for his gun because there upon his chest, shining like the brightest star, was a silver badge. 'I'm a U.S. Marshal, and I'm here to save you.'

"The children cheered and they all lived happily ever after."

Judith and Mary clapped and cheered. "Bravo!"

"You're a born storyteller, Rick," Mary said, praising him.

"I always knew you were born for something," Carter interjected.

"Ah, you're just jealous because I outshined you," Rick shot back with a smile.

"Boys, boys," Judith said. "That was a grand story. Now let's see what you think of the music I've picked out for my program." She rose and went over to the piano situated in front of a large window.

Judith started playing Stephen Foster songs while Mary stood by the piano listening. The beautiful music soon swept Mary off into the melody. Next Judith played "Beautiful Dreamer." Mary began to hum softly.

Judith stopped playing and looked up at Mary. "You know this song?"

Mary nodded.

"Let's start again so that you can sing. Your voice is beautiful, my dear."

The music began. Mary shut her eyes and sang. Her crystal clear voice filled the room as she felt herself relax and float with the music. She'd never felt quite like this, so free and light.

Flabbergasted that such a small woman could have a voice like that, Carter could only sit in awe of her. Her voice was magical, and it made him feel things he really didn't want to feel about the woman. For the moment, he just sat back and enjoyed.

All too soon the music ended, and Judith looked at Mary with a radiant smile. "That was lovely. Where did you get such a voice? You must have sung professionally before."

"Thank you. I don't think so," Mary replied, shaking her head.

"I insist, you must sing with me at the concert hall," Judith said, touching Mary's hand. "Everyone will love you. It will be a special treat for the folks of Windy Bend because this time of year, we don't see many outside folks."

"Do you really think I should?" Mary asked. What if somebody saw her? She bit her lip and then decided she was being paranoid; besides, she didn't want to insult Judith.

"I most certainly do." Judith stood, pulled the lid over the piano keys. "We'll practice tomorrow.

But for now, I believe I'll turn in. I'm feeling a little tired tonight."

"Could I borrow a book from the library?" Mary asked. "Maybe it will help me sleep."

"Of course you can." Judith leaned over and kissed Mary on the cheek. "It's at the other end of the house. Carter will show you and help you get a volume down. Some are quite high."

"I—I don't—" Mary's bluster was cut off by Carter.

"It isn't a bother. Come on."

He was already standing, but Mary hesitated. She wasn't too sure she wanted to be alone with Carter. Something about him scared her. She knew it was silly. She'd been around men all her life. But there was something about this man . . . She looked to Rick, but he was already heading toward the stairs with Judith.

"Are you afraid?" Carter asked in a low voice that sounded more like a challenge.

Mary stiffened and jutted out her chin. "Of course not," she told him. She wasn't afraid of any man.

# Chapter 6

Staying at least one step behind Carter, Mary followed him down the hallway. She preferred to keep him in view.

He opened the library door, and to her surprise the lamps had already been lit and the room was bathed in soft light, making the walnut paneling shimmer. The scent of oak burning in the black marble fireplace made for a cozy room. That was, until she glanced around the room. It was anything but cozy—it was huge and richly decorated.

"Oh my," Mary breathed as she strolled into the room.

Carter turned and smiled. "My family likes to read, as you can see." He raised his arm in a sweeping gesture to show off the surroundings. "There are many books to choose from."

"I should say so," Mary said as she glanced around. Three walls were nothing but bookshelves from floor to ceiling, stuffed with rich leather-bound books. She could remember the bookshelf back home that contained maybe thirty books; Mary had thought that was a lot, but this room must contain thousands.

The hardwood floors were covered with a burgundy and cream-colored rug. The fragrance of lemon oil floated in the air and gave freshness to the room. There was a long sofa in cream and two overstuffed chairs in the same rich burgundy, matching the rug perfectly.

"Help yourself to any of the books," Carter said in that deep rich voice she was becoming accustomed to and liking more each day. "What do you like to read?"

Mary's back was to Carter, so he couldn't see her smile. He was testing her, she decided, trying to trick her into revealing something about herself. She thought deep down Carter was already suspicious that she knew more than she was letting on. Slowly, she turned and looked at him. "I don't know. What do you suggest?"

Carter actually smiled, showing Mary how handsome he really was. Masculine strength was carved into his strong chin. Those black eyes of his were piercing and gave no hint what he was thinking. But Mary would have loved to know what Carter thought about her. Did he think she was even a little attractive? Probably not. He didn't seem to notice she was a woman at all.

"I'm not good on suggestions unless you want a book on firearms. The other day, Mother said that she'd read a book she liked very much." Carter shut one eye as he tried to remember the title. "Let me see"—he leaned against the desk and folded his arms across his chest—"the title was . . . little something." He thought for another moment. "*Little Women* or something similar.

"I tell you what." He shoved away from the desk.

"You start at that end and I'll start at this end, and we'll see if we can spot the title."

"All right," Mary agreed. She looked at the many books. She still couldn't comprehend having the time to sit and read them all. Her life up to now had been filled with work, and at the end of the day she had always been too tired to think about reading. Come to think of it, she really hadn't had much of a life over the last two years. Oh, she'd accomplished her goal of making the mine successful, for all the good it did her now. Other than that, she had nothing but rough hands to show for her hard work. But all that was in the past.

If she could clear her name, she would turn the mine over to someone else to run. Then she'd try to start a new life, a real life, somewhere. There must be some man out there for her, someone who could hold her interest. However, if she were anything like her mother, she might be destined to live alone. Her mother had always been sure that some man was going to fall in love and rescue her from the whorehouse, but all she'd ever gotten were empty promises.

Mary didn't want to live like that. She didn't want to ever be dependent on anyone. It was the uncertainty of giving her heart to someone that scared her most of all. She didn't want empty promises from a man, nor did she want her heart broken.

"You're quiet," Carter said, startling Mary so much that she jumped.

She blinked a couple of times, then realized she'd been staring at the same book for the last few minutes. "I was just wondering what my life was like. Somehow I don't think it was very interesting."

"That isn't something we'll know until your memory returns," Carter said, but he didn't bother to turn her way as he searched for the book. "You could have a husband desperately searching for you."

"I doubt that," Mary automatically replied. "Unless he is the one who dumped me in the snow." She couldn't help laughing aloud.

*Must keep Carter off track,* she reminded herself.

She looked over her left shoulder and found Carter looking her way. "I think I'd know if I were married." She held up her left hand. "See, there is no ring, and no sign that one has been there."

Carter arched a doubtful eyebrow.

Mary ignored him and went back to looking, running her fingers across the leather-bound tomes as her gaze traveled over each title in search of *Little Women.* Was that it up above her head? She took a step backwards to see better and bumped into Carter; she hadn't realized he was standing right behind her. She felt his hard chest against her back and her pulse leapt with excitement.

He was so tall she felt as though he could swallow her up if he wanted to. "I'm sorry," she apologized.

She didn't dare turn around to look at Carter. He radiated vitality that drew her like a magnet, and if he could do that without her looking at his face, into his eyes . . . heaven help her if she faced him.

"I think I've spotted your book. Hold still," he said in that deep voice that made her breath catch in her throat.

It was a darn good thing she wasn't attracted to him or she'd be in real trouble.

Carter loomed over her as he reached two shelves up to extract a fat brown book. His body was pressed against hers, causing shivers of excitement to run up and down her spine, and an even more terrifying realization washed over Mary—she had been lying to herself, for she was very attracted to this man.

She could feel his warm breath on her cheek, and if she turned just so, she had no doubt that she'd be able to feel his lips.

*Oh God, the temptation.*

As soon as she'd thought about turning, Carter stepped back, and Mary was dismayed at the loss of his heat burning against her—and at the magnitude of her desire. She wanted to yield to the burning sweetness she'd felt by his mere touch. She wasn't sure why. She didn't care anything about the man, she told herself. Surely, this attraction must be mere curiosity. But curiosity could get her into more trouble than she was already in.

She had to control herself. So she drew a deep breath for courage and turned.

The expression in Carter's eyes was so galvanizing that it sent a tremor through her. For a long moment, they just stared at each other, saying nothing.

What would it be like to be kissed by Carter? To feel his lips on her neck? She wondered as Carter's dark eyes held her. She wasn't sure what to do or say, but someone had to say something.

Mary thought she'd seen something very inviting in Carter's gaze. Too inviting, and considering the strange way she felt at this moment, it was better that she not accept his invitation. "Th-thank you for getting the book for me," Mary finally managed to get out.

But invitation to what? She didn't know.

"No problem," he said in a voice that sounded

as raspy and strained as her own. "Are you going to your room now?"

"I—if it's all right, I'd like to stay here and read until I get sleepy."

"Help yourself," Carter replied as he turned to go. "I'm going to get some shut-eye. See you in the morning."

After Carter left, Mary had to take several deep breaths just to regain her composure. She wasn't certain what had just happened between them, but it was something she'd never experienced with anyone else. It was almost frightening—like she'd been caught in an erratic summer storm.

Finally, Mary snapped to and took her book to the couch. She placed several pillows on the end, plumped them, then settled down with a small sigh into the comfort of the goose down pillows.

It sure beat a seat in a covered wagon. Mary closed her eyes and thought back for a moment. There had been days she'd believed she'd never get off that wagon, and as she thought back she realized that time had actually been one of the more interesting in her life.

Mary shivered in the chill of the big, empty room, so she slipped off her shoes and tucked her feet under her on the couch, then pulled the cream-colored afghan over her. The fleecy blanket warmed her, and she wondered what it would have felt like to have Carter tuck that afghan around her.

The fire crackled in the fireplace, and somewhere in the hallway a grandfather clocked chimed at the same time as the clock over the mantel announced the hour. She counted each chime. It was ten o'clock, and aside from the clocks, the rest of the house was quiet. She assumed that the servants had gone to bed, too.

She thought back. She really couldn't remember when she'd ever been completely alone, except maybe when she'd been with her mother. When her mother had entertained gentleman callers, Mary had been forced to stay in the kitchen. She'd had one small corner that was all her own. Several patched quilts were placed on the floor and that was where she played with her imaginary friends until she got sleepy. Those blankets had been her world for a long time. She could remember grabbing the satin edge of one of the blankets and rubbing it between her fingers until she fell asleep.

Mary shook her head to dislodge the memory. That was the past. Looking around the room, she had to think that things could only get better.

Opening the book, Mary began to read page after page, trying to engross herself in the crisp black words on the yellowish paper, but after a while she gave up. Her mind had too many thoughts running through it to concentrate on the story. Finally, she rested the book on her chest and leaned her head back against the fluffy pillows.

Here she was lounging in comfort while Big Jim was dead. She felt bad that she wasn't any closer to figuring out what had happened than she had been several days ago. She'd been so confused ever since she'd awakened in the arms of the marshal.

Now that was something she could write a book about—waking in the arms of a strange cowboy.

What made the marshal tick? Mary wondered. She had learned that he was a man of principle, but would he ever consider compromising? Could he ever look the other way and not arrest her?

She didn't think so.

Mary wasn't even sure what she was doing here,

living with people she barely knew. At first, she had convinced herself that it was because she needed time to heal. She'd been here over a week and the knot on her head had gone down. But she was still here, having made no plans to leave.

She couldn't just ride out. Carter would want to know where she was headed. And what could Mary tell him when she wasn't supposed to know her identity? Yet, she couldn't stay either. Her dilemma overwhelmed her every time she thought about it, so as usual she put off thinking about it.

Right this minute, Mary's eyelids were so heavy that she could barely keep them open. Maybe if she could close them for just a minute while she tried to remember the pieces of her last day at Gregory Gulch, she'd feel better.

Slowly, Mary began to drift off. Drowsiness claimed her, and the warmth of the blanket made her feel secure. Deeper and deeper she sank until she could see Gregory Gulch in her mind's eye.

That morning had begun like most mornings. She'd fixed gravy and hot buttermilk biscuits with black strap molasses for breakfast. After the third helping, Big Jim had asked, "How long you gonna do this, gal?"

Not understanding what he meant, Mary had given him a confused look and asked, "Do what?"

Jim licked the molasses from his fingers before answering. "How long you gonna keep hiding in these mountains working yourself to death?"

"But you're here," she pointed out.

"Reckon you're right, gal. But I'm an old man. You, on the other hand, are a right pretty filly that some man should make his wife."

"I suppose I have worked a lot. But what else do I have, Jim?" Mary replied.

"That's the point, gal. You'll never know what you can have as long as yer working up here with old men. Before long you'll be as old as I am."

"I think you're trying to get rid of me," Mary teased.

"Naw. Just want what's best for you. True enough, I'd miss you once you were gone." Jim tore a biscuit apart and sopped up some molasses. "But I've seen you work your hands until they bleed, and I don't want to see you break the rest of your body until they match your hands." He looked up at her. "You're still young."

"I know you're right, but I need a little more money before I call it quits."

Jim let out a long, audible breath. "There's never enough money to be had when the prospect of more money is out there."

Mary shook her head. "It's different with me. I've never had anything of my own. I always wore clothes the people from town didn't want anymore. My sister has money, but that is hers. I want my own. I want to be independent and in control of my own destiny. I'm not going to wait around for some man to discover me."

"And what are you going to do with your money?"

"I want to live like everyone else and be normal. I want a small house." She smiled, then added, "One with a little white fence running around it."

"I hate to tell you, lass, but I just can't see you as being ordinary." He chuckled. "How about kids?"

"I'm not sure. I've never thought about them. I can't imagine getting married." Mary sighed.

"Ah, gal, do you not realize how lovely you are? One day a man will simply take your breath away, and then you'll be wanting to get yourself hitched."

"I couldn't count on that, Jim. But if there is

someone, he's going to have to be one hell of a man to turn my head." Mary laughed. "I'm pretty headstrong, in case you haven't noticed."

This time Jim laughed. "He's out there somewhere, and I bet when you first meet him, you won't like him one dang bit," Jim said as he stood. "Let's go find some gold so you can find your cowboy."

"I'll just settle for the gold," Mary grumbled, following behind Jim.

As they trudged toward the mine, Jim said, "Did I tell you that sorry brother of mine thinks he wants to start working the mine? Got a letter from him the other day. Said business was slow and he needed something to do."

"Are you going to let him?"

"Don't know. He always tends to take the easy way out of things. We've never really got along, but I guess he is my brother—or I should say half brother—so I gotta consider it. Reckon kin is kin."

Mary punched Jim in the arm. "Maybe you'll be lucky and he won't show up."

As her thoughts drifted, she could see herself and Jim working in the mine. Her next memory was of her entering the front door of their cabin. Jim had gone ahead of her. When she entered the cabin a stranger stood up, but he was in the shadows and she couldn't see his face.

"Mary, I have a surprise for you," Jim had said.

Mary's dream faded to black. She couldn't remember any more of what happened until she woke up with the knife in her hand. She saw the blood. She saw Jim. Dead. Lifeless. No, Jim, no!

She began to scream, "I didn't do it. I didn't do it. You must believe me, I didn't do it!"

Someone was shaking her, and Mary fought

against the restraining arms. "No! No!" she yelled over and over again.

For Carter, sleep was elusive. For some reason, he couldn't get Mary off his mind. Every time he closed his eyes, he could hear her voice, and worse, he could picture her sitting across from him with that golden mass of hair tumbling over her shoulders, begging him to touch the silken strands.

That was enough. He tossed the covers aside and slid out of bed. He slipped on his breeches and his shirt but didn't bother with his boots. Maybe he'd just check on Mary. He shouldn't have left her all alone.

Carter had just entered the downstairs hallway when he heard Mary cry out. Alarmed, he ran to the library and shoved the door open. He'd kill any sidewinder that hurt her, but what he found wasn't a sidewinder. Mary was on the couch thrashing about and yelling she didn't do it.

Do what, he wondered.

He strode across the room in no time and sank quickly onto the sofa. He shook her shoulders, gently at first, but Mary was sleeping so soundly that she didn't wake. Instead, she fought him and cried out, "Please, I didn't do it!"

Carter wrapped his arms tightly around her and crushed her against him, forcing her to be still. "Wake up, Mary." Carter tried to sound calm, but he realized he was breathing hard from his struggles. "It's Carter. I won't hurt you. You're having a bad dream."

Mary still struggled, which made him wonder what terrible thing had happened to her that it lurked just beneath the surface waiting to be released. "Wake up, Mary."

Finally, she stilled. Her eyelids fluttered open and she leaned back to look at him. Tears streamed down her cheeks and she appeared truly to be frightened. The fear was plain in her eyes as she blinked at him, totally confused.

"Shh. It was just a bad dream, I'm here," Carter soothed as Mary trembled in his arms. "Everything will be all right."

Mary cried harder, and Carter cradled her face between his palms, forcing her to look at him. "Look at me, Mary. Look at me. I promise I won't let anyone hurt you."

She managed a small nod and then threw her arms around him. He enfolded her in his arms, soothing her as he shifted around until his back was against the couch and Mary was pulled across his lap. He held her, rubbing his hand over her back to calm her down. Every once in awhile, he leaned down and brushed her cheek with his lips while he whispered, "Hush. I don't want you to cry."

Some time later she finally calmed down, but she didn't try to pull away from him and he didn't push her away. Mary evidently had a lot of pain and fear that had been penned up in her for a long time. Carter knew she'd be exhausted after such a crying spell. He probably should leave her— but he couldn't. He was well aware of the intense hunger that devoured him with every passing minute. But he swore he'd never let her see the depths of his passion. Yes, he should probably leave this room immediately.

But he didn't.

Mary waited for her breathing to return to normal. She couldn't remember ever crying like that before, but she couldn't seem to stop herself, either. She couldn't hold in the grief any longer, and being able to get it all out was a relief. All the same, she was embarrassed that Carter had to find her this way. She pulled back to apologize, but stopped when she saw the expression in his eyes. He had tipped his chin down to look at her, and what Mary saw took her breath away. It wasn't a look of impatience. He wore a tender expression on his face as if he felt her pain.

She tightened her hand around Carter's neck and lifted her chin so that her mouth would meet his lips. She wanted to forget her pain and experience something, though she wasn't sure what. She brushed his mouth slightly, and he pulled her closer, kissing her softly at first before becoming demanding. It took Mary by surprise. A sudden flood of tenderness overwhelmed her. When his tongue touched her lips, she gasped, and he took advantage of the opening.

She had been kissed a couple of times in her life, but never like this. It was so different from anything she'd ever known. She was lost in pure sensation, and she forgot about Carter being the enemy. He was flesh and blood like herself, and Mary sensed a need in him that matched her own. She saw in his eyes a haunted expression. Could he be looking for something he didn't have, just as she was?

This was the first sign she'd seen that Carter possessed any kind of emotions at all. He'd always seemed so cold, so in control. Mary might be naive but she felt that he was experiencing something more than just lust for her.

Carter was experiencing something . . .

He felt as though he'd been slammed in the gut with a sledgehammer. For the last few years Carter had visited the local whorehouse when his needs arose, a process that had worked well for him. It had been a quick, simple relief and there had been no emotions involved.

But once he pulled Mary into his arms, he hadn't been able to turn on that numbing feeling that he had always been so good at. He felt every inch of her. He smelled her scent. Her heart beat in a rhythm that matched his, and somehow he was slipping rapidly under her spell. Even at the height of passion Carter had never experienced the hot, intense longing that he did now. What would it feel like to bury himself deep into Mary until she was clinging to his shoulders, whispering his name over and over again?

It was something he'd probably never know.

Finally Carter realized he had to put a stop to this. It was the right thing to do. For all he knew, the girl could be married, and he still had two outlaws to catch before be could even consider a future with her. Or anyone.

"I'm sorry, Mary," Carter finally said, pulling back even though his body ached for more. He could see her passion-filled eyes that turned his blood into liquid fire. "I took advantage of you."

It took a moment before Mary could think straight. Then Carter's words sank in. She was pretty sure she'd just been insulted. He was sorry for kissing her, and that meant he felt nothing for her. So what else should she expect? She didn't deserve love.

"I'm sorry, too," Mary said in a low voice. "But I was so scared . . ."

"I know," Carter acknowledged, pulling her closer. "We'll just forget that it happened."

Carter said one thing but did another, Mary noticed as he kept her snug within his arms. She placed her head on his chest and her eyes drifted shut. What would it feel like to one day have someone who cared about her?

Mary had always believed that she would never find out. This brief moment might be all she'd ever have.

Because she'd lose what ground she gained as soon as Carter linked her to the murder.

# Chapter 7

So now what?

Those were the words screaming through Mary's brain as she opened one bleary eye. All right, so she'd had a moment of weakness last night, but what part of last night was real and what part was a dream?

She sat up in bed and brushed the hair out of her face. Touching her lips, she knew from their tenderness that the kisses had been very real— sleeping with Carter had been the dream. All night she had dreamed of the man and his caresses.

She supposed there wasn't any harm in dreaming. As long as she didn't act upon those dreams, she'd be all right. Then she realized how stupid it was to let her thoughts wander down that path when they would only bring her nothing but trouble.

Someone needed to knock some sense into her. How could she have even thought about sleeping with the man? And how was she going to face him this morning? Especially now that he knew she was mere putty in his hands.

And why him?

She'd never desired any man. She loved Billy, she always would, but now she realized what she felt for him was different than what she felt for Carter, so why did she have to pick a man with a badge?

Maybe she was going crazy.

At least, when they both had come to their senses—all right, so it was Carter who'd come to his senses. She probably wouldn't have.

He'd said it was a mistake, and she had agreed. Well, what else could she have done? She had believed that the kisses were enjoyable, but he apparently thought it had been a mistake. It must have been a completely different experience for him. He did promise that it would never happen again. And now in the bright light of day, she knew she'd never kiss him again. It was just plain foolishness.

However, Mary couldn't help wondering if he'd felt any pleasure. Was she a complete failure as a woman?

She shook her head. Not that it mattered. Maybe it was better that she didn't know. What would knowing do?

She swung out of bed convinced that she really needed to get out of Windy Bend. She was becoming much too comfortable at the ranch. But how could she get away? She had no money or at least not with her. If she took a horse, they could hang her for horse thieving, and she had enough trouble without adding anything else on top of it.

Maybe there would be some way she could be alone and go to town. Then she could wire Brandy and Thunder to send her some money.

She'd just have to be patient for once in her life.

\* \* \*

Mary shouldn't have worried about what Carter would say. When she saw him at breakfast, he acted as if she didn't exist. It sure wasn't anything like he'd acted last night.

He didn't even look at her. In fact, as soon as she came in, he excused himself and left the dining room.


Carter couldn't get out of the house fast enough this morning. How had he let that girl get to him? Maybe he'd been too long without a woman and it would probably have happened with any woman. That was it. There. Now he felt much better as he walked out onto the porch and the cold, damp air cleared his head. Since it was raining, he slipped his slicker on over his head, then settled his Stetson securely onto his head and headed to the stables.

The rain would wash away the last of the snow and show them all that spring was just around the corner. Maybe when he could get out and do some physical labor, he could expel some of this pent-up energy he'd built up over the winter.

Rick had already ridden into town. Now Carter was glad that he'd sent Rick ahead. It would give him some time alone, and this morning he needed the time to think. He just couldn't shake off last night.

When he'd left Mary and returned to his room, all he'd done was toss and turn because Mary kept intruding on his sleep. But it wasn't just the lack of sleep that was bothering him today. Nothing seemed to bring him any satisfaction. It was as if there were a restless animal within him. He was tired of chasing bad guys and never being in one place longer than a week or two at the most. Coming home had made him take a good look at his life . . . and there wasn't much to it, he decided.

Maybe he could let Rick take over the town and then he could go after Sammy Carson. He was the one who'd snatched his sister. Once that score was settled, then maybe he could rest easy.

*And the girl?* his conscience asked.

All right, so he couldn't keep the girl completely out of his thoughts. Last night had been a moment of weakness, but she had looked so—so damn innocent and scared that the need to comfort her had overwhelmed him. She'd felt too good in his arms. That he couldn't deny.

Mary was a beautiful woman, but it wasn't just her beauty that drew him to her. There was something different about her. That inner spark he'd glimpsed lurking beneath the surface intrigued him.

What made Mary tick?

He might never know, and since he had just ridden onto Main Street, he didn't have any more time to think about Miss Mary Noname.

Carter guided his horse, Blue, over to the livery to keep the animal out of the heavy downpour. There wasn't any need to make his horse miserable—one of them was bad enough.

Carter kept his head down against the driving rain as he made his way to the jailhouse, letting the rain run off the brim of his hat and down his slicker. He opened the door and sought out the promise of a dry room.

"Sleep late?" Rick asked with a grin.

Carter grimaced as he slipped off his hat, hit it a couple of times against his chaps to shake off the water, then hung it on a chair post. Next, he pulled his slicker over his head and draped it over the other chair back. They should dry quickly near the potbellied stove. "I'm not that late," he finally grumbled.

"I heard you up walking last night. Figured something must be on your mind, keeping you awake," Rick said as he reared back in his chair and popped a piece of straw in his mouth.

Carter ignored Rick's needling and glanced at Hank. "I see you're out of bed."

"Darn tootin'," Hank O'Tool said with a weak grin. "Two weeks in bed is enough to drive any man plumb loco. How about pouring you and me a cup of coffee?" He held up his tin cup.

Carter took the cup then grabbed another off the shelf before going over to the potbelly stove where the silver coffee pot was percolating. He grabbed a rag and picked up the pot to pour the coffee. A little spilled on the stove with a loud hiss as the bubbles danced along the hot surface.

Hank still looked a little peaked, Carter thought, but he guessed that was to be expected after what the man had been through.

Hank still had the kind face that Carter remembered from when he was growing up. Hank's heavy mustache was a little grayer to match the gray in the sides of his hair, but he was still a tough lawman and held the respect of the folks of Windy Bend. When Hank did decide to retire, he'd be hard to replace.

Carter handed Hank a cup of strong, black coffee, then took a seat in front of him. "You probably should be careful not to overdo it today."

"Now you sound like your ma," Hank grumbled, though his grin countered his gruff voice.

Carter chuckled. "You should know by now that she's always right."

"Kind of like her son," Hank said with a smile. "How is the old gal? Haven't seen her in a couple of weeks."

"She's pretty happy at the moment." Carter looked at Rick and gave him a sly wink. "Wouldn't you say so?"

Rick nodded in agreement. "Heck, yeah. She's sure been smiling a lot."

Hank sat up a little straighter and drew his brows together. "How come?"

Carter shouldn't be pulling Hank's leg since he'd been so sick, but he knew that Hank had been sweet on his mother for a very long time. "Well, Hank, it's like this." Carter leaned forward, propping his elbows on his knees. "I brought someone home with me and Mother has taken a real liking to them."

"She hardly noticed me and Carter at all," Rick added as he let his chair fall back to the floor. "Sorry, Hank, you've been replaced."

"It ain't fair," Hank stated. "Just let me get laid up a little bit and she forgets all about me. Just like a blamed woman. Once she gets you interested, then she moves to greener pastures."

Carter couldn't hold his smile any longer. "I didn't say she'd forgotten about you."

"Well, what would you call it? Who is the fellow?"

Carter waited for a moment until Hank's face was good and red. "Mary," he said, struggling to hide a grin.

"What the hell?" Hank swore, and slammed his cup on the desk, splattering the coffee over the old, brown wood, then swore some more as the hot coffee hit his hand.

Carter and Rick laughed as Hank glared sourly at both of them.

"You good for nothing mangy dogs!"

"Ah, come on, Hank, where's your sense of humor?" Carter asked, rocking back on two chair legs.

"So who is this Mary?"

"The prettiest little thing you've ever seen," Rick said.

"Does this mean Carter—" Hank paused.

"No, it doesn't. This is a girl we found lost in a snowbank," Carter said. Then he filled Hank in on the rest of the story.

Hank finally said, "So what are you going to do about her?"

"I don't know," Carter said. "I can only hope that her memory comes back soon."

The lovely green gown hung invitingly on the wardrobe door. Mary had never seen such a pretty dress, and she was reluctant to try it on. It was the one Judith had picked out for her to wear tonight.

As she stood in front of the dress feeling the texture of the fine material between her fingers, someone knocked on the door. "Come in," Mary called over her shoulder.

"The dress will do you no good hanging on the door," Judith scolded with a smile. "You need to be dressing, so you can charm everyone at the opera house."

"It's so lovely, I'm afraid I'll mess it up," Mary said.

"Nonsense. It's just cloth and material. It will wash. Now come along and put on your bustle."

Mary slipped off her plain brown skirt and placed it on the bed. "I've never worn a bustle before."

"Then it is time for you to start," Judith told her as she picked up the contraption. "You see"—she squeezed the humped-looking thing—"this is nothing but gathered silk taffeta. It's lightweight and sits behind you like this." She demonstrated the proper sitting technique, flipping the bustle up to keep from squashing it, then wrapped the ribbons around Mary's waist and tied them. "There we go. Now your gown will hang much prettier."

"It feels funny." Mary laughed as she wiggled her hips. "Why do I need one?"

"It's known as fashion, my dear." Judith cast an eye over Mary. "In many ways you're very much like a child who's never dressed up before."

"I'm not sure I ever have," Mary admitted. She held her arms up so Judith could slip the dress on over her head.

The silk slid with a rustle down Mary's body. It felt so soft and smooth against her skin. The only clothing she had ever known was made of cotton and wool.

Judith brushed the skirts down and jerked at the pleats until she had the dress just right. Then she announced, "It fits perfectly. Now, let me pin your hair up and we'll be ready. Sit down here." She pointed to a stool.

Mary took a quick look at her reflection in the mirror as she sat down. The woman who stared back looked nothing like the Mary she was used to seeing. The color of the gown made her complexion look soft and creamy. "This is such a vivid color. What is it called?"

"Dragon green," Judith replied as she rolled Mary's hair around her fingers. "See, it has a cuirass bodice." Judith pointed at the dress. "And a pronounced train on the skirt. It was designed in France and brought over here for Lisa. Unfortunately, she never got to wear it. However, green becomes you, my dear. You look very fetching. See how gold your hair appears? There will be many men's hearts fluttering tonight."

"I doubt that, but thank you just the same," Mary said, trying not to look skeptical. "Are Carter and Rick going with us tonight?"

"Most certainly. They are waiting downstairs for us right now. There." Judith patted Mary's curls. "Perfect."

Mary tossed her head and a cascade of ringlets fell over her left shoulder. She had to admit she did feel pretty. What would Carter think about the transformation? She shrugged. Well, she really didn't care what he thought.

Judith sighed and seemed suddenly to sag. "I believe I'll sit down for a moment." She walked over to a chair and sat down, then she leaned back and rested her head.

Mary stood. "Are you feeling all right?" She noted that Judith's color was very pale. "Maybe we shouldn't go out, after all."

"Of course we should. I'm just a little dizzy, probably from all the rush and excitement. Just give me a moment and I'll feel fine. If you'll look at the far end of the wardrobe, you'll find a winter cloak to keep you warm." She gestured in the direction of the wardrobe.

Mary located the dark brown garment and folded it over her arm. "Are you sure you're up to going out tonight?"

"I wouldn't miss it," Judith said as she rose and headed out of the room with Mary following her.

When Mary rounded the corner, she spotted Carter with his elbow propped upon the mantel, talking to Rick.

Carter looked magnificent. His black suit and crisp white shirt made him appear extremely dashing. His bright red vest provided just the touch of color he needed.

When he caught sight of Mary, he made no effort to disguise the look of admiration in his eyes. He stared at her quite openly, with the same hungry look she'd seen just before he'd kissed her. Was he thinking of that kiss? She felt her body flush at the memories as she returned his stare, unable to look away. Slowly Carter lowered his eyelids, until his eyes seemed hooded and she could no longer read his thoughts. Just what did Carter think of her, she wondered.

Rick didn't bother to hide any of his emotions. He stood with a grin and gleam of admiration in his eyes. "Ladies, you look grand indeed."

"Thank you, sir," Judith said. "You gentlemen look mighty fine yourselves. I can't remember when I've not seen you with guns strapped to your sides."

"Rest assured they will be close by," Rick said.

Judith turned to Carter. "We should probably be going now."

Carter pushed away from the fireplace. "The buggy is out front."

Mary slipped on her cloak, assisted gallantly by Rick, while Carter opened the door. "You have a buggy?"

"Yes," Judith answered as she preceded Mary out the door. "What do you think?"

"It is very nice," Mary said. Parked in front of the house was a sleek black buggy that had two seats instead of one. The backseat was completely covered by the canopy; the front seat was partially covered. Rick and Judith climbed into the buggy first, so they could sit in the rear.

Mary didn't have much of a choice but to sit next to Carter. He helped her up, then walked around to the driver's seat and took his place. Someone had heated bricks for their feet, and they felt good against her toes as she rested her kid pumps on the bricks. Carter tossed a quilt over their legs and picked up the reins. He looked at Mary. "Are you ready?"

Mary nodded.

Carter flicked the leather straps and the buggy lurched forward. There were three ranch hands riding in front of them. Mary looked at Carter, arching an eyebrow in question. Carter explained that since they lived a ways from town, there was always safety in numbers. She knew firsthand how harsh the West could be.

She felt the red velvet cushions beneath her and marveled at the very smooth ride. "This is a very nice buggy," Mary commented. "The only thing I've ever ridden in is a buckboard. And it doesn't ride anything like this."

Carter glanced quickly at her and Mary realized too late that she'd slipped again. She did everything she could to keep from looking guilty at the slip as she looked away from him.

"My husband, Thomas," Judith said from behind Mary, "insisted that I have a buggy. He said he didn't want to see his wife driving a buckboard. And with Thomas, everything had to be the best."

It was the first time Mary had heard any mention of Carter's father. She wondered what had happened to the man, but figured it was none of her business. "He certainly had good taste."

"In all things," Judith admitted with a sigh. "I still miss him a great deal, but at least I have Carter. He looks so much like his father that, at times, I feel as though I'm staring at Thomas."

"I'm sorry I didn't get a chance to meet him," Mary said. "Was he a lawman, too?"

"Thomas was a cattleman," Judith said. Mary could hear the pride in her voice. "He was killed in a stampede the year before Lisa's death."

"Those years must have been hard," Mary said.

There was a moment of silence before Carter said, "Now that the weather is clearing"—he paused as he maneuvered the buggy around a hole—"you'll get to see some of the cattle we own."

"Really?" Mary glanced at Carter and felt all warm and tingly inside. There was something seductive in the way he looked tonight. She could feel his leg pressed next to hers, and she could sense the tension coiled in him as if he wanted to leap up at a moment's notice. She wondered if the man ever relaxed. Was he always on alert, watching, waiting for the next incident to occur? If so, Carter's life was as boring as hers. Maybe they were more alike than she realized. "How many head of cattle do you have?"

"A few thousand," Carter answered.

"That sounds like a lot to me."

"Not really, but it is a good start."

"Would you believe that Carter prefers to chase bad guys than cattle?" Rick asked.

"No, I can't," Mary said, "but I'm sure he has his reasons."

Carter couldn't explain the strange feeling that swept over him. She had actually taken up for him, and he appreciated it.

"I'm hoping one day he'll come home for good," Judith said.

Mary glanced at Carter from beneath her lashes and she could see him tensing up as if he were fighting a battle within himself. How could she penetrate the deliberate blankness of his eyes? She reached over and placed her hand on his arm. For some unexplained reason, she needed to touch him.

Carter didn't turn her way, but he did take her hand in his, causing her stomach to flutter as if a thousand butterflies had been released.

"What are you going to do once the sheriff is on his feet again?" Mary asked. She really hadn't thought about Carter leaving, but she knew he couldn't stay here forever. But would he take her with him? There would be no reason for him to stay in Windy Bend unless he was going to work the ranch, and the way he felt about his job more than guaranteed he wouldn't be staying.

"I'm not sure," Carter admitted. "There's been some trouble at Pikes Peak. Heard tell that they are having a hard time solving a murder. May mosey up there and help out."

"I—I see," Mary managed to get out as each little butterfly in her stomach died. What was he going to do when he discovered that the solution to the mystery was sitting next to him? She bit her lip and stared straight ahead. She didn't want to know the answer.

"What happened?" Judith asked.

"A murder. It seems one partner got greedy for the gold and murdered the other partner. Carved him up real bad," Carter explained.

"Are they sure that's what happened?" Mary

blurted out. If Carter thought that way, then so did everyone else. "Sometimes things look one way but are not what they appear."

Carter turned to her, and Mary was thankful that it wasn't broad daylight. "Possibly," he finally admitted, then added, "a good lawman always checks out every possibility."

"Glad to hear it," Mary said, and then cursed herself silently for not keeping her mouth shut. Up ahead, she could see the town lights and not too soon, for her. At least the topic of conversation would change.

As they drove down Main Street, Mary was surprised at how large Windy Bend looked. It wasn't as big as Denver, but it was a good-sized city compared to most little towns. "What is that?" Mary asked.

"It's the Victor, our newest five-story hotel," Carter told her.

"It boasts one hundred fifty guest rooms," Judith added.

Mary gazed at the hotel. "It is hard to believe that you have so many visitors to this small town."

"After the gold strike two years ago, the town has been growing," Judith said.

As they continued down the street, Mary noticed the lampposts with gaslights on top of each one. They lit up the entire street. In the middle of town the Butte Opera House stood, an impressive three-story brick building nestled between all the wooden structures.

Carter pulled back on the reins. "I'll help you ladies out, and then I'll park the buggy down at the livery." He jumped down and walked over to his men. "You boys enjoy yourselves for a few hours. Just be sure you stay out of trouble."

"Yes, boss," they said with a nod, and rode off down the street.

"Carter, you go with the ladies, and I'll park the buggy," Rick suggested.

"Fine," Carter replied as he reached up to help Mary down. She hadn't taken one step before she was jerked roughly back. Her skirt had caught on something.

She tugged on her skirt. "I'm afraid I'm stuck."

Carter chuckled. Then he reached around Mary and pulled the material free. "There you go."

His closeness heated her face more than any fire could. "Thank you," Mary murmured.

Carter offered his arms to both women, "Ladies." One on each side and holding his arms, they walked into the building past a man taking up money.

Mary looked around Carter to Judith. "People are paying good money to hear us sing?"

"Yes, they are, a whole thirty-five cents. The money goes to keep the opera house in good condition," Judith said. She glanced up at her son. "Did Hank say that he was coming tonight?"

"Yes, he did. He's still moving a little slow, but I'm sure he will perk up when he sees you after the performance."

"Well, then." Judith stopped and turned toward a hallway that seemed to lead behind the stage. "We'll see you after the performance."

Carter leaned down and kissed his mother on the cheek. "Good luck. We'll be in the fifth row."

Mary sighed. "Good. I might need rescuing if the audience starts throwing things."

Carter and Judith both laughed, and then Carter said, "Not a chance. I've heard you sing."

Mary watched him walk away. He'd actually given her a compliment, but he hadn't kissed her on the cheek. She quickened her steps to catch up with Judith. Carter probably hadn't realized what he was saying.

Mary followed Judith as she walked down a short hallway to the back of the stage, growing more nervous with every step. She prayed she wasn't going to embarrass herself when she stepped out on stage.

She also prayed that no one would jump up and holler, "Murderer!" And at that thought, she realized she was doing a very foolish thing.

# Chapter 8

Backstage, Mary stood next to Judith while she chatted with some of the locals who acted as stage-hands during performances at the opera house. Judith explained what she and Mary would be doing, and two of the men moved a piano into place.

The murmur of voices grew on the other side of the curtain as the auditorium filled. Mary thought about peeking out between the curtains to see how many people were out front, but then reconsidered. She was already nervous enough. She just might flee if she saw a bunch of strangers staring at her.

"How many seats are out there?" Mary asked.

"A thousand," Judith said without a second thought. Then she had the stagehands push the piano again, to where Judith thought that they would have better lighting.

Mary wished she hadn't asked. She clasped her hands together to keep them from shaking as she glanced around, trying to keep her mind off her jitters. The theater was impressive. It looked like something she imagined one would find in a city like Boston or New York. Mary had read about such places, but never dreamed she'd be performing in such an impressive building.

There were several men milling about, checking on the curtains. She was watching them when she caught a glimpse of a stranger in a green plaid coat standing in a corner, apparently doing nothing but staring at her. His hair was slicked back with pomade and he was smiling at her.

*A plaid coat?*

Her heart raced. Quickly, she looked away. What was it about the plaid coat that nagged at her memory? It was true that one usually didn't see such brightly colored material, but that wasn't it—it was something that she couldn't put her finger on.

She glanced at him again. His hand started toward his face. Her stomach tightened. A box fell with a big crash, drawing her attention away. She jumped and swung around.

Mary gasped and reached for Judith. "W—who is that man over there?"

Judith turned in that direction. "Who, dear? I don't see anyone."

Mary looked again, but the man was gone. She sighed. "Perhaps I just imagined him."

Judith shrugged, then returned to her conversation. Mary didn't really listen because she knew she'd seen the stranger and something about him made her feel very sick. What a strange reaction to have, she thought.

*Green plaid.* She squeezed her eyes shut to help her remember. Where had she seen a coat similar to the one he had on? In the back of her mind, there was a vague memory just out of reach. Again she tried to bring the picture forward, but the image of the coat was replaced with blood.

Her eyelids popped open and her breathing quickened. She tried to keep her fragile control. *My God!* It matched the piece of fabric she'd found in the cabin. She'd forgotten all about it. Could that stranger have been in the cabin that night? But who was he?

When she returned to the ranch she was going to search the pockets of her old dress for the scrap of material. Maybe holding the slip of fabric would help her remember who the man was.

Judith touched Mary's arm. "This is Mayor Higgins. He will introduce us," Judith explained. "Mayor, this is our houseguest, Mary."

"Welcome to our town," Mayor Higgins said with a smile. "Folks are mighty pleased to have you perform for us."

Mary returned his smile and some of her tension eased. "They haven't heard me sing yet, Mayor. They could change their minds."

The mayor's eyes twinkled with amusement. "As long as you don't sound like you're calling cows, they'll love you."

"Take your places," the tall stagehand on the far left called out.

The mayor ducked in front of the curtain to announce the upcoming performance. A flicker of apprehension coursed through Mary as she nervously clenched her hands again.

Judith moved around the piano and took her seat on the piano bench. "Mary, I want you to stand to my left beside the piano. I want our audience to hear that lovely voice loud and clear."

Mary began to tremble. "I like that idea because

it will give me something to hold on to," she said. "I feel like I'm going to faint."

"I know you're nervous, Mary, but once you begin to sing you'll forget all about it. Just remember the folks from Windy Bend are simple townsfolk, and they will be happy to hear your beautiful voice. This concert is a real treat for them." Judith sighed. "I'm feeling a little queasy myself, so I must be just as nervous as you are."

"Your face is a little flushed." Mary peered at Judith. "I know I asked you before, but are you sure you're feeling all right?" And then a thought occurred to Mary. What if Judith was sick and couldn't perform, leaving Mary to sing by herself? That was a quick and disturbing thought which made her stomach clench tighter.

Judith gave her a slight smile, one that really didn't reach her eyes. "I will be fine. I'm just a little tired from getting everything ready. Besides, if something happened to me, I know you'd be glad to entertain our audience." She had a sly smile on her face.

Mary laughed, easing the tension for the moment. "I wouldn't count on it." She didn't think Judith was telling the truth, but the curtain had started to rise and Mary couldn't say anymore.

Judith began playing as the curtain slowly rose and they glanced out at the audience. Mary was so glad that she didn't have to sing the first song because if she wasn't holding on to the piano, she'd have crumpled to the floor in a heap. Her legs were shaking so badly, they could hardly hold her up. Where was the brave adventuress she used to be?

Not only did she see a sea of people with all eyes focused on them, there were three stories of seating, and four box seats with hand-painted angel medallions on the front. The two balconies were something she'd never seen before. She took a deep breath and shut her eyes as Judith led her into the next song.

Mary opened her mouth to sing but nothing came out. She stood there, blank, amazed, and very shaken. Her gaze darted to Judith, who smiled and nodded to her. She played the opening phrase again.

Mary shut her eyes and began to softly hum the melody. Then she grew more confident and began to sing. Her voice came out clear and crisp, showing none of the nervousness she felt. As she lost herself in the lyrics, she discovered that she enjoyed singing. Funny, she'd never sung much, but she found it was different from anything she'd ever done before and she was surprisingly good at it.

And, thank God, the audience wasn't throwing anything at her—yet.


Carter watched Mary closely. She appeared scared to death, and for a moment he thought she was going to be sick. When she opened her mouth and nothing came out, his heart ached for her. He was certain she was going to dart behind the curtain.

But she didn't.

And for some reason, he felt his chest tighten with pride. The girl had gumption. She stood proud. Mary was breathtakingly beautiful, and it was really hard not to watch every move that she made.

"I've never heard a voice like that," Rick said from beside Carter. "She could be a professional singer for all we know."

"Could be, but I doubt it. If she were experienced, she wouldn't be so nervous. Instinct would kick in. However, I do agree the woman can definitely sing. It is almost like we're listening to an angel."

The audience oohed and aahed through several songs, and finally, after the last song, the audience leapt to their feet for a standing ovation. The clapping continued until Judith agreed to one more song.

When the final note had been played, Judith held out her hand to Mary, and they both went to center stage to take their bows.

The clapping and cheering were very loud and seemed to go on forever. Mary couldn't believe the reception that they were receiving. She wanted to share her happiness with someone. She searched the first few rows for Carter, and there he was. He was smiling at her as if he were very proud.

Mary smiled with sheer pleasure. She was so happy to have not made a fool of herself. The applause was still thunderous as Mary looked further to the back. There, she glimpsed a man in the very back of the center aisle wearing a green coat.

"There he is again," Mary whispered to Judith as they took yet another bow.

Suddenly, two loud explosions rang out, drowning out the applause. Mary screamed as a burning fire entered her body. She reached out for Judith as she crumpled to the floor.

Mary looked around in confusion. What was happening? Somebody had shot her. Panic was rioting within Mary, but she wasn't quick enough to catch Judith because Mary was slowly sinking to the floor. Her legs refused to hold her up any longer.

The audience panicked.

Mary heard the commotion all around her. She tried to hold on, but she was slipping fast. "Somebody help me," she whimpered as she sank to the floor.

# Chapter 9

Carter leapt out of his chair.

His heart had lodged somewhere in his throat, but his gaze never left the prone forms of Mary and his mother. From where he stood, he could see blood on Mary. My God, had someone just shot them both?

He had to shake himself out of this stupor he seemed to be in. He hadn't even looked for the shooter as any good lawman should because he wasn't able to take his eyes off the people he cared for on the stage.

*Don't let them die,* he prayed silently.

There was a sea of people between Carter and the stage, and everyone was shouting and pushing as they surged toward the back of the theater. Every one of them was in his way.

"They're dead!" someone in the crowd shouted.

Carter's panic soared.

One woman screamed as she was pushed to the floor in the panic to escape. "Calm down," Carter shouted, "so no one gets hurt."

He had to get to the stage. "Rick. You try to find out where the shots came from if you can get through this damn mob. I'm going to make my way toward the stage."

"God Almighty, I can't believe this happened," Rick yelled, trying to be heard above the crowd. "You don't think . . . ?"

"I don't know," Carter snapped as he shoved his way down the aisle and into the sea of people. "Make way, I'm coming through." He felt like a fish swimming upstream. "Settle down, folks," he said as he pushed his way through the crowd. "Everyone will get out safely if you remain calm."

It seemed like an eternity passed before Carter finally reached the far end of the stage and climbed up the steps. To his surprise, he found Mary sitting up. Carter breathed a great sigh of relief. Thank God, she was alive. He whispered a silent prayer of thanks as he rushed to her.

"Someone tried to kill me," Mary said, a little dazed. "I think it was the man in the green coat."

Carter noted the blood on her sleeve. "Are you hit anywhere else?" He looked her over, frantic that he'd let someone else he cared for be hurt. "I'm sorry I let this happen to you."

"I don't think I've been hit anywhere else," Mary said. "Carter, there wasn't anything you could have done to prevent the shooting. You were not on duty." Mary looked toward Judith and gasped. "Y-your mother."

Fear gripped Carter around the throat as he turned toward his mother. How could he have forgotten her? He leaned over her.

He'd already lost his father and his sister; God couldn't take his mother, too. Carter felt for a pulse and prayed that he'd find one as his gaze quickly swept her body. He didn't see any blood, but he knew two shots had been fired.

Thank God, her pulse was strong. So why was she on the floor? "I don't see any wounds," he said, puzzled. "Maybe she fainted from the noise. But that doesn't sound like something my mother would do."

Mary placed her hand on Judith's forehead. "My God, she's burning up with fever. I asked her earlier if she felt bad, but of course she denied that she did. She must be sick."

A man dressed in a black suit climbed the steps up to the stage. "Can I be of help, Carter?" he asked as he slipped on his spectacles.

"Doc Moore. It's my mother."

"Don't know what this town is coming to," Doc Moore fussed as he stooped down to examine Judith. "Shooting in the opera house. In all my born days, I've never heard of such a thing." He pulled up Judith's eyelids and looked into her eyes. He searched over her body with his hands. "No wounds." Then he felt her forehead. "Yep, that's it."

"What, Doc?"

"I suspect your ma has finally gotten herself a first-class case of influenza. Bit surprised she hasn't been retching." Moore straightened. "And this young woman might need a bullet taken out of her arm, or if nothing else, to have it bandaged. Get both of them to my office so I can work on them with the proper equipment."

Carter helped Mary stand. Just the sight of the bloody sleeve made his jaw tighten. He wanted to find the bastard who would dare shoot a woman. And he railed against himself. How could he have been so careless to let his guard down? For one night, Carter had just wanted to be an ordinary citizen, so he'd left his gun in the buggy. He hadn't even bothered to scan the crowd as he would usually have done because he'd grown up with these people. Why hadn't he looked for strangers?

He noticed that Mary's face looked pasty and pale. If she fainted on him now, he'd have one hell of a mess. Doc Moore was too old to carry anyone. "Can you walk by yourself?"

Mary held her arm, which blessedly had gone numb for the moment, tightly against her chest. She knew the numbness would disappear later and she'd feel it like the devil, but for now she was all right. "I think I can manage."

Carter removed a handkerchief from his breast pocket, wrapped it around her arm just above the wound, then tied it tight. "That should slow the bleeding until Doc can look at it."

Mary waited for Carter to lift his mother into his arms and then Mary followed him out of the theater. Thankfully, the crowd had cleared inside, but most of them milled around outside, waiting to find out what had happened. Carter didn't take the time to tell them anything as he hurried past everyone to the doctor's office, two doors down from the opera house.

Mary felt dazed and a little confused. Everything had happened so quickly. Had somebody tried to kill her? Why? Could it have been the man in the plaid coat? And the big question was, would he try again? It now became a necessity for her to remember the man before he tried the next time.

Doc Moore unlocked his office door and held it open so Carter could go through. Carter turned to get his mother through the door, then looked back to make sure Mary was right behind him.

"Carter, why are you carrying me?" Judith's groggy

voice broke through the silence as they entered an examining room.

Relieved to hear her voice, Carter glanced down at her. "Because you didn't seem to be able to stand on your own two feet. And dragging you out of the theater was out of the question," he teased.

"That's ridiculous. I was just a little dizzy, that's all. I heard some loud noises which sounded like gunfire, and then I simply fainted. I must have been too excited."

"Enough, Judith," Doc Moore said in a very firm voice. He turned to Mary. "Sit up here." He patted a table. "I'll be with you in a moment." Then he turned his attention back to Judith. "I'm going to give you something for that fever of yours, and then I want you to be quiet and lie on the table while I look at the girl's arm."

"You're so bossy," Judith stated in a very weak voice. "I'll be just fine. Nothing a little rest won't cure. And what is wrong with Mary?"

Carter helped his mother seat herself on the table. "She was shot."

"Shot?"

Doc Moore shoved a spoonful of medicine at Judith. "Here, swallow this. It will help you sleep."

"But—" She shook her head and tried to push the spoon away. "I don't want to sleep. Who shot Mary?" She turned toward Mary. "How are you, dear?"

Doc Moore frowned. "Do as you're told, woman." He shoved the spoonful of medicine into Judith's mouth when she opened it to protest. "There is more than one way to get something in you," he said, smiling.

A commotion sounded in the outer office, and then Rick and another man rushed through the door. Rick glanced at Mary, and the older man strode over to Judith. "What have they done to you?" the older man said.

Doc Moore swung around to the intruders. "Well, Hank O'Tool, you finally done and gave Judith the grippe."

Hank frowned at the doctor. "She wasn't shot?"

Doc Moore looked over his glasses. "Nope. Were you not listening? She's got the grippe."

"I warned her to stay away, but you know how hardheaded she can be." Hank looked down at Judith. "Do you feel poorly?"

"I do not appreciate you calling me hardheaded, but I will admit that I've felt better," Judith said. "I'm sure I'll be fine by tomorrow. Should you be out of bed so soon?"

"Just like you"—Hank smiled as he took her hand—"to worry about others. I hope to get back to work by the end of the week."

Judith yawned. "I'm so drowsy. I can't seem to keep my eyes open," she mumbled, then twisted around to try and see what was happening with Mary. "Are you all right, child?"

"I'll be fine, Judith. You should get some rest," Mary told her as Judith's eyes drifted shut. Hank held Judith's hand and Mary could see the affection that he felt for her. But she'd also heard Hank say that he would return to work soon. Did that mean that Carter would be leaving, as well?

Mary looked around. She noticed that the doctor's office was very neat and clean. A cabinet with a glass front held most of his instruments. Two shelves in the corner held bottles of various shapes and colors; she assumed that was where he kept his medicine.

"Let me see what we have here," the doctor said, placing a pan of hot water on the table next to her. Mary winced as he touched the wound and felt down in the hole. He wasn't very gentle. "I think the bullet went straight through," he said, more to himself than anyone else. "You were lucky."

"I was very lucky," Mary agreed.

"Well, I'm going to have to cleanse the wound, bullet or no. And it's going to need a few stitches." He poured a brown liquid over the wound as he spoke. Mary cried out and tried to jerk her arm away, but the doctor had a tight grip for an old man.

Her arm felt like it was on fire. She breathed rapidly and gritted her teeth as she tried not to cry. She could feel the tears pooling in her eyes, but she fought them because she didn't want to embarrass herself by behaving like some silly, weak female.

Finally the sting eased, and Mary saw that Doc Moore was threading a needle—a very big needle, she thought. Panic set in. Her desperate gaze darted toward Carter, and she tried to say, "I—I—"

"Do we have any whisky?" Carter asked Moore.

"Nope, just used the last on her wound. If we can get her to hold still, it will only take a minute. I'm afraid I'm fresh out of ether—expecting some in next week—but it won't do the girl much good tonight."

Carter stepped up to the table where Mary was sitting. "Why don't you lean on me and hold my hand," Carter suggested.

Mary bit her lip and nodded as she took his hand. It looked so small in Carter's big hand, but being near him gave her more strength than she had on her own.

"This is going to hurt, little lady, but I promise that I will be as quick as I can," Doc Moore told her.

Mary didn't think that he sounded sorry at all.

"You'll have to hold very still," the doctor cautioned her.

Mary took a deep breath and squeezed Carter's hand as hard as she could. She pressed her head against his chest while he tightened his other arm around her. The needle pierced her skin, and she bit down on her lip, hard. She felt the thread sliding through her skin ever so slowly. Oh God, it hurt. She squeezed Carter harder.

When the doctor took the second stitch, Mary felt the blackness settling in over her, and she thankfully left the pain behind.

"She passed out," Carter said.

"Good," Doc Moore replied. "It will be much easier on her now." After a few more stitches he said, "There." He finished tying off the thread. "Well now, looks like you are going to have two patients on your hands for the next few days. I believe Mary will feel better by tomorrow, but your ma is going to take a week."

"Maybe more," Hank added. "I sent Rick for the buggy and the men. I'll help you get the women outside." Hank scooped Judith up in his arms. "Do you need me to ride with you to the ranch?"

Carter lifted Mary, her head resting limply on his shoulder. "Thanks, Doc."

As they left the office, Carter said to Hank, "You know, I brought some men with me so we would be safe, but it didn't help, did it?"

Hank shook his head but said nothing.

"I'll be back tomorrow to see if we can figure out who did this. Do you have any ideas?"

"Not a one," Hank admitted. "I did catch a glimpse of a stranger in a green coat, but it was only a glimpse. I could have been mistaken."

"Green coat? Mary said something about seeing a green coat when I reached her on stage."

"Good heavens," Rick said as he opened the door to the buggy so Hank could place Judith on the rear seat. "This isn't the way I pictured us going home. I didn't get a chance to ask before. How is your ma?"

"She has a case of influenza, but she wasn't shot," Carter said as he placed Mary on the front seat. "Mary was wounded, but it was minor. She passed out when Doc started stitching her up." Carter leaned on the buggy. "What did you find out?"

Rick shrugged. "Actually, the answers I got were damned strange. A few men said they thought they had seen a stranger standing in the doorway, but they couldn't remember what he looked like. They would start to say, 'He looked like . . .' and then they stopped right in the middle of their sentences and got the most puzzled looks on their faces. It was as if they knew what he looked like but couldn't remember, so I basically got nowhere. Sorry."

"Strange." Carter leaned against the buggy. "I shouldn't have let my guard down," he muttered, shaking his head. "I couldn't have imagined that something like that would happen in Windy Bend. I guess I know better now." He frowned. "I keep seeing the scene over and over in my head, and now that I'm thinking about it, when I first reached Mary she said someone was trying to kill her." Carter looked-ed hard at Rick. "Maybe she was right."

"We haven't had a shooting in six months until I got shot," Hank spoke up. "I thought I'd pretty much cleaned up the town, then somebody shot me and now the girl . . . Well, I'll tell you, I'm not going to have this kind of thing going on in my town." Hank swore. "We will find out who did this. Whoever it was had all gurgle an' no guts."

Carter placed a hand on Hank's arm. "Tomorrow will be time enough. You get some rest, and we'll see what we can figure out in the morning."

Carter climbed up into the buggy, reached under the seat, and placed his gun next to him on the seat. Just in case, he thought. "Boys, you ready?"

"Yes sir, boss."

"If you see anything strange, shoot first and ask questions later."

"Yes sir," Stanley said. "We heard what happened, and we'll be sure to keep our eyes open."

Carter urged the horses forward. As they started back toward the ranch, Carter glanced over at Mary. She looked so innocent in her sleep. He'd placed her head on his lap so she wouldn't bang her head on the side of the buggy as they rode. He liked feeling her scant weight against him.

Carter wondered if someone really was trying to kill Mary, and if so why. It had been his experience over the years that men killed for three reasons: revenge, greed, and because someone knew too much. Mary didn't appear to have any money. One could look at her hands and tell that she had worked hard, so that left him feeling that Mary knew something she shouldn't.

Lord, it would help if he knew what.

He wasn't sure how he was going to protect her from the unknown. But he sure as hell was going to try, because he'd realized something tonight that surprised the hell out of him.

Mary had come to mean something to him, whether he liked it or not.

He cared for her—maybe he even loved her. Wouldn't that be a hell of a note?

# Chapter 10

By the time Thunder and Forester reached Gregory Gulch, they had struck up a mutual trust of one another.

Thunder observed the rough sod mining camp as they rode through. There were two rows of rough-hewn log cabins on each side of the road. A young man who looked to be about eighteen, tall, broad-shouldered, with heavy black hair hanging shaggily about his face and head, was trudging down the road. He was wearing a big, floppy hat pulled down over his head. He looked up as they passed and said, "Howdy, Marshal."

"Are you going to the mine, Daniel?"

"Yep. Had to go buy a new rocker. My other one got busted up."

Thunder couldn't imagine why Mary had ever wanted to live in such a place. The cabins' windows were grimy and a few cabins didn't even have windows. He had lived in places like this, but Mary was different.

Today was the first day of May, and the ground

looked it with the muddy puddles in the ruts in the road. Thunder was thankful the snow had almost melted away. Nothing was left except the dirty stubborn spots in the shade that refused to leave. So far, the weather this year had gone from bitterly cold to warm with nothing in between. Crazy weather, he admitted. Thunder's Cheyenne grandfather had once told him when one season is skipped, trouble is on the horizon. Now Thunder realized how true his grandfather's words were.

"Here we are," Forester said as he dismounted in front of a log cabin that looked slightly bigger than the rest.

Thunder followed the marshal into Mary's cabin. It was dark inside and smelled musty, so they had to stop and light several kerosene lamps. After the last one was lit, Thunder picked up a kerosene lamp and looked around. The first thing he saw was blood—on the table, on the chairs, everywhere.

Forester pointed to a spot in front of the fireplace. "We found him right here."

Thunder nodded. A large red stain indicated the spot where Big Jim had died. This didn't look like a simple shooting or a simple argument. It appeared more like cold, calculated murder. There was so much blood in too many places. "Did you find a weapon?"

"Nope."

Thunder held the lantern down toward the hardwood floor where the scene looked even more grisly. "These look like bloody footprints." He glanced up at Forester.

"Same thing I thought. They're headed that way." Forester pointed to his left.

Thunder followed the footprints into a small bedroom where the scene looked even worse—

blood-soaked sheets, blood on the pillow, blood on the blankets. "My God," Thunder finally said as a chill ran over him. It had been a long time since he'd seen a man's blood. "Was this Big Jim's room?"

Forester shook his head. "It was Mary's. I found Big Jim's things in the other room."

Thunder stared at the bed. "I sure hope that Mary is alive, but from what I see, she could very easily be dead."

"Why leave one body and not the other?" Forester asked.

"Good point." Thunder looked back to the fireplace and then the bedroom. "It appears that she killed him, and then stumbled to bed." Thunder turned to make eye contact with Forester. "You did notice that I said *appears?*"

When Forester didn't say anything, Thunder continued. "I know Mary wasn't capable of doing something like this unless she was attacked, and from what you tell me of Big Jim, he wouldn't do such a thing. So what else could have happened?"

"That's what I've been asking myself over and over again," Forester admitted. "I asked everyone who was around both of them that day to see if anyone had heard any arguments. No one did."

Thunder searched all around the room trying to find some clue. Next to the wall, he spotted something that looked like a nightgown. He bent down and picked up the garment. Under it was a box, and beside the box, next to the wall, lay something shiny. "You said that you haven't found the murder weapon?"

"That's right."

"Well, I think we have now," Thunder told him as he reached down to retrieve the knife, still covered with blood.

Forester frowned. "That's Big Jim's knife. He carried it with him everywhere. See the 'J' on the handle?"

"So why would the killer leave it behind?"

"Good question."

Thunder contemplated the knife. "I have two thoughts. First, it would take somebody pretty strong to take this knife from Jim. Second, perhaps the knife was left behind to frame Mary."

"That's what I'd like to think," Forester admitted. "But we have no proof. We gotta find somebody with a motive to kill Jim." Forester contemplated for a moment. "I almost forgot," he said thoughtfully, "right after the funeral, Jim's brother came over and asked me questions about the mine."

"Do you know him?" Thunder asked.

"Nope. Just showed up in camp the day before the murder. He said that Jim had asked him to come work in the mine."

"The day before?" Thunder arched his brow. "Interesting. Where is he now?"

"Gone. I had no reason to hold him, and he needed to make a living. Seems like he's some snake oil salesman, but I told him to swing back by this way."

"I don't know about you, but I'd like to talk to him. What's his name?"

"John."

"I'll find him. But I think the best way I can help you is to find Mary." Thunder sighed. "And hopefully alive."

"How are you going to find her? I'm sure the trail has gone cold by now."

Thunder smiled. He draped his arm across Forester's shoulder. "I grew up with the Cheyenne. I'll find her."

* * *

John McCoy was going to get damned good and drunk, but not in Windy Bend. He wasn't stupid. He'd managed to hypnotize the two men in the back of the theater so that they could never identify him, but he didn't want to take the chance of staying in town and having someone ask who the stranger was. His best bet was to lie low and then return once everything had blown over.

Propped upon the Alamo's brown, wooden barstool in Mountain City, McCoy called for a second bottle of whisky. While he waited for the bartender, he tried to form a plan. He might not have succeeded in his last attempt, but he wasn't giving up so easily. He was a man of many disguises, and he'd make sure he used a different one when he returned to get the girl.

Hellfire. He'd had a clear shot of her, but she'd moved at the last minute, so he was pretty sure he hadn't killed her. If he had, all his problems would have been over by now. Then he could head back to claim the mine as his.

The next time he wouldn't fail.

The girl needed to die. He was pretty sure that he could control her mind if he could get to her. Hypnotism was one of his many talents, and he was damn good at it.

The problem was getting to her.

Of all the confounded luck for Mary to end up with a U.S. Marshal who evidently had no idea who she was or that she should be in jail.

"Damn Carter Monroe," McCoy grumbled before snatching up the shot glass and spilling whisky on his hand.

"Are you a friend of Monroe's?"

"What's it —" McCoy cut short his question

when he turned and saw it was a gunslinger who'd asked. He'd seen the man before. He was tall and spare and stood about six feet, two inches. Dirty auburn hair fell to his shoulders and his face was covered by a full beard. "You're Sammy Carlson?"

"What of it?"

"Just like to know who I'm talking to," McCoy said, then shoved the bottle toward him. "Have a drink."

"Obliged. This here is my brother Randy," Sammy said as he reached for the brown bottle. "And who might you be?"

"Nobody as famous as yourselves. Name is John McCoy."

"Well, now that we know each other"—Sammy gave him a slight smile—"how about answering my question about Monroe."

"Hell, no, I ain't no friend of Monroe. Don't even know him. But the fact that he's a marshal lends to the fact that we ain't never goin' to be friends. It's just that he's got something I want."

"He's been a thorn in our side for the last few years," Sammy said, jerking his head toward his brother. Then he tossed the whiskey down in one gulp. "Last time I seen Monroe was in Texas. Ain't sure where he's lurking nowadays."

John laughed. "Try the next town, Windy Bend."

Sammy turned to look at John. Sammy had a hard, cold-eyed smile. "What do you say we call the marshal out? He's been dogging our tracks for a couple of years now."

"Sounds good to me. But I figure we need a plan. Maybe I can help both our causes," McCoy added. He raised his glass in a toast. "Do you want to just kill the lop-eared mule or make him sweat a little?"

Sammy chuckled. "You're faster than a lizard giving up its tail to a hawk."

McCoy smiled at them. "Let's see what we can come up with."

Three days had passed and Judith's fever still ran high. But today Mary and Maria, the house-keeper, had gotten Judith to drink a little chicken broth.

"At least she stayed awake long enough to eat," Mary said as she placed the bowl on the night-stand.

Maria nodded. "I believe I'll bathe Miss Judith with some cool water and change her gown when she wakes up," she said as she straightened the sheets.

"I'll help you," Mary told her.

"You have been in here every day since you've been injured, senorita," Maria said as she plopped down in the chair beside the bed. "I think you need to get some rest. Your arm is still sore and needs to heal." She gave Mary a knowing nod. "I saw you wincing a couple of times earlier. Now, you go—run along, and I'll stay right here with Miss Judith."

Mary smiled. "If you insist. I will be in my room if you need me." Maria had been correct. Mary's arm was sore, but it felt much better now than it did the night of the opera. She was thankful that whoever had tried to kill her was a sorry shot.

As she climbed the stairs to her room, Mary felt so weary that her legs were like stiff sticks. She'd spent the last two nights sitting at Judith's bedside, because she'd been so sick to her stomach that neither of them had gotten any sleep.

When Mary entered her room, she went to the wardrobe and found her old dress. She searched the pockets for the piece of material. That was the clue that would lead her to the real killer.

She pulled out what looked like a piece of green wool and held it up to the window. She'd only glimpsed the man at the opera house that one time, but she could swear he had on something very similar to this plaid fabric.

Mary slipped off her dress and placed it on a nearby chair, then slipped on a comfortable silk robe.

Wearily, she lay down on the bed. She was still holding the material as she shut her eyes and drifted asleep.

Again horrible dreams filled her, but this time she saw a man with red hair holding his hand out to her and she began to scream. However, he kept coming at her, holding out his hand. She began to run. But she wasn't quick enough. He caught her. "Who are you?" she screamed. He didn't answer. Instead he shook her.

Startled, Mary's eyelids flew open and Carter was sitting on the bed, shaking her. "You're dreaming again."

Mary calmed down enough to recognize Carter, and when she did she clung to him. She was actually trembling. "It was such a horrible dream, but I never get to see the face."

Carter's arms encircled her, one hand on the small of her back. She noticed from the shadows on the wall that it must be late. Had she slept through dinner? She hadn't realized how tired she was, but it was easy to forget everything when she was in Carter's arms. Her head fit perfectly in the hollow between his shoulder and neck, and she felt safe.

"Are you ever going to tell me what your dreams are about?" Carter murmured from above her. His voice was so husky that it felt like a sensual caress.

"I wish I could." Mary sighed. And this time she meant every word. She wanted to tell Carter what had happened. She wanted him to believe her and help her find the killer.

But she couldn't take the chance of him hating her. With Carter, everything was either black or white. Mary knew Carter was a disciplined man who might never believe her. And still, she fought a battle with herself because she could no longer deny herself his touch.

Big Jim had told her that one day she'd find a man she couldn't so easily dismiss. Why did he have to be a lawman? Mary leaned back and gazed into Carter's dark eyes, realizing he could very well destroy her, and even with that knowledge, she now knew that she loved him.

She hadn't meant to love him, but she did. The admission was dredged from a place beyond logic and reason, and no matter how hard she tried to talk herself out of making a foolish mistake, she realized she was doomed.

Obviously love was something that couldn't be controlled.

Carter recognized the desire in Mary's eyes and, damn it to hell, he couldn't let her go. What was a man supposed to do when he found himself wanting a woman so badly that he couldn't sleep, and no matter how hard he tried, he couldn't quit thinking about her? What did Miss Mary No Name taste like? Was her skin like silk?

Those dark sapphire eyes told him that she wouldn't resist his kisses. Each time he saw her, the pull grew stronger. Was he man enough to walk away from her before it was too late?

Evidently not, because he lowered his head, seeking to touch her skin. Mary's breath was warm and moist against his face as he kissed the pulsing hollow at the base of her throat. God, she tasted good, he thought as he nibbled on her neck.

His arms seemed to move of their own will. Instead of pushing her away, he was gathering her closer to him, and that was when he heard her moan his name.

Carter's blood surged through his body as his lips sought hers in an urgent kiss that left him throbbing and wanting her so badly that it scared the shit out of him.

And she wasn't pushing him away.

That was the problem. He could feel each luscious curve of her body.

However, even that didn't stop him as he moved his mouth over hers, devouring its softness while his fingers deftly untied the sash to her robe. He slipped the robe down over her shoulders, followed by her chemise. A small gasp escaped Mary's lips when he cupped her breast, but again she didn't pull away.

He grazed her earlobe and whispered, "You're so beautiful."

Mary had never had anyone tell her she was beautiful. She basked in the glow that Carter thought so. He was doing marvelous things with his hands and there was a dreamy intimacy to their kisses. He cupped the soft warm flesh, pushing it upward until her nipple rose in the air, then he took her breast into his mouth. She couldn't believe how wonderful it felt. Small shivers of delight followed everywhere his hands touched.

He left her for a moment to remove his clothes,

and as the cool air swept over her, Mary wondered if she should put a stop to this, but she couldn't find the words to stop something she wanted. She knew Carter must feel something for her. She could tell by his tender touch.

And then he was back, stretching out over the top of her, his warmth feeling good against her skin, his body rubbing all her sensitive places. Slipping his arms beneath her, he pulled her close to him, and Mary could feel his desire as he gave her a fiery kiss, his tongue caressing hers, his lips rough and tender—a kiss that left her breathless and wanting something more.

Mary's passionate response was driving Carter crazy. He wanted so much to sink into her warm flesh that he could hardly hold back. She kissed much better than the whores he'd been with, but there was also a hesitancy.

He positioned himself between her thighs. Mary's eyes were blazing with desire, inviting him when he finally entered her. She cried out at the same time he realized how very inexperienced she really was.

"Christ, Mary! Why didn't you tell me?"

"Tell you what?"

Carter stopped. He realized he'd sounded harsh. His breath was raspy as he said, "I'm sorry, Mary. I—I didn't know."

Mary didn't understand what he was saying. "You hurt me."

"I know. Lie still and the pain will ease," he said tenderly, kissing her face.

After she'd had time to adjust to Carter, he started to move again. "Is that better?"

She nodded and wrapped her arms around his neck as she began to move with him.

"Ah, Mary. You have such fire and you're all mine," he murmured into the side of her neck.

All Mary's doubts and fears disappeared into the night. Nothing mattered but the moment. Something stirred within her that she could only describe as both torture and pleasure. She felt nothing but the swift rapture that enveloped her, lifting her toward a peak of something more. As her excitement rose, her hips began to move with his, tentatively at first, then with more confidence.

He moved faster and faster until he'd taken her to a frenzied state that made her feel as though she was falling off a cliff. "Carter," she gasped as he thrust one last time and squeezed her so tight that Mary thought he might have broken her ribs.

A sudden flood of tenderness overwhelmed her and tears filled her eyes, escaping in spite of her efforts to hold them back.

Carter rose and looked at Mary. Seeing her tears, he wiped them tenderly from her cheek. "Was it that bad, Mary?"

She smiled. "Quite the contrary. It was wonderful. I never knew—"

Carter rolled to his side but kept Mary wrapped in his arms. "It was good for me, too. I'm sorry I hurt you. If I had known . . ."

Mary let his words sink in. What had she done?

Did this mean she was no better than her mother? Mary knew that all good girls saved themselves for marriage. Somehow she'd forgotten all that tonight. She had made love to Carter because she loved him, and she thought that he loved her, but as the aftermath of lovemaking wore off, she couldn't remember him saying anything about love.

Again she thought of her mother. Could she have

been so naive the first time, and given her love to someone who didn't love her in return?

But Carter was different—Mary knew he must love her. He had to.

She liked snuggling in his arms. She loved having her head rest on Carter's shoulder. Maybe if she fell asleep in his arms, the horrible dream would stay away. She closed her eyes, but sleep wouldn't come.

Carter hadn't said anything after they'd made love, and she wondered what he was thinking. "Carter?"

"Mmmm?"

"What happens now?" she asked.

"We go to sleep."

That wasn't the answer she'd wanted, especially when she felt so unsure of everything. "I mean, what happens to us?" The moment she asked the question, Mary felt Carter tense.

"Ah, Mary," Carter said with a sigh. He squeezed her a little tighter. "I don't have an answer for you. Until we find out who you are, there can't be much of a commitment."

He sounded so businesslike . . . so distant. Yet, he still held her tenderly. *But I do know who I am. If only I had the nerve to tell you.* "Do you care anything at all for me?" she blurted before she lost her nerve, her hand resting on his chest.

"I care," he said tenderly. Then he added, "Let's get some sleep, and we'll talk in the morning. I'm expecting some important information to arrive tomorrow by Pony Express."

At least he wasn't hopping out of bed like her mother's "callers" had, Mary thought. "What kind of information?"

"It's a flyer from Marshal Forester at Gregory Gulch. It's a wanted poster with the picture of the person who murdered Jim McCoy."

"I see," Mary said in a rush of breath. Sooner or later, she'd known the day would come.

*At long last it was here.*

There would be no tomorrows for them because she was leaving in the morning. Just as soon as Carter left the ranch. She would flee and forget about the perfect world she'd gotten to see, if only for a little while. She'd forget Judith's motherly touch. She would forget everything.

Forgetting Carter wouldn't be so easy, however.

# Chapter 11

Thunder rode into the town of Appleton. He figured it would be the best place to start since Appleton was the first town one came to when leaving the mountain. He wouldn't have stopped this soon if he had been the one running, but he could hope that Mary had.

The way he saw it, Mary's horse was missing, so she either rode off because she was scared or because she was forced to. He couldn't imagine Mary in the middle of that gruesome scene, and he prayed that the blood he saw in her room hadn't come from her.

He would always picture Mary as the defiant brat who had wanted to know who he was. Thunder knew that she could be stubborn, hardheaded, and difficult to get along with, but she was family, and that was what mattered. He smiled, remembering the bedraggled girl he'd first met.

As his horse trotted down the main street of Appleton, Thunder spotted the telegraph office and veered his mount in that direction. The first thing he needed to do was send Brandy a telegram letting her know that he was still searching for Mary. How could he be blessed with two such females? Talking about hardheaded, his wife was another one who was definitely hardheaded. He smiled again. Maybe that was what made her so lovable. Or, at least, made him love her.

After Thunder finished at the telegraph office, he asked for the best place to stay and was told the Stratford Hotel.

He strode down the boardwalk past the saloon and then past the local whorehouse, where the girls were hanging out on the balcony. A busty woman looked over the rail and hollered, "You looking for a good time, honey?"

Thunder glanced up. "Not tonight."

As he entered the Stratford Hotel, he thought a hot bath and a good night's sleep would help his disposition.

But then, finding Mary would do that, too.

"Need a room," Thunder informed the clerk, who was behind the counter reading a newspaper. The young man jumped at the sound of Thunder's voice.

The young man looked over the paper and frowned at him, and Thunder's temper became even shorter. He knew his hair had grown long, although he kept it tied back with a leather strap, and he probably looked pretty damned savage with his dark complexion, but no matter who he was he didn't care for discrimination.

"We don't give Indians rooms."

"I'm not an Indian. You should be glad, because if I were I'd have your scalp for that last statement," Thunder gritted out.

The boy looked startled, but he stood and said,

"No offense, mister. How many nights you staying?"

"One. And I'll need a bath drawn."

The clerk pointed to the book for Thunder to sign. When he turned the register back around he read, "Thomas Bradley."

"But you can address me as Thunder."

"Odd name."

When Thunder made no comment, the clerk handed him the key. "Hope you have a nice stay, Mr. Thunder."

"It's just Thunder, kid." He leaned forward on the counter and said matter-of-factly, "Tell me, kid, do you remember seeing a young woman, about this tall?" Thunder held his hand up to his chest. "She has blond hair and blue eyes and maybe came through here about two months ago."

"Nope," the clerk said, then changed his mind. "Wait. A young woman with blond hair was brought in here about that time, I think, but I never did get to see her eyes because she was unconscious."

"Unconscious?"

"Yes, sir. A man carried her in here and demanded a room. They spent the night, and then he carried her out the next morning."

Imagining what the man could have done to Mary, Thunder stiffened, his lips thin with anger. "What did he look like?"

"Mean-looking cuss," the clerk said. "And very demanding, but then sometimes U.S. Marshals are."

Thunder stared at the clerk, baffled. "He was a marshal?"

"Yes, sir. Let me see." The pages snapped as he flipped back in the book. "His name was Carter Monroe."

Thunder nodded. He had no idea what she'd

be doing with a marshal, but it was better than her being with the murderer. "Can you tell me anything else about the girl?"

"Nope. But I bet the doc can. He was called in to take a look at her. She looked real bad off."

Thunder thanked the clerk and then headed to his room. He waited impatiently for the clerk to send up the maid with buckets of hot water. He needed to get clean. The clerk had told him Doc Elliot always ate in the hotel restaurant, so Thunder decided he'd go talk to him tonight.

And being clean would make him a little more acceptable in the restaurant. He really needed a haircut, too, but that would have to wait.

Thunder felt better after cleaning up and changing clothes. One night in Gregory Gulch had been enough for him, he thought as he walked downstairs. He wasn't sure how Mary had been able to bear it. The girl had more grit than he'd given her credit for.

It was about seven when Thunder entered the dining room, prepared for an argument but getting none. The room was small. Eight pine tables draped in white cloth were scattered around the room, and only half of those were filled so it made it easier to find who he'd come to see.

He immediately spotted a man who looked like a doctor, and he wondered why doctors always looked so unkempt. The man was sloppy, like he'd been in a hurry to put on his clothes. "Are you Doc Elliot?"

The man took a bite of his steak, placed his fork on the plate, then looked up from beneath gray, scraggly eyebrows. "Yep," he said, his mouth full. He finished chewing then added, "What's ailing you?"

"I'm fine, but I would like to speak with you after you've finished your dinner."

"I'm not one to waste time, son. If you haven't eaten yet, pull up a chair and we'll talk while we eat."

"Obliged," Thunder said as he sat down. A girl hurried over to them and Thunder ordered a steak.

Doc leaned back in his chair with his cup of coffee. "Now what can I do for you?"

"I understand that you treated a young woman who was brought in by Marshal Monroe. Can you tell me anything about her?"

"Depends," Doc said, then took a swallow of coffee. "What's it to you?"

Thunder looked at the ornery old coot and wanted to shake the answer to his question out of him, but figured the man was probably just being cautious, so he let it ride. For now. "I think she might be my sister. Mary disappeared about the time the girl was brought through here."

"What did she look like?" Doc fired back.

"She's pretty. Long blond hair and dark blue eyes," he added. "And she's about so tall." He held his hand up to the appropriate height.

"That pretty much describes the girl I saw. 'Course, she was unconscious so I really couldn't judge her height, but when I looked in her eyes they were the dark blue you described. Very rare color, indeed."

Thunder cut his steak. He was grateful that it looked like he was finally going to get the man to talk. "Did she say anything? Was she hurt or cut?"

"She was pretty much unconscious. Had one hell of a lump on her head, but she seemed pretty healthy otherwise. The marshal said they found her upside down in a snowbank."

"Other than that she wasn't hurt?"

"Nope. I figure she was thrown from a horse. She never did regain consciousness while she was here."

"What did they do with her?"

"Since they didn't know who she was and she couldn't talk for herself, they took her with them. I warned both of them she probably wouldn't be able to remember anything when she woke up. It was a very nasty bump. But the marshal seemed real reluctant to leave her here."

"They?"

"There were two marshals with her."

"Have any idea where they were headed?"

"Nope, but maybe the sheriff can tell you."

When Thunder finished his meal, he thanked the doctor then paid a visit to the local sheriff, who told him where the Monroe fellow was headed.

It wasn't exactly the answer Thunder wanted to hear. Windy Bend was a day's ride from here, but at least it was something. Maybe he could find her faster than he'd first thought. However, he couldn't start out in the middle of the night, so he had no choice but to wait until morning.

Thunder climbed into the lumpy hotel bed, which only offered a little more comfort than sleeping on the ground. He smiled, thinking he'd grown soft, preferring the dry room to the wet ground.

Tomorrow would be soon enough to head out for Windy Bend. If his luck was good, he'd find Mary safe and he'd bring her home.

\* \* \*

Mary watched as Carter dressed. She would miss seeing him every day, and she'd miss what they'd shared last night. It could have been the start of something new for her.

Maybe one day her life would be back to normal—not that it ever had been. Of course, she wasn't sure she'd know how to behave if everything were to be completely normal.

When Carter finished dressing, he came back over to the bed and sat down on the side. He stared at her for a long moment before he spoke. For an instant a wistfulness stole into his expression. "How do you feel this morning?"

She longed to say scared to death, but she didn't. She was keenly aware of his scrutiny. Instead she replied, "I'm fine."

"Last night . . ." He didn't finish what he had to say.

Mary's stomach tightened with the anticipation of Carter's next words. She knew he was going to say it had been a big mistake, and of course, he would be sorry.

*They were always sorry.*

"—Last night was very special," Carter finally said, then surprised her by pulling her into his arms. He kissed her gently, then he drew back and looked at her with what Mary thought might be tenderness. "You're something, Mary No Name. I care for you a great deal."

Mary's heart flipped over at his tender words. Trembling with emotion, she touched his cheek. "I love you," she said softly, realizing the minute she said the words that it was a mistake. But she wanted him to know the truth. At least that much of the truth.

Carter didn't say anything else. She felt her flesh

color as he kissed her again, quickly, passionately, and then he left her.

Tears welled in her eyes. Mary stared at the closed door, willing it to open and for Carter to come back. "If only things were different," she mumbled as she slid out of bed, wincing at the tenderness in her private self, the reminder of what had happened last night.

Carter hadn't said that he loved her, but then Mary knew better than to fall for softly spoken words. After all, she'd been taught by her mother, who believed anything the men promised her. She used to think that her mother had been such a fool. Now, Mary realized how easy it would be to fall in such a trap. She tilted her chin stubbornly forward. Well, she was stronger than that.

She drew in a deep, fortifying breath.

Mary didn't need Carter, she told herself.

She didn't need anybody.

And with that firm resolve, she marched over to the washstand and began to take a birdbath, erasing all traces of Carter's touch. As she scrubbed each part of her body, numbness seemed to settle in. It felt good, compared to the emptiness that would come later. It was exactly what she needed now.

When she'd finishing dressing in her old gray dress, she felt much like the old Mary. It was as if the past two months had never happened. But they had. Mary knew they had, and so did Judith and Carter. Mary couldn't leave without writing a note to Judith, thanking her for all her kindness and explaining that she'd remembered who she was and had to leave to settle some unresolved issues. Then she signed her name, Mary Costner.

She also left a note for Carter, saying she was

sorry. She signed her name, too. She knew that as soon as Carter saw that poster, he'd know who she was and he'd come after her anyway. After all, it was his job.

She had to hurry.

Mary handed the note to Maria and told her to give it to Judith when she was feeling better. Mary longed to see Judith and explain, but Mary knew she'd break down if she did. She couldn't risk losing the numb feeling that she had worked so hard to achieve.

When she reached the stables, Mary explained to Stanley that she was going for a ride and would be back soon. Since she wasn't taking anything but the clothes she'd arrived in, it looked perfectly normal.

She supposed it would appear as though she'd stolen the horse, but she would return it. She was merely borrowing the animal for a while. However, she doubted that Carter would see it that way.

As Mary rode away, her heart ached. She had truly loved it here on the ranch, but she knew she was doing the right thing. She was heading home to the people who would believe her. Carter never would unless she had proof.

Until he did, she couldn't stay here.

Mary had to admit something she'd thought she would never do. She had been wrong.

She did need somebody—she needed her family.


Carter shook himself out of his stupor and blinked as Windy Bend came into view. He didn't remember the ride into town, and that wasn't a good thing for a lawman. He should have been on the alert, watching.

He must be slipping.

First at the opera house and just now, he warned himself. That was a good way to get himself killed. He'd never been one to daydream or lose his concentration. He had to do something to get his mind off Mary, because when he thought of her, he lost all his focus.

And last night he'd lost not only his focus, he'd lost what sense he had. He'd never before done anything without thinking it through—until last night. Mary had made him feel things he'd never felt before, and he'd lost all thoughts of anything but her.

He couldn't possibly love her; he tried to convince himself that it made absolutely no sense. He would have to know a woman for a long time before he could feel anything for her. He'd have to court her and get to know her family because there was no such thing as love at first glance.

He knew nothing about Mary No Name other than he desired her more than he ever had wanted any other woman. He couldn't deny his lust. He'd definitely proved that last night. He hadn't expected Mary to be a virgin, and when he'd learned it, he was too far gone to stop. Why hadn't she stopped him? He shook his head and sighed.

Carter guided his mount to the hitching post and tied him in front of the sheriff's office. He was still frowning as he mosied into the office.

As soon as he opened the door, he asked, "So, did we find out anything?"

"And a good morning to you." Rick chuckled. "No, we haven't found out anything."

Hank poured Carter a cup of black coffee and handed it to him. "Here. The way you look this morning, you must need something damned strong."

Carter accepted the cup with a nod. "Obliged," he said, and inhaled the rich aroma of the dark brew.

Hank sat back down at his desk. "It's the damnedest thing. A man marches into the opera house with a gun and everybody becomes deaf and dumb. Surely somebody had to have seen him."

"Maybe they're afraid," Carter said.

"Nope. That ain't it," Rick said. "It's like they can remember, but they can't say it. They get this odd look on their faces and then they tell me they didn't see anybody."

"Maybe, I'll go back to the opera house and see if I can find some kind of a clue."

"How's your ma?" Hank asked.

"Better, but she is still running a slight fever. Mary has been a big help taking care of her."

"How is her arm?" Hank asked.

"She's sore, but getting better." *And she feels absolutely wonderful in my arms.*

"Mary sure has a pretty voice," Rick said. "Funny how she can remember how to sing, but not her last name. I sure thought she'd remember who she is before now. Somebody, somewhere, must be worried about her."

*She has a lovely body, too.* Carter knew he needed to get the thoughts out of his head so he said, "I'm sure they are." He just hoped it was not because she had committed a crime.

The jailhouse door swung open and a man strode in with a couple of leather pouches slung over his shoulder. "Hello, Hank," he said, nodding to Carter and Rick. "Heard you got yourself shot."

"Yep." Hank nodded, flexing his shoulder. "Must be getting slow."

The messenger looked through one of the bags and fished out a handful of letters. "Here you go." He handed the letters to Hank.

"Obliged," Hank said, reaching for the bundle. "How you doing, Virgil?"

"My ass hurts," he answered. "I've been in that damned saddle too long."

"Why don't you rest a spell?" Rick suggested.

"Better not. I'm late. Ran into the Carlson gang a few miles outside of town and had to swing around another way. Figured if they saw me, they'd go for the mail just for meanness."

Carter frowned. "You sure it was the Carlson gang?"

"Dang tootin'. I had the misfortune of bumping into them before." He held up his right hand to show he was missing half a finger. "Last time I only lost a finger," Virgil said as he turned to go. "Sure don't want to lose nothin' else. I hope you folks don't have no trouble."

"Me, too," the sheriff said. "See you next time, Virgil."

After Virgil had left, Rick looked at Carter, who was staring out the window. "Well, you've been chasing the Carlsons. Looks like you're not going to have to chase much longer."

"I'd say they are looking for a fight, all right," Carter said.

"And you are going to oblige them," Rick concluded.

"Damn right."

Hank had been opening the mail as they talked. He unfolded a piece of paper and held the sheet up. "I think this is our new wanted poster," he said. He looked at it closer, his eyes growing wide. After a moment, he said, "I'll be damned."

"What is it?" Rick asked, taking the paper out of Hank's hand. Rick's eyebrows shot up in surprise. "Jumping jacks!"

Carter took a deep breath and asked, "So, who is it?"

Rick carried the poster over to Carter. "Maybe you can tell us."

Frowning, Carter jerked the poster out of Rick's hand. Why were those two were acting so strangely? They acted like they'd never seen a wanted poster before.

Carter glanced at the poster and froze. They had been right. This poster certainly was different from any other he'd seen. He stared at the picture in the middle and he began to grow cold inside. From lowered lids, he shot a commanding look at the two men staring at him. His mouth was set with annoyance.

"Wanted dead or alive for the murder of Big Jim McCoy," he drawled with distinct mockery for all to hear. There was a picture with the name printed under it. His face became a glowering mask of rage. It didn't say Mary No Name. It said in plain black and white, Mary Costner.

# Chapter 12

Carter felt numb as he stared at the poster.

He closed his eyes and took a deep steadying breath, then he thought back to the first night when he'd found Mary. She'd had blood in her hair. Even then the hairs on the back of his neck had told him something wasn't right. He'd also had the feeling that she was running from something.

He had been right.

The girl had played him for a fool the entire time, and worse, he'd let her. To think that he could have felt something for Mary stunned him. His shock yielded quickly to fury. His eyes darkened like angry thunderclouds. He'd been foolish to let his guard down.

When Carter looked up, Hank and Rick seemed to be waiting for him to say something. "I guess we now know Mary's last name." A thin chill hung on the edge of his words.

Rick was frowning as if he were trying to figure it all out. "I find it hard to believe that the Mary we know could have killed anyone."

"That's for a judge to decide," Carter said in a voice that sounded as ice cold as his heart felt. He went to the desk, placed his coffee cup down with a resounding thud, and grabbed his hat.

"Where you going?" Hank asked.

With an impatient sigh, Carter replied, "To arrest Mary."

"She's too young to be in jail," Hank protested. "Maybe there is something more about what happened that we're not seeing."

"What's the matter with both of you?" Carter snapped. His curt voice lashed out at them. "She might be a woman but she is accused of murder." He looked at Rick. "We simply overlooked the clues. Remember when we found her? She wasn't all that far from Gregory Gulch and her hands were rough for a woman, but we were too caught up in the helpless female appearance to pay attention to our jobs." Carter nodded curtly to both of them. "Gentlemen, she could be a cold-blooded murderer who wrapped us around her little finger," Carter told them. For all he knew, she could be back at the ranch having a good laugh about the fool he'd been.

"What about the Carlson Gang?" Hank asked.

"If they want me, they will have to wait their turn," Carter gritted out, feeling all his anger bubbling like a cauldron inside of him. "You did notice that poster said dead or alive. I'd like to see her brought in alive," he said, then slammed the door on his way out.

"Strange," Hank commented.

"What's strange?" Rick asked. "Carter's always been hotheaded."

"Well, that might be true"—Hank chuckled—"but the Carlson Gang has been a thorn in that man's side ever since I can remember. Getting every last one of them was all he seemed to live for. Now, suddenly they're not so important." Hank scratched his head. "I think Carter cares for Mary, but he'll never admit it. 'Cause if he did, he'd have to question himself about upholding the law."

Rick laughed. "Maybe he doesn't know he cares. He sure hasn't admitted it to me. Until he does, I'd say Carter is in for a rough ride."

When Carter arrived at the ranch, his anger was barely held in check. He strode into the house and demanded Mary's whereabouts.

Maria was coming out of the kitchen when she ran into Carter. "Señor."

"Where is Mary?"

"She's gone. At least two hours now."

"Gone where?"

Maria shrugged. "I do not know, senor."

He didn't say anything else as he strode across the main room. So she had run. It figured that she'd just up and leave with not so much as a good-bye, the ungrateful bitch. Of course, why would he expect her to say good-bye, considering what he knew about her now?

She'd been using them all along, pretending not to remember her past when she'd only needed a place to hide. Carter climbed the steps two at a time, heading for her room to see if she had cleaned it out. If she'd left her belongings, maybe it meant she was coming back.

He shoved open the door and glanced around. It looked exactly the same as it had this morning, only the bed had been made. A note was propped up on the pillows.

He snatched up the paper and then went to the

wardrobe. All the clothes were still there as if Mary had never been here. But her old dress was gone, he noticed. His brow lifted with surprise. "Well, I'll be damned. At least, she isn't a thief. Just a murderer," he said to himself. He looked down at the paper he had crumpled in his hand. He unfolded the note.

> *Carter,*
> *I know you won't believe anything I have to say, but I have come to care a great deal for you and your mother. That is why I'm leaving. I love you both, and I don't want to hurt you with my problems.*
>
> > *Love,*
> > *Mary*

She called murder a problem? Carter crumpled the note and tossed it on the dressing table, then stormed out of the room. He couldn't stay there. The whole damned room smelled like Mary. He clenched his jaw. When he passed Maria in the hall, he told her gruffly, "Have somebody clean that room right away."

Carter took a deep breath before he opened the door to his mother's room. She lay swaddled in bedclothes, her eyes shut. But the minute she heard him, her eyes opened. Carter thought she looked pale, but that was to be expected since she'd been in bed a few days.

"How do you feel?" he asked as he took her hand in his.

"Maria says my fever has finally broken," Judith said. "And my head doesn't hurt half as bad as it did. I hope I'm at least sitting up by tomorrow."

"I'm sure you will be, Mother." Carter knelt beside her bed. "I'm glad to hear that your fever has broken. Hank said he'd be out to see you tonight," Carter said as he pushed himself to his feet. He wanted to give his mother a reassuring smile, but couldn't. "I have to ride out, and I don't know when I'll be back. I'll see you when I return." He turned to leave.

"She's left us," Judith said, simply.

Carter glanced back at his mother. He saw the tears in her eyes and he heard the sadness in her voice. He wanted to choke Mary for making them care about her. "I know."

"Mary left me a note saying she'd remembered her identity," Judith told him. Carter was surprised that Mary had been so thoughtful.

Judith took a deep breath before she could continue. "I will miss her," she whispered, then gave her son a soft smile. "But I have the feeling she'll come back to us."

Carter couldn't bring himself to tell his mother the truth, not while she was sick. "Maybe she will," he said, hoping he sounded convincing. "Get some rest so you can get well, and don't worry about Mary," he said.

Judith rewarded him with a smile, but Carter could see the tears she was trying not to shed. It was the same look she'd had after his sister's death. It only added fuel to the fire burning in his chest.

Carter went straight to the stable and retrieved his horse. Then he went in search of Stanley. Carter found him pitching hay. "Have you seen Mary?"

Stanley stabbed the pitchfork into the ground and leaned against it. "Yep. She took the gray out for a ride. Should be back before long, I expect."

Carter mounted his horse. "Which way did she go?"

Stanley pointed. "That way."

Carter swung his mount around and rode off, but he did manage to hear Stanley say, "Don't think she's in trouble, do you?"

Carter could only laugh to himself at the last remark. "Trouble," he said as he rode. "The girl invented the word." Now he could add horse thief to her other charges. As he settled his horse into a canter, he shook his head.

The stupid woman was headed in the wrong direction.


The mountains Mary rode through were beautiful, and the Ponderosa pines a lush green. She felt almost peaceful riding along surrounded by God's beautiful land. She really wouldn't mind living somewhere like this, she thought. Maybe one day, if she could clear her name, it might be possible. The road finally opened up to a wide expanse of prairie covered in a rainbow of wildflowers, making her want to stop and breathe in the beautiful fragrance. And then she realized how stupid that thought was.

She was running for her life, not out for a lovely ride.

She'd pushed her mount hard for the first couple of hours, but she finally eased up, not wanting to exhaust the horse. She had discovered she had no idea which direction she needed to go, so she just rode in hopes of seeing anything that might look familiar.

By now Carter must have seen the wanted poster, and he'd know she'd been lying. She wondered if there was some small chance that Carter might think she was innocent. Or did he think like most lawmen, and could only see what appeared to be the truth?

She longed to stop and rest for a while. She was tired. It was as if all the problems resting on her shoulders were crushing into her. She couldn't hold her head up. With that thought, she purposely straightened her back and lifted her head, determined that she wouldn't be beaten.

Suddenly, the peace in the valley was broken by a horse's whinny.

She heard hoofbeats.

Twisting in the saddle, she looked behind her and saw a lone rider headed toward her. He wore a light-colored Stetson. Even at a distance, his identity was unmistakable.

*Carter!*

Mary nudged her mount into a full gallop. The wind whipped at her hair, and she had to shove it out of her face to see. Then she glanced behind her again. Carter was gaining ground. His mount was faster than hers.

The ground began to tremble, and Mary knew it had nothing to do with Carter, but she wasn't sure what the cause was. As she reached the top of the next rise, she found the reason. She jerked her horse to an abrupt stop.

A herd of buffalo was stampeding toward them, and in a few minutes she would be directly in their path. Her spooked horse reared, his hooves pawing the sky. Mary tried to hold on but she lost her seating and fell to the ground. There was no time to think as she scrambled to her feet. She turned and started running toward Carter. Her horse was racing that way, too. Of course, he didn't stop when she called to him since she didn't know his name.

Panic threatened to cut off her air supply, but Mary couldn't stop because if she did, she'd be trampled. She looked up and would have laughed if she could. She was getting closer to Carter. Who would have thought she'd be running toward the law instead of away?

But her choices, at the moment, seemed slim. Carter would only shoot her—the buffalo would kill her inch by inch.

Carter couldn't believe what he was seeing.

Not only was Mary running toward him, there must be a thousand buffalo bearing down on her. The woman seemed to court danger in everything she did.

This time, she'd bitten off more than she could possibly chew.

He saw the black storm clouds in the distance and realized what had spooked the herd.

Mary didn't stand a chance.

Buffalo were faster than horses, they could run longer than horses, and they never backed down unless they were frightened. That was Carter's only hope. He had to scare them.

He didn't stop his horse. Instead, he looped the reins around the saddle horn and braced his knees so he could get a good shot. Then he drew his Winchester rifle and fired up into the air. Slowly, the herd began to shift and run to the right of Mary.

For a moment, Carter couldn't see Mary for all the dust. He kept riding toward the point where he'd last seen her. Finally, he saw her. He leaned down and reached for her, yelling, "Give me your hand."

She grabbed his forearm, and Carter swung her

up behind him, kicked his horse in the flanks, and then took off after her mount now that the danger had passed.

Carter felt Mary's heavy breathing on his back as she tried to catch her breath. He hated to admit it, but it took a few minutes for his breathing to calm down, too. That had been a close call. Mary easily could have been killed, a thought that made him sick. But she was safe now, with her arms wrapped tightly around him.

By the time they reached her horse—or should she say Carter's horse—Mary had quit shaking. She had never run so fast in her life. Knowing she was going to be trampled to death had given her wings. Somehow, she'd managed to escape without a scratch. It reminded her of the time she had almost drowned in the Missouri River. She looked heavenward. Maybe somebody up there was watching out for her.

Carter stopped his horse, then reached behind him and grabbed Mary's arm to help her dismount. She slid effortlessly to the ground. Mary started to thank him for saving her life, but the look on Carter's face stopped her.

And he had yet to let go of her arm.

She gazed up at him.

He warned her with a voice that gave her chills, "Don't make me chase you again!" With that remark he released her.

Mary actually didn't know what to say to him. After last night, when everything had been wonderful, it had been hard enough. But today, nothing was the same. She felt as if she were dreaming. Nothing had been normal for her since Big Jim's death. But she was determined to say something to Carter or bust. Mary could see the disgust in his eyes, and she didn't like it. She had to hang on to the slim hope that he might listen to her.

"Is that all you have to say?" Mary asked.

"There is one more thing," Carter said, shaking his head, "You're under arrest, Mary *Costner,* for the murder of Jim McCoy."

Mary flinched at the hardness in Carter's eyes. So much for him listening to anything she had to say. She could tell by looking at Carter that he'd already made up his mind. She hadn't been able to miss the way he'd stressed her last name to reveal that he now knew who she was. Her anger simmered as she glared at him.

How could he judge her when he knew nothing at all about her?

Carter was so mule-headed that he'd never listen to her side of the story. Mary drew a deep breath and shook her head. Why should she waste her breath? She jerked around and mounted her horse, determined not to say another word to him.

But once she was seated, she lost the battle with her mouth. "You're not going to add horse thief to the charges?"

Carter almost smiled, but caught himself. He'd expected a river of tears. He'd expected her to tell him that she hadn't murdered her partner. That she was innocent. He'd love to know how many times he'd heard a crook utter those words.

But Mary hadn't said any of that. Instead, that spirit of hers had kicked in, and Carter realized that she would never plead or beg for mercy. And she would always challenge him as she was doing now, so he said, "And horse thief."

They rode silently, side by side, for a long time before Mary asked, "Does your mother know?"

"My mother is still very sick," Carter drawled.

"And yes, she knows that you are gone and is very upset that you ran out on her, too."

Mary glared at Carter. "Only because I knew *you* wouldn't listen."

Carter grabbed her horse's bridle and stopped both their mounts. He had murder in his eyes as he snapped, "What was there to listen to, Mary? More lies? You came into our home and pretended you didn't know who you were, and I must say you were a damned good actress." He saw the hurt in her eyes, but then again, it could all be an act.

Carter had thought he knew her, but he didn't. "What. You have nothing to say?" he taunted.

"I was brought into your home with little choice," Mary shot back. "I wish the hell you'd left me where you found me."

"That makes two of us, my dear." Carter slid from his horse, then jerked Mary from hers. He was so angry, he shook her, demanding, "Why did you lie to me?"

Mary shoved against his chest and shrugged her arms to get Carter to loosen his grip. Her temper rose. She was tired of taking the blame for everything. "Think hard, Carter," Mary exploded. "Did I lie to you? I don't think so." She paused for a moment, breathing hard. "I just never told you the complete truth, and the reason I didn't was because I knew you would act exactly like you're acting now," she said in a rush, having to get the words out as quickly as possible to keep him from interrupting.

Then she went on, "You don't want the truth! You couldn't handle it if it hit you right between the eyes. You just need a prisoner to bring in so you can say you've done your job. Because that is what a good lawman does, isn't it? He captures the bad guys. Or at least the ones he *thinks* are the bad guys."

Every word Mary threw at Carter stung as if she'd slapped him. He was a damned good lawman who went after the slimy lawbreakers who threatened good people. How dare she challenge his motives!

Carter dragged Mary up against his body and glared down at her. A cynical inner voice cut through his thoughts. *Why do you let this damned woman get under your skin?*

But it was too late.

The admission was dredged from a place beyond logic and reason as his eyes raked boldly over her, stopping at her eyes. They glistened with anger. He saw the fire that made her who she was along with the passion smoldering just beneath the surface.

And the next thing Carter knew, he was kissing her. He wanted to punish Mary for making him feel all the things he felt for her.

He'd made three mistakes in his life.

The first one was letting his sister remain in that wagon. He'd paid for that mistake. Second, he'd picked this woman out of the snow. He was still paying for that one. But his third mistake was making love to a woman who could possibly hang for murder.

What would he do if they hung Mary?

He wanted—hell, he didn't know what he wanted, and therein lay the problem.

Finally, Carter gentled his kisses and kissed her with a fear that he'd never kiss her again. He felt as if he were losing something very precious and there wasn't a damned thing he could do about it.

Mary had made her mistake when she'd taken

someone else's life. And, knowing this, he still held her.

Thunder rumbled all around them, but neither noticed until the first fat raindrops began to fall.

Carter's mouth seized hers, stealing her breath and making Mary forget that he'd just arrested her. It was raining harder now.

Neither of them noticed.

All she could think about was what had happened last night and how wonderful she'd felt in Carter's arms. Why couldn't she have the one thing she wanted?

And then she remembered Big Jim's words . . .

*"Ah, gal, do you not realize how lovely you are? One day a man will simply take your breath away, and then you'll be wanting to get yourself hitched."*

*"I wouldn't count on that, Jim. But if there is someone, he's going to have to be one hell of a man to turn my head." Mary laughed. "I'm pretty headstrong, in case you haven't noticed."*

*Jim laughed. "He's out there somewhere, and I'll bet when you first meet him, you won't like him one dang bit."*

As Mary savored the wild kisses, she now knew Jim's words to be true. She didn't like Carter. Unfortunately for her, she loved him, and there wasn't anything she could do about it.

Carter finally tore his mouth away. For one unguarded moment, Mary thought she saw something heartwarming in Carter's eyes, before that hard mask settled over his features again.

Carter didn't know what the devil he was doing. He was supposed to be arresting the woman, not kissing the hell out of her. What was it about Mary that flamed his desire until he couldn't think logically? He was a trained lawman, for Christ's sake, but the minute he touched her, it was an explosive combination that drove him beyond anything logical.

He pushed her rain-soaked hair from her face. "Tell me, was last night a lie, too?" Carter asked.

She didn't answer.

He dropped his arms and stepped away from her. Mary could feel his warmth leaving her body as the rain plastered their clothes to them.

She started back, trying to show her defiance, but she couldn't maintain it. Finally, Mary broke down and cried. And then she hated herself for showing Carter her weakness.

The damned man!

Mary wanted to hurt Carter just as badly as he had hurt her. She had opened her heart and told him how she felt, but he'd offered her nothing in return. He only wanted to think the worst, and now he wanted to use her to make him feel more like a man.

Looking at him through tears that blurred her vision, Mary said, "That is something you'll never know."

The thunderstorm passed as had their passion, and now they were both standing on the open plain shivering with the cold the rain had brought. There seemed to be an emptiness in both of them that neither of them knew how to handle.

Then they remounted and started back toward town. Cold, miserable, and lost in their own thoughts, they passed the rest of the journey in silence.

Mary felt the gulf between them widening, and she wasn't sure if she wanted that, but there wasn't much she could do to change things. Carter was a marshal and she was his prisoner. Nothing would change the fact that they were enemies.

When they arrived at the sheriff's office, they dismounted and Carter pushed her in front of him as he escorted her into the jailhouse.

As she preceded him, Mary wondered if he thought she'd really make a run for it with him wearing a gun. What he didn't know was that if *she* had a gun she probably would have made a run for it, because she was pretty damn good with a gun.

Inside the office it took a few minutes for Mary's eyes to adjust from the sunlight to the darker interior, then she looked around. Sheriff O'Tool was sitting behind his desk talking to a man who had his back to them. Rick stood with his arm propped on the window ledge, watching the two men at the desk.

It was the perfect humiliation, Mary thought. Not only were the two people she knew going to see her locked up, but now a perfect stranger, who was slowly turning her direction, would witness the whole thing.

# Chapter 13

"Thunder!" Mary cried out.

She ran to him, throwing her arms around his neck. "I'm so glad to see you."

"It's all right, kid, I'm here now," Thunder said.

Carter watched as Mary draped herself all over the stranger who had his damned arms wrapped around her in a very familiar way. Hank was still seated at the desk, and Rick was still propped in his favorite spot by the window. The stranger didn't seem to be bothering either of them. Carter's jaw tightened. "Who the hell are you?"

The man stepped away from Mary. "You must be Monroe. I heard you were ornery."

Carter hadn't moved. "Among other things," he said, his tone as cold as ice. "You still haven't answered the question."

"That's right, I didn't introduce myself. I'm Thomas Bradley, but I'm called Thunder." Thunder didn't extend his hand. He could see that Carter definitely had a burr under his saddle, and somehow he figured Mary was that burr.

"Strange name," Carter said.

"I was raised by the Cheyenne."

"Hmmph," Carter grunted then asked, "What can I do for you?"

"Mary is Thunder's sister," Rick said.

Carter glanced at Rick, then back to Mary. "Is that true?"

She nodded.

Carter started toward Mary but his eyes were on Thunder. "I hate to tell you this, but your sister is under arrest for murder," Carter informed her brother. "I never did hear anything about her family since she pretended to have amnesia while she was with me."

Thunder glanced back to Mary, his brow arched. "Did you do that?"

"Afraid so," she admitted with a sheepish smile.

Carter unlocked the cell and held the door open. "It's time to lock you up."

Thunder stepped in front of her. "Before you lock her up, I should advise you that I'm also Mary's attorney. As such, I need to talk to her."

"You're a lawyer?" Carter asked in a disbelieving tone.

Thunder did his best to hold his temper. However, the marshal seemed to be shoving mighty hard toward a fat lip. "You doubt what I just told you?"

Hank jumped into the conversation. "I received a telegram from Marshal Forester about an hour ago saying Mister—I mean, Thunder—might be stopping by. Said they have been working together to help find the killer."

Carter grimaced. "Sounds like our Mary has an interesting family," he said, but he thought, *One that I know nothing about*. What was she doing working in such a rough conditions when her brother was a lawyer? Carter motioned for Mary to enter. "You can talk in here since this is where Mary will be held until I can take her back to Gregory Gulch."

"I don't suppose you'd release her into my custody?" Thunder asked.

"You supposed right." Carter gave him a smirk. "I don't know you, mister, so I'm afraid the trust isn't there. You'll have to talk in there," Carter said with a nod to his left.

Thunder gave Mary a small shove forward. She walked right past Carter into the cell and never once glanced Carter's way. Thunder followed.

"I'll need a chair," Thunder informed Carter as he passed.

After the chair had been placed in the cell, Thunder sat down across from Mary, who was sitting on the bunk.

Hank shoved away from his desk and looked at Rick. "Let's go get some grub. I'm hungry."

"Sounds good to me," Rick said, grabbing his hat off a peg. "How about you, Carter?"

"I'll stay here with the prisoner," Carter said, then slumped down. "Bring me back a plate of stew. Better make that two plates. We'll have to feed the prisoner."

Mary cut her eyes sarcastically toward him. *Now, isn't that nice of him?*

She wanted to throw something at Carter, but then she wondered, what was the use? He wasn't going to change, no matter what she did. Or didn't do.

Mary watched Carter just as he watched her.

Trying to look casual, Carter leaned his chair back against the wall, propped his feet on the desk, then pushed his Stetson down over his eyes. He didn't seem worried about anything, especially her, but then why should he? Carter was on the right side of the bars. She wasn't.

And Mary knew he would be listening to everything she and Thunder talked about.

"Well, young lady," Thunder said. He sat down in the straight-back chair and folded his arms across his chest. "This is some mess you've gotten yourself into."

"It seems that way," Mary agreed.

"Can you tell me what happened?"

Mary shook her head. "I wish I could. But the truth is . . . I really don't know what happened."

"Jesus Christ, Mary," Thunder yelled. "There was blood everywhere—how could you not know what happened?"

"You don't have to shout," Mary informed. "It doesn't make sense to me, either. Why do you think I ran?" She didn't wait for him to answer. "Because I knew no one would believe I didn't do it." She frowned, then added, "I don't believe it, and I was there!"

"All right, all right," Thunder said, holding his hands up. "Calm down. Let's start from the beginning and tell me everything." He leaned forward and propped his elbows on his knees. "I heard you and McCoy struck a rich vein of gold."

"I'd almost forgotten that. It seems so long ago. I went from being very happy to scared to death in a matter of a few hours." She smiled ruefully. "Jim and I were heading home from the mine when he told me he'd invited his half brother over to eat with us. He said his brother had just arrived at camp."

"What did he look like?"

"I don't know," Mary admitted with a disgusted shake of her head. "I remember going into the cabin and poking up the fire so I could start dinner, but I don't remember anything else after that until I woke up the next morning."

Mary went on to explain how she'd awakened that morning covered in blood and gripping the knife. She told Thunder what she'd done that morning before she left and about her rush to leave town, only to be thrown from her horse. "And that is how I met Carter and his family."

"That's some story," Thunder said. "Somehow we're going to have to get you to remember what you can't. There is probably a good reason why you can't recall certain facts. We'll just have to find the answer." Thunder grew serious. "I do have one question for you."

"What?"

"Why didn't you come home?" Thunder asked. He'd said it in such a quiet way that Mary felt guilty.

"Because I didn't want trouble for our family. I thought I could remember on my own. However, it hasn't happened so far."

"I have a hunch that Jim's brother had something to do with this, but why you can't remember him is still a puzzle to me," Thunder said, rubbing his jaw. "I'll figure it out, though."

Mary relaxed. She could always count on Thunder. "Well, now that you're here you can tell me what's going on at home. How is everybody doing?" she asked.

Thunder smiled. "It was a real battle leaving them behind," he told her. "They all wanted to come help."

Feeling better already, Mary smiled. "Have you heard from Billy?"

"Claire is doing fine and expecting the baby anytime. Billy did have three more colts born in the last few weeks. One he declares is going to be a great racehorse."

Thunder rose. His powerful, well-muscled body moved with easy grace. "Guess I'll go to the hotel and think about what you've told me. I'll be back in the morning. Is there anything you need, kid?"

"Yes, another dress to change into would be nice."

"I'll do what I can. See you tomorrow," Thunder said. He turned toward where Carter was still lounging at the desk. "You can let me out now," Thunder called.

As he waited for Carter to unlock the door, Thunder glanced at the marshal as he strode past him. "I assume my sister will be well protected tonight."

"I'll stay right here," Carter assured Thunder. "I assume *you* will be back tomorrow."

For some reason, Thunder found the marshal's displeasure amazing. "You can bet your life on it." He stepped out and closed the door firmly behind him.

Carter frowned at the door, then dropped back down into the chair behind the desk. He propped his chin on his hand and thought. He wasn't sure how he felt about the story Mary had told her brother. Even though it sounded far-fetched, it really seemed like the Mary he'd come to know. Maybe she was telling the truth.

He'd heard the desperation in her voice, and that made him wonder. But Mary not being able to remember puzzled him. Could someone have drugged her? It was definitely a possibility, but surely she would have remembered seeing the man beforehand. Damn, his head hurt.

He shoved himself to his feet and grabbed the

coffeepot. Coffee. That's what he needed. He ducked into the back where the sink was located and pumped some fresh water for a pot of coffee.

Mary might be charged with murder, but Carter had a hard time believing she could do anything to harm anyone. It was just a gut feeling, but he'd need proof, because he'd learned in the past that looks could be deceiving.

When Carter returned with the old tin coffeepot, he placed it on the potbellied stove, then stoked the fire. The nights still got cool after the sun went down, and since they would be spending the night here, they might as well be comfortable.

Carter glanced over at Mary. She looked much like a child sitting on the crude jail bunk with her knees drawn up and her arms wrapped around them, watching him. "Is there anything you need?"

Her eyebrows arched mischievously as she looked up at him. Her dark blue eyes glistened like rare jewels. Then she answered him, "A key."

Carter chuckled. "Nice try." No matter how angry he was with her, there was something about Mary that made him smile. Perhaps it was the defiant little spark that lay just beneath her alabaster skin or that volatile nature that dared him to provoke her.

Rick shoved the door open and marched in, two plates of stew in hand. He slammed the door shut with his foot. "Hank has gone to get the horses, but we didn't forget your supper." Rick placed the tray on the desk and removed the dishtowels that had been covering the plates. Fragrant steam wafted up into the air and Carter's stomach growled.

"It was mighty good tonight," Rick commented as Carter took a plate of stew. Rick went over to Mary's cell and unlocked the door. "You'd better eat while it's hot."

"What the hell are you doing?" Carter snapped.

Rick looked at Carter as if he'd lost his mind. "You didn't expect her to eat in there." Rick jerked his head toward the cell. "Did you?"

"She's a prisoner."

"But she's a special prisoner," Rick said with a smile. He hung the keys on the peg before addressing Carter. "Now, if you don't think that you can handle her, I'll be glad to stand guard for you. Otherwise, I'm headed back to the ranch."

"Get out of here," Carter muttered. He rubbed the muscles in the back of his neck.

Mary realized then that Carter was very tense. And she was sure she was the cause. The silence lengthened between then, making her uncomfortable. "Look, if you don't want to eat with me, I'll go back into my cage."

Carter pointed to the chair across from him. "Sit down, Mary," he ground out.

He didn't even wait for her to do so before he grabbed up his fork and started eating. Then Mary remembered she wasn't a guest, but a prisoner. What did she expect, a tablecloth and candles?

She took a bite of tender meat and admitted it was wonderful. However, the company left much to be desired, and she was determined not to be the first one to speak. She'd just enjoy the food and then go back to her cell.

"If that was your brother," Carter said out of the blue, "then how come you have different last names?"

"I don't have any real brothers or sisters."

"Aha! I knew he was lying."

"If you'd let me finish," Mary snapped, a little irritated that Carter would always think the worst where she was concerned. "I grew up in an orphanage. There were six of us," she said in a soft voice. Then her pride kicked in and she spoke with more confidence. "Somehow, we managed to become a family, but it wasn't easy. When the oldest, Brandy, married Thunder, he became my brother, too, or you could call him my brother-in-law."

"That's interesting," Carter said as he picked up his cup of coffee. "Thunder was one of the orphans?"

"No. Thunder was raised by the Cheyenne. If you think he looks savage now, you should have seen him then. He scared all of us. When we met him, he was a scout for a wagon train. Since we didn't have a man with our wagon, Thunder took care of us."

Carter leaned back and propped one booted foot on his leg. "He actually volunteered?" Carter asked with a grin that was irresistibly devastating. "After meeting him, I find that hard to believe."

Mary started laughing and Carter actually smiled. She reached for her cup of coffee. She chuckled, then swallowed her smile. "No, he didn't volunteer," she admitted. "He was roped into taking care of us, and he didn't like it any more than we did." She smiled as she remembered all the interesting times they'd had.

Mary went on with her story because every time she paused, Carter would prompt her to continue, much like a child hearing a bedtime story. So she told him all about the journey until she came to the part where Brandy had murdered Sam Owens. She hesitated, then with a resigned sigh she related the tale.

"It must run in the family," Carter said nonchalantly.

Mary placed her cup on the table, her eyes feeling like they were spitting sparks. Why had she bothered to tell him anything if he was going to make fun of her? She stared at him long and hard. Instead of exploding like she wanted to, she didn't say anything.

"Are you going to finish your story?" he asked.

She arched her eyebrow. "I don't appreciate your comment," she informed him.

"But it's the truth," Carter argued.

"Only on the surface. That is your problem, Carter," she snapped. "You never bother to look beneath the evidence. You only accept what's right on the surface." Mary pushed herself to a standing position. "Sometimes, things are not as they seem. Let me tell you why Brandy shot the man. It was because Sam was trying to rape Ellen, my younger sister, and when Brandy tried to stop him, he turned on Brandy."

Mary leaned across the table so she could see Carter at eye level. She wanted him to know she was serious about Brandy. "If Brandy hadn't shot him, I'm sure I would have. So you can arrest me for thinking about it!"

Mary straightened, then gave him a sarcastic look. "Oh, I forgot, you've already done that." She flung the words at him, turned, and went back to her cell.

"Where are you going?"

"I'm a prisoner, Marshal, or have you forgotten?"

Carter sauntered over to the cell, rubbing the back of his neck. The woman made his head hurt. He had been enjoying the conversation, figuring it was a good way for him to get to know her. And he'd been surprised at what he'd found so far—

this was one hell of a woman who also had one hell of a temper.

"Look." He grasped the bars as he leaned against the door. "Why don't we call a truce tonight and just talk? It's going to be a long night, and we may never get another chance."

Mary wasn't sure she wanted Carter to know anything about her. But then again, his opinion couldn't be much lower. "All right," she finally agreed. "You can sit over in that chair, but make one more sarcastic remark and I'll throw you out on your ear," Mary warned him.

He chuckled and seated himself leisurely, stretching his long legs out in front of him. What was it about her that made him feel so good? "Your family is definitely interesting."

Mary nodded. "You could say that. They would probably tell you that I was very hard to get along with."

"They wouldn't have to tell me." Carter smiled devilishly. "I know that firsthand."

Mary shook her finger at him. "I hate to tell you but you're no prize yourself."

"Maybe it's because we're both so alike."

Mary smiled. "Perhaps."

Carter shifted in the chair. He realized he liked it when she smiled.

"What happened to your parents?" he asked.

"I never knew my father," Mary said, her smile immediately disappearing. "My mother worked in a brothel, and that is where I was raised until I was put in the orphanage."

Carter frowned. "I'm sorry. Sounds like you had it rough."

Mary thought he really looked sincere. "Thank you. I guess we can't help where we come from, but we can help where we're going. I swore I would never be like my mother, but I'm definitely not as good as your family. I'd never even seen such pretty clothes until I wore your sister's things," she said.

Carter leaned over and touched her hand. "Don't put yourself down. No matter what clothes you have on the outside, you are still the same person inside."

She laughed sarcastically. "Yeah, I'm no good."

"I didn't say that."

"It's kind of hard to believe in yourself when you're accused of something you didn't do."

"I can see your point."

Mary held up her hand. "Enough about me. Tell me about your father," Mary said. "I can't imagine having a father."

"I won't deny it was nice having loving parents. I guess I never realized how fortunate I was until hearing your story. According to my mother, I look a lot like my father. Everyone looked up to him." Carter shifted to a more comfortable position. "And he doted on my mother."

"I could hear the affection in your mother's voice when she spoke of him. How did he die?"

"He came up on some rustlers hotfooting calves. Instead of going for help, he went charging up the hill toward the men. He was determined to run them off. You see, my father wasn't afraid of anything."

"What's hotfooting?"

"It's when rustlers take a hot iron and burn the calf between the toes, making its feet too sore to walk."

"How cruel. Why?"

"So they will get lost from their mothers. It makes

the strays easier to rustle. Anyway, my father must have surprised the four men. They all turned and fired at him." Carter's eyes flashed with sudden anger. It still made him angry to think of his tragic death. "He never stood a chance."

"I'm so sorry," Mary whispered, her hand on her chest as if she felt his pain.

"It taught me a very valuable lesson," Carter said as he rose. "To always be cautious." He glanced at the oil lamp, which gave off only the dimmest light. "The oil is getting low. I guess we should turn in."

Mary's eyes were the darkest sapphire color. "Thank you for not leaving me locked up tonight. You've made it easier."

Carter looked down at her upturned face. He saw the heartrending tenderness of her gaze. "I wish things were different."

With their faces only inches apart, she whispered, "I do, too."

When Carter's gaze fell to her lips, Mary felt her heart race. She tried to stop the dizzying current racing though her as his hands slipped up her arms, bringing her closer. She wound her arms around his neck in response.

*This is a mistake,* she thought.

She felt Carter's breath against her face as he pressed his lips to hers, causing her to moan. Even though she knew Carter was the enemy, it was as if her mind shut down completely when he touched her.

She trembled with the need to be held. She fitted herself perfectly to his body. A burning desire was building inside of her, creating an aching need for him. His lips crushed down on hers, parting them with a hungry urgency, and she responded, mating her tongue with his.

He kissed her again and again until her breath became his. Mary knew she should pull away—save what dignity she had left—but she craved his affection even now, after he'd arrested her. She hadn't been lying when she'd told him that she loved him. She couldn't deny herself his touch any longer.

Lifting his head, Carter gazed down at her. "What is it about you that makes me forget every other thought in my head?"

"Tell me last night wasn't a lie," she said—the same question he'd asked her.

"It wasn't a lie," Carter admitted. It was an awakening experience that had left him reeling. Then he knew he was going to do something that he shouldn't. "I want you just as much now as I did last night. I want to feel your naked body next to mine, to hold you in my arms once more."

"Sleep with me tonight," Mary whispered in his ear.

Carter's eyes darkened as he pulled her down on the cot. The soft light was so dim she could barely see the desire in his eyes, but she knew it was there.

His mouth caught hers in a kiss that was both rough and tender, and Mary gave in to her swirling emotions. The last thing she remembered was Carter whispering, "I don't want to lose you."

# Chapter 14

The only sound coming from the cell was the even breathing of the couple entwined in a lovers' embrace as they slept on the small cot.

The first rays of sunlight slipped through the high cell window and cast a warm glow into what was usually a cold room.

Carter stirred, waking Mary. Her head was resting on his shoulder with her arm draped across his chest. She really didn't want to move because, once she did, the contented spell she seemed to be in would vanish, reality would barrel back into her life, and she'd be on her own again.

"Did you sleep well last night?" Carter asked.

"Yes, I did. No nightmares," Mary murmured, wondering if he felt as wonderful as she did this morning. "How about you?"

"I did sleep well," he said, looking down at her. "We should get dressed before we have company, and I have to explain why I'm in a cell with you without my clothes on," Carter murmured, absently rubbing her arm.

Mary laughed as she looked up at him. "Even though the answer would be obvious, I suppose you're right." She traced her fingers across his chest, swirling circles in the thick hair. "Thank you for staying with me last night. You seem to chase my demons away."

"If only I could keep them away." Carter pulled Mary up and kissed her. "But you don't have to thank me. I guess by now you've figured out that there is something between us. You're very special to me. I—I don't know what else to say," he said hesitantly.

Mary sat up and reached for her blouse. *You could try saying I love you.* Somehow, his words were irritating this morning. Then she remembered her mother and another woman talking. At the time the words had meant nothing to Mary, but now . . . The woman had said, "You mustn't mistake a man's attention for anything other than what it is. Just because he desires you don't mean he loves you. You have to hear the words."

And Carter hadn't said the words.

"Well, maybe one day you'll figure everything out," Mary snapped at him.

Carter got up and grabbed his breeches. He stepped into them quickly and reached for his shirt.

Evidently, her barb had bounced off him like water, which irritated her even more.

When Carter had finished buttoning his blue shirt, he glanced at her. "You realize I have to take you back to Gregory Gulch for trial."

Mary stood across the cell, her arms folded, damning Carter with her eyes as he locked the door. Maybe he didn't love her at all. If he did, would he lock the door? Could it be nothing more than lust that he felt?

Had she been a fool, just like her mother?

He said he cared for her, but hell, he cared for his horse, too. Well, he wouldn't kiss her again so easily. She might love him, but she wasn't a fool. "I realize you have to do your job, Marshal."

Carter narrowed his eyes and stared at Mary. He started to say something but changed his mind. Instead, he walked over to the potbelly stove and opened the small door. Taking a poker, he stirred the coals, then chucked some small pieces of wood into the fire to take off the morning chill. This time of year, they only needed the heat in the morning and at night now that the weather was turning warmer.

Grabbing the tin coffeepot, he went out back and dumped the grounds and old coffee. He felt lower than a snake, but the fact remained that Mary was accused of murder and he had a job to do.

Whether he liked it or not!

Carter heard the front door open as he headed back toward the front. He heard Rick say cheerfully to Mary, "Good morning. Carter run off and leave you?"

Thunder followed Rick inside, carrying a big tray of food.

"No, I didn't leave her," Carter informed him as he entered the room. "I'm making coffee."

Rick smiled. "Good, I brought you both some breakfast. And it sounds like you need some of that coffee. Fast."

Thunder strolled over to the cell. "How did you sleep last night?"

Mary knew her cheeks heated to a soft pink as she said, "Fine."

Rick opened the door, and Thunder removed a plate of biscuits for the three of them, then took the tray with the remaining plate of hot biscuits and gravy in to Mary. "Hope you're hungry."

"Thank you. I am."

Thunder handed her a package that had been tucked under his arm.

"What's this?"

"I believe you asked me to get you a change of clothes."

"Thank you," she said, and kissed him on the cheek. Then she placed the package on the end of the cot. She wasn't sure how she was going to change clothes without any privacy, but that was something she'd worry about later. Mary sat back on the bunk with her legs pulled up so she could place the plate on her lap. She buttered her biscuit.

Thunder dragged a chair into the cell. "I need to ask you some more questions," Thunder told her. "Do you feel up to it this morning?"

Mary nodded since her mouth was full.

"Good," Thunder said. He turned the chair backwards and straddled it. "I want you to think real hard. There had to be somebody else in that cabin. Is there anything you can remember?"

At first Mary shook her head, then she remembered the piece of material. She fumbled in the pocket of her skirt and withdrew the green plaid material. "This." She waved it at Thunder.

He took the fabric and examined it. "This is fine wool, the kind that comes from England or Ireland. I saw plaids like this when I lived in Boston, but what does it have to do with Jim's murder?"

"I don't know. When I woke up I found that small piece of material on my bed, and since I've never seen it before I wondered if I might have torn it off of whoever was there."

"That's a good point."

Mary picked up the linen cloth and wiped her mouth. "The night I was shot—"

Thunder gripped the back of the chair. "You were shot?" his voice boomed.

"Right here." She pointed to her arm, then went on to explain that she'd been singing and why. "I saw a man backstage with a green plaid coat. That's what made me remember the piece of material. He seemed to want my attention, but when I pointed him out to Carter's mother, he was gone. And then I thought I saw him at the back of the theater before I was shot."

Thunder smiled. "I think somebody is trying to kill you, kid, because you know something you shouldn't."

"But why can't I remember?"

Rick moved over to the cell. "I'm sorry for listening, but what Mary said sounds like the same thing several other folks said when I questioned them after the shooting. They thought they saw someone, but when I asked them to describe the person, it was as if their memory had been wiped out."

"That's interesting," Thunder said. "There has to be a clue that we're missing." He turned his attention back to Mary. "Can you remember what the man looked like?"

Carter had been listening to the entire conversation. Could it be that someone had framed Mary? But it still didn't make sense why she couldn't remember anything at all.

Mary placed her empty plate on the tray. "He was tall, very thin, and he had black hair."

"Did you ever see Big Jim's brother?" Thunder asked.

"No. Jim mentioned his brother was supposed to come to camp, but I never saw him," Mary replied.

"Well, he told Marshal Forester that you cooked supper for him, and then you and Jim got into an argument," Thunder told her. He watched as her face paled.

Mary stormed to her feet. "That is not true! I remember cooking supper because he was supposed to come to eat, but he never showed up, and I don't remember anything after that." She looked at Thunder and frowned. "That doesn't sound good, does it?"

Thunder stood. "No, kid. It doesn't. But we'll find out what happened."

Hank, breathing hard, stormed in through the door. "We got trouble."

"What kind of trouble?" Carter asked.

"The Carlsons are down at the saloon. They stopped me on the way in and told me to tell you they'd meet you on the street in two hours. If you don't show up, they'll start shooting anybody walking down the sidewalk."

Mary moved toward the bars. She could see every muscle in Carter's body tense. This was what he'd always wanted—revenge for his sister's death.

"I'll be there," Carter said.

"How many?" Rick asked.

"Five altogether," Hank told them. He reached for the coffeepot. "Two Carlsons and three new guns. However, there could be more that I didn't see. The last I heard, the gang had grown to ten."

"There are three of us. It shouldn't be bad," Rick reasoned.

"Sounds like you boys have trouble," Thunder said. He leaned back against the wall. "Who are the Carlsons?"

Rick spent the next half hour telling Thunder about the gang while Rick and Carter cleaned their guns. When Rick had finished, Thunder said, "Let's make that an even four."

"It's not your fight, Thunder. You don't really have to," Hank said.

Thunder studied the sheriff for a moment. "I think it evens up the numbers."

Carter looked up from loading his gun. "Can you shoot?"

Thunder smiled slowly. "I believe I could hit something if it were big enough."

Carter looked skeptical.

Thunder wasn't surprised. But he was finding he liked Carter's surly attitude. He just might be man enough to handle Mary—and even then it wouldn't be easy.

"If you have doubts, why don't you just draw on Thunder?" Mary suggested from her cell. She wore a devious smile that Thunder recognized well.

Carter stood up and holstered his .44-caliber Remington. "That isn't a bad idea. I don't want to have you getting killed on my conscience just because you can't handle a gun."

"You boys unload your guns first," Hank told them. "Just in case you forget this is practice."

They both emptied their chambers. Thunder leaned casually against the wall. Carter was across the room. Rick stood in the middle.

"All right, on the count of three, both of you draw. Those guns are empty, aren't they?" Rick asked.

Both men nodded.

"One. Two. Three," Rick shouted. "Well, I'll be

damned," he said when Carter's gun had only half cleared the holster.

Mary smiled as Thunder said, "You lose."

"All right," Carter agreed, his brow arched. "I guess you can go with us. Where did you learn to shoot like that?"

"When you've been called a half-breed all your life, you learn real quick how to handle a gun."

"Hell, I want him in front of me," Rick said with a chuckle.

As Thunder reloaded his Colt, he asked, "When do you intend to leave for Gregory Gulch?"

"Just as soon as I kill the last two Carlsons," Carter said nonchalantly.

"Revenge drives many men," Thunder commented. "If someone had killed my family, I'm sure I would probably feel the same way. Just remember, there comes a time when you have to let the past go and start living."

"You sound like somebody who has been there," Carter said.

"That's right. I was driven by my own demons for a long time," Thunder admitted. Then he changed the subject. "I will probably catch up with you later. I'd like to find John McCoy. Supposedly, he's headed this way. That is, unless you feel that you need my help in getting Mary safely back to Gregory Gulch."

Carter shot him a withering look. "I think I can manage. Nobody will harm her."

"Good. Make sure they don't, or you'll answer to me." Thunder didn't even pretend to smile.

Hank finished his coffee. "I think both of you could stand a strong cup of coffee." He held up the coffeepot and motioned to both of them. "Be-

ieve I'll do a walkabout and warn folks to stay off
he streets."

"Better take someone with you," Carter suggested.

"I'll go," Rick volunteered.

Hank placed his hat on his head. "After seeing
Thunder draw, I'd rather have him."

"Thanks a lot," Rick grumbled. "Guess I'll go
get more ammo at the hardware store."

"No offense, son," Hank said.

Hank and Thunder were still laughing at Rick
as they walked out the door. Then there was quiet.
Mary wasn't used to just sitting around, doing
nothing, and she felt restless, like a caged animal.
She cast a glance at Carter. It appeared he was
going to be her only source of entertainment, so
she might as well talk to him.

"Couldn't you just arrest that gang so no one
would get hurt?" she asked.

Carter glanced up at her with a look of disbelief.
"I could issue them an invitation, but I doubt they'd
take it. They were brought before a judge once,
but they got off because the evidence presented
didn't hold up in court."

"I was being serious," Mary insisted with a
frown. "One of you could be hurt."

Carter moved over so he could see her through
the bars. "You would worry about me?"

Mary wasn't going to give him the satisfaction of
hearing she'd be worried sick, so she simply said,
"Of course, I don't want a stranger to drag me
back to Gregory Gulch. I'm used to you."

She received a frown from him that really pleased
the ornery side of her. But she managed to keep a
straight face. Then she added the final blow to his

ego. "I was worried about Hank. He isn't as young as the rest of you."

"Hank is pretty fast, so don't let that graying hair fool you," Carter told her. He shifted and propped his shoulder against the wall as he talked to her. "Want to hear how Hank got his job?"

Mary went back to the cot and sat down. Better to keep her distance from him. "Sure. I've got time."

"I'm not sure I can tell it the same as Hank, but I'll give it a shot," Carter said with a smile. "Seems like a cowboy came in off the range one day and proceeded to celebrate at the Golden Lady. As the rotgut began to take over his body, he began to shoot out the lights. Guess he needed something to do. He started demanding that people drink with him and generally making life unpleasant, but that wasn't enough—this cowboy started roughing up a couple of patrons. So Hank, who had been sitting in the corner playing cards, strolled up to the cowboy and said, 'I'll give you five minutes to get out of town.'"

"Did Hank have a gun?" Mary asked.

"Nope."

"So what happened?"

"The cowboy put up his gun, walked out of the saloon to where his horse was hitched, and rode out of town."

Mary came back over to the bars and gripped them. She waited to see if Carter was teasing her. "Just that easy?" she asked.

"Yep. Hank was asked what he would have done if the cowboy refused to go. And Hank said, 'I'd have given him five more minutes.'" Carter chuckled.

Mary laughed. "I like that story. Thank you."

Carter shoved away from the wall and covered her hands on the bars with his. "You're welcome. I wish I could let you out of there," he admitted.

"I do, too."

"Mary, if anything should happen today . . ."

Ignoring the mocking voice inside that wondered why she cared for this man, she begged, "Please don't do this. Just arrest them."

"I don't intend to have a gunfight if I don't have to, but it will be hard to arrest that many men without it. You'll be safe in here."

"It's not me I'm worried about," she said in a choked voice. She cleared her throat before she asked one last time. "Don't leave me locked up! I promise I won't run. Just don't leave me locked up."

Carter touched her hand in a gentle caress. "I can't break the law, Mary. Not even for you."

She could only stare at him. She knew all along that Carter believed in his principles, so how could she blame him for not breaking them? *Not even for her.* She would hear those words forever.

*Not even for her.*

Because those words would remind her that Carter didn't love her. She'd been fooling herself all along.

*Not even for her.* Mary wanted to cry for being such a fool.

Rick barged through the door. "It's time. They just shot Hank."

Carter grabbed his gun off the desk. "Is Hank alive?" he asked as they raced out the door.

Mary didn't realize that tears had started to tumble down her cheeks. She was left alone clinging to the cold bars, praying that no one would be killed, and wondering if Hank was still alive.

# Chapter 15

The Red Eye Saloon was buzzing with activity. It was just past noon and the place was already crowded as the Carlsons ambled through, winding around the tables and making their way toward the mahogany bar in the back of the building.

A honky-tonk piano player was playing a tune in the corner, but no one paid him any attention as they were either drinking or playing cards.

Sammy spotted McCoy's back at the bar and headed toward him. Sammy sidled up to the bar on one side of McCoy with Randy on the other side. "See you had to have a drink, too," Sammy said and then ordered whiskey. "What have you heard?"

McCoy tossed down a shot of red-eye before replying, "They have more help. Sheriff Hank came in earlier. He had a tall gunslinger with him. I heard Hank call the man Thunder. If that is true, you boys are in a lot of trouble."

"Pretty fast, huh?" Randy asked.

"Damned tooting. Haven't heard anything about him for a few years. But trust me, he's fast. I saw him take a man down in Independence before his victim had a chance to clear leather."

Sammy refilled his shot glass. "I'm not so bad myself."

"Let's hope so," McCoy said. Turning sideways to look at Sammy, McCoy asked, "What's the marshal after you for?"

Sammy chuckled. "Not too sure other than he's a lawman with a burr under his saddle about something. Don't ever remember meeting up with him face-to-face even though he's picked off most of the old gang."

McCoy wiped his mouth with the back of his hand. "Are you boys still going with my plan?"

"Yep. Although I'd rather shoot the marshal down in the street, I like the way you think about making Monroe suffer for the years he's dogged my tracks."

"I think McCoy's idea ain't half bad," Randy chimed in. "This way we won't get charged with nothing since we aren't doing the shooting. We'll come out of this whole mess lily white."

"Good." McCoy smiled. "Now remember to keep them busy, so I have time to carry out my end." He slapped his coins on the bar. "Give me half an hour to get set up before you call them out."

Randy watched McCoy as he left. "Something about that guy makes my skin crawl."

"Yeah. Mine, too, but we have the same goal this time, so it works," Sammy said before he tossed down another shot. "Don't know if I believe what he's talking about. Putting somebody to sleep or whatever the hell he called it."

"Me neither. We'll have to see if he can do what he says." Randy grabbed a cigar off the bar. "Reckon it's worth a risk or two."

"Give me one of those," Sammy ordered. "If he don't, we'll just put a bullet in him." He shrugged. "No big loss."

"Ah, shit!" Randy swore. His gaze fixed on the big looking glass over the bar. "Here comes the local sheriff."

"Good," Sammy said. "I ain't going to take no sass off him. Not today."

The telltale smell of burning tobacco hung in the air as Hank strolled through the saloon.

"Look, boys. I don't want any trouble."

Sammy leaned back on the bar. "Our fight is with Monroe."

"But it's in my town," Hank pointed out. He wasn't a man of violence, but he wasn't a man to back away either. "I won't have you shooting up the town," he informed them.

Sammy straightened, his hands on his hips. "This has been a long time coming, Sheriff. Don't even know why Monroe has dogged my tracks, but I'm real sick of it. If you don't want nobody hurt, I suggest you get them off the street."

Hank looked at the outlaws long and hard. If he'd been ten years younger, he'd have already slapped these two in jail. But age had a way of making one cautious. "You boys are going to regret this," he warned them one last time, then made his way to the front where he'd left Rick standing by the bat-wing doors.

"Not as much as you will," Sammy muttered under his breath to Randy. "Get one of the boys to take old Hank out."

Randy nodded. "He's a mouthy old coot."

"He also made a big mistake when he killed our brother a few years back," Sammy said tightly, then motioned for the bartender to bring another bottle. "We're going to get revenge big-time today."

Hank and Rick sauntered out of the saloon and onto the street. What they didn't see was Randy giving a signal from the saloon doors.

Hank rubbed the back of his neck as they walked. The clinking of harnesses and the squeak of saddle leather sounded pretty normal at the moment. "I got a bad feeling about this. Those two are shifty-eyed scoundrels—can't trust them."

"I agree," Rick said. "I think they intend to shoot up the town."

"Yeah. Me, too. And we don't have enough guns to defend it." Hank pulled out his pocket watch; the sun glinted off the gold. "We got fifteen minutes. Better start warning folks to stay inside."

"I'll take this side of Main Street," Rick said as he started across the dirt.

They both knocked on doors and warned the citizens that there was going to be a gunfight and they needed to stay inside. Most folks nodded, but none volunteered to help out.

Rick was getting ready to step off the sidewalk to meet Hank when he saw a flash and heard a shot. He crouched down and fired at the rooftop, sending the outlaw toppling over the side of the building and down to the ground with a bone-crunching thud. Rick didn't pay any attention to the body because Hank lay sprawled out in the street, and he wasn't moving.

Rick ran to Hank's side, then dropped down on

his knee. He saw that Hank's eyes were open and he breathed a sigh of relief. "How bad is it?" he asked, helping Hank to a sitting position.

"Pretty darn bad when you get shot in the back," Hank grumbled.

"I got the slimy bastard who did this," Rick told him, then he grasped Hank's arm. "Here, let me help you to your feet. We need to get you to Doc's before they start shooting some more." Rick looked at Hank's arm. "Appears to be in the shoulder."

"Yeah. The same damn shoulder I was shot in two and a half months ago." Hank grimaced as he stood. "I don't have time for the doc. You boys are goin' to need help."

Rick steadied Hank. "You're in no condition to be in a gunfight. I think one bullet hole is enough for one day," Rick told him while guiding Hank in the direction of the doctor's office.

"You saying I'm no good?"

"Just not at your best. At least you have one good arm," Rick cajoled as they hobbled across the street. He constantly scanned the buildings to make sure someone else didn't take a shot at them before they could get to safety.

"My shooting arm is still good," Hank admitted. "But I'm beginning to wonder if I ain't too dang old for this job."

"You've just been down lately. First the flu and now two new bullet holes." Rick opened the door to the doc's office. "Hey, Hank has been wounded!"

Doc Moore sauntered out to meet them, took one look at Hank, and said, "Again?"

"Yep. I'm getting slow," Hank admitted.

"I'm going to leave him here," Rick said on his way out the door. "There might be more coming."

Rick ran all the way to the jailhouse, burst through the door, and shouted, "Hank's been shot!"

Carter paused just outside the jailhouse door and strapped down his gun. He straightened and looked out at the now deserted street. There were no riders or children playing, only quiet and the wind whipping down the street, causing a whorl of dust. He felt the tension; his long awaited day had arrived.

Carter, Thunder, and Rick shuffled out into the dirt street. At the far end they saw five men; Carter knew two of them had to be Sammy and Randy Carlson. They were spread across the street, poised, ready.

"Does it strike you as odd that the Carlsons are at the far end of the street instead of in front of the saloon?" Carter asked.

"Maybe they wanted to get away from the townsfolk," Rick suggested.

"I don't think so," Thunder said.

Carter glanced to his left. "Let's hear what you're thinking."

"Could be an ambush," Thunder told them as he adjusted his black Stetson over his eyes. "Only white men are stupid enough to walk down the middle of the street and shoot at each other."

Carter cleared his throat. "Should I point out the fact that you *are* a white man?"

"Ah." Thunder smiled. "But I was raised by the Cheyenne."

"Are we going to stand here and jaw-jack all day," Rick asked, flexing his hand impatiently, "or get on with it?"

"Youth," Thunder said. "Why don't you two go ahead, and I'll even out the fight by seeing who's lurking on the rooftops."

"Good idea," Carter agreed.

Thunder darted into the alley so quickly, he seemed to have disappeared before their eyes. Carter and Rick started walking, making sure they didn't take their eyes off the enemy.

"You think we can take them?" Rick asked.

"They're pretty fast," Carter drawled. "But I think we can take them. I especially want Sammy—he's the one who rode out with my sister, and he's always escaped my grasp in our previous encounters with the gang."

As they passed the saloon there was a noise. Both men crouched down and swung to their left. They saw Thunder wave briefly before he disappeared again.

"I believe Thunder is still a little savage," Rick said as he straightened and they started forward again.

Another sudden thud followed the first, catching their attention for a moment. Carter realized that Thunder was making good on his promise. They hadn't heard any shots so he was either knocking them unconscious or slitting their throats.

*Maybe Thunder truly was the savage.*

"As I was saying. What are you going to do when you no longer have to worry about the Carlsons?" Rick asked.

"I don't know," Carter answered truthfully.

They stopped about thirty feet in front of the outlaws. They were within easy speaking distance of the men and could see them clearly. All five of them were spread out across the street, feet apart, fingers flexing, waiting for someone to make the first move.

"I think we're a little outnumbered," Rick commented.

"Will one more help?" Thunder called from the boardwalk before strolling over to stand with them.

"What took you so long?" Carter asked sarcastically.

"The last guy was pretty stubborn."

One of the Carlsons shifted his stance. "Our fight ain't with you, mister."

Thunder's mouth spread into a thin-lipped smile. "It is now."

"Suit yourself." The taller one sneered.

"Which one of you is Sammy Carlson?" Carter asked.

The taller one spoke. "I am."

"Then you are under arrest," Carter told him.

"I heard you been lookin' for me, Marshal." Sammy's words were directed at Carter. "What for?"

"You're under arrest for the murder of my sister," Carter snarled.

"Just who the hell is your sister? And how do you know I killed her?"

"Think back five years when you were in this very town." Carter spoke in a hard, strong voice. "You were drunk and shooting up the town. However, that must not have been enough because on your way out of town you picked up a young woman who was sitting in a wagon—long blond hair, blue eyes."

"Oh yeah, I remember now," Sammy said with a slow smile. "Fine little piece, too."

Carter's gun cleared the leather in a flash. But he was so angry his bullet only hit Sammy in the arm. He grunted and grabbed his wound.

Then all hell broke loose.

A bullet caught one of the men just about the belt buckle; blood sputtered as he went down.

Bullets were flying as both of the Carlsons ran into the dry goods store where they could hold off the law. Seeing this, Carter, Rick, and Thunder dove behind a wagon and water trough.

Shots were heard from within the store and Carter knew they had killed Mac McBride, the store's owner.

"Christ," Rick swore. Wood splintered off the trough and nicked his arm.

"You all right?" Carter asked.

"Yeah," Rick grumbled.

"I'm going around the back of that building," Thunder called from his position. "If we don't do something, we'll be here all day."

"Look," Rick shouted at the same time, but was ignored as the outlaws opened fire.

Rick and Carter returned the gunfire, covering Thunder as he dashed across the street in a blaze of bullets. Remarkably he made it to the other side of the street without a scratch.

A bullet whizzed by Carter's head just as he ducked behind the wagon. He reloaded his gun while Rick continued firing. Carter had thought this was going to be a fair fight in the street. He should have known better.

"Look," Rick said again in between shots.

"That is the second time you've pointed that way," Carter told him. "The fighting is the opposite direction."

"No shit. However, the town is burning down the other way."

Carter eased up and looked over the barrel. A gust of wind whipped by him as he eased up to see flames coming out of the top of the building. The smoke was strong. The citizens were running out in the streets, screaming and yelling for water.

"What are we going to do?" Rick asked.

"Finish the outlaws," Carter said, turning back around. "They'd love nothing more than to shoot at those innocent people." He clicked the chamber of his gun shut and got back on his knees. "Listen! The shooting has ceased."

"They're gone!" Thunder yelled just before he came out of the building. "Christ! There's a fire."

Carter and Rick came from behind the wagon. "I guess we're going to have to go after them," Carter said.

"That fire is getting near the jail!" Rick yelled.

Carter swung around, the blood draining from his face. "Mary. She's locked up. I'd forgotten about her," he admitted.

Thunder frowned.

Carter took off, then stopped. "The Carlsons." They were within in his grasp—all he had to do was ride after them. It was what he'd always dreamed of, what he'd always wanted.

However, not when Mary's life was endangered.

Carter turned and started running toward the orange sky. It appeared as if the whole damn town was burning. The wind seemed to be whispering for him to hurry as it whipped up, causing the flames to soar higher and the dense smoke to become thicker. The wind was helping flames jump the street. They landed on top of the dry goods store and other buildings. Several bucket brigades had already been formed. They were trying to save the opera house.

When he reached the jail, smoke was pouring out the windows and panic like Carter had never experienced before threatened to take his breath away. He didn't think twice as he barged through the door with his shoulder into black-gray smoke that sucked all the air out of his lungs and sent him to the ground. He sputtered and coughed until he could catch his breath, then got to his knees.

The heat was unbearable as Carter crawled along the fire, praying the entire time. He was so damned scared that Mary would be dead, his hands were shaking. It was all his fault. He shouldn't have left her alone, just like he shouldn't have left his sister alone. Evidently the years hadn't made him any wiser.

The smoke burned his eyes as he blundered through the smoke until he finally felt the hot metal bars, but the door was locked.

His heart sank—she hadn't gotten out.

After he got the keys and unlocked the door, he called, "Mary! Make a noise so I can find you."

Nothing.

Part of the roof caved in and Carter had to roll to the side. He jerked the handkerchief from his neck and covered his mouth. Then he searched the cell, moving toward the bundle in the corner. The bundle wasn't moving.

"Mary." Carter coughed, having taken in the bitter smoke. Tears streamed down his cheeks as he felt the bundle.

Nothing. His brain screamed that it was all his fault.

The flames were too intense to go any farther. Carter was forced to stumble back though the smoke until he fell out the door.

He felt someone drag him off the porch and into the street. He coughed, gasping for fresh air, but he really felt like dying.

When he finally got his wind, he looked up at Thunder. Tears blurred Carter's vision as he whispered, "Mary is gone."

# Chapter 16

Thunder yanked Carter up by the shirt, which was no easy task. "What do you mean, she's gone?"

"I just told you. I found Mary's clothes in the corner, but not Mary! And I'd suggest you get your hands off me," Carter growled through clenched teeth.

Thunder let go of Carter, but still gave him a hostile glare. "That doesn't make any sense. Was the door open?"

"No. I had to unlock it."

Something cracked behind them. They both swung around just in time to see the roof of the jail cave in, making both of them jump back as sparks flew high in the air and landed like raindrops around them.

Thunder ran a hand through his hair. "If she were dead, you would have found her body, so let's don't think along those lines. She's alive. She's gone through too much in her life to die now."

Evidently Carter didn't heed the warning, because as he gazed at the fire he said, "Maybe she went to the back room and couldn't get out."

"I told you to quit thinking like that!" Thunder snapped.

Carter had had enough. "I'm getting pretty damn sick of you right about now, so you'd better tread softly." His voice was quiet, yet held an undertone of cold contempt as he finished. "You think that I'm not upset about Mary? Why, she means ..."

"Yes," Thunder prodded, his arms folded across his chest as he waited for Carter to finish his statement.

"She means a lot to me," Carter snapped. His expression was one of mute wretchedness.

Thunder had to keep from smiling.

"But *you* locked her up."

"For Christ's sake! She broke the law. It was my duty."

Hank came storming up to them. His shoulder had been bandaged, but other than that he looked fine, just angry. "What the Sam Hill is the matter with both of you? The town is on fire, and both of you are standing out in the middle of the street arguing when you should be helping folks fight the fire."

"We can't find Mary," Carter said as if Hank should understand that nothing else mattered. "Did you let her out by some chance?"

"Nope." Hank shoved back his hat. "But when I was walking out of Doc's office, I saw her riding out of town. Almost didn't recognize her because she had on different clothes."

"Who was she with?" Carter and Thunder asked at the same time. It was getting to be a damn annoying habit, Carter thought. They were too much alike.

"Don't know," Hank said with a shrug, then he winced at the pain in his shoulder. "Figured it was one of the boys from the ranch. Once I saw the fire, it made sense that you wanted her safely out of town."

"But Mother didn't know Mary was here," Carter quickly pointed out. "So I doubt it was a ranch hand. But who?" Carter glanced at Thunder to see if he had any answers.

Thunder shrugged. "I have no idea, but at least we know Mary got out of the blaze. Let's help with the fire now, maybe we can figure it out later."

Carter insisted that Hank help to direct everyone where they should go, thinking it would be much easier on him. Then Carter and Thunder worked with the citizens trying to save precious belongings, because there was no help for the buildings.

In the end the only things left standing were the saloon, the dry goods store, the livery, and the funeral parlor.

The rest of Windy Bend had been burned to rubble.

The men gathered to stare at the smoking haze as the sky turned to dusk. The red embers looked like glowing eyes staring at them.

Doc Moore was the first to speak. "What in the hell could have caused such a fire?"

"Good question," Hank said. "If there had been lightning, we would have known the cause. Maybe somebody set the fire."

Just then a rider came barreling up behind them, stopping about fifty yards away from the group of men.

Carter and Thunder both swung around and drew their guns, but wisely held their fire, waiting to see what the rider said. The man threw something in their direction, then rode off.

Carter retrieved the leather pouch. He peered inside the pouch, saw a piece of paper, and withdrew it. Quickly, he scanned the writing in the dimming daylight. "The Carlsons have Mary," Carter finally said. He handed the slip of paper to Thunder.

Hank blew out a disgusted sigh. "Now I'm sure that fire was set. First they kept you busy in a gunfight while the rest of the gang grabbed Mary. The Carlsons have plagued this town for too long."

"Yes, they have," Carter agreed, his voice hoarse with frustration. "Let's get the horses," he said, turning to Thunder.

As they marched to the stable, both men were quiet. Carter's thoughts were on the note. The instructions were to ride to King's Canyon and make camp, then wait. Mary would be sent to them. Something was wrong. It was too simple. He knew that the Carlsons were up to something. But what?

He realized that his heart was slamming against his ribs. He was much more scared not knowing about Mary than he had been in the gunfight. He just prayed they didn't hurt her.

"This could be a setup," Carter said, finally expressing his thoughts.

Thunder nodded as he tightened the cinch of his saddle. "You're probably right. We'll have to be on guard."

"They're using Mary for a bargaining tool, so right now she's safe. But if they've hurt her . . ." Carter's curt words trailed off.

"You'll what . . . arrest them?" Thunder asked with a sardonic smile.

Carter gave him a sidelong glance as he mounted his horse. This time, he could truly say that he'd have no regret for what he would do to them. "I thought more along the lines of killing them."

Thunder's smile was without humor. "Then count me in."


Mary couldn't believe that Carter and Thunder had left her locked in the cell like a common criminal. It was so like Carter, but she'd thought otherwise of Thunder. She had to smile at that thought, but the smile quickly vanished when she remembered that Carter hadn't even bothered to look back at her as he'd stormed out the door.

It was a helpless feeling to be confined and without any control of her situation, but there wasn't anything she could do about it now except sulk.

She glanced at the package on the cot. At least she could change her clothes now that she had a little privacy. She unwrapped the bundle and found a white blouse similar to what she'd seen Mexican women wear.

Mary pulled her old dress over her head and tossed it in the corner. She never wanted to see the threadbare garment again. After wearing the nice clothes that Judith had provided, Mary realized that she enjoyed dressing well and would like to have fine clothes of her own someday.

She shook out the garments, then slipped the blouse on over her head. The white ruffle fell nicely around her shoulders. It was a perfect fit and very comfortable, as well.

The dark blue skirt was simple and fit snugly around her hips, flaring out toward the hem. It was a little short, but that didn't matter. At least her skirt wouldn't drag in the dirt. Once she had the waist hooked, she ran her hands over the material to smooth it out.

Now she was all dressed up with no place to go, so she sat down to wait. A gun blast sounded in the distance. She gripped her hands, praying that no one she cared about had been killed.

Then there were more shots.

And still she waited for word.

The waiting was miserable. She didn't know what was going on. She wanted to see what was happening.

What if Carter had been killed? Her stomach clenched. Mary couldn't bear the thought of not seeing him again. No matter how angry she was at him, she didn't want him hurt.

Something smelled funny. She sniffed. It smelled a lot like smoke. Mary hurried to the bars of her cell and peered over at the potbellied stove, but she didn't see anything unusual. Yet the smell seemed to be growing stronger.

Something was burning.

She glanced up at the window and saw small wisps of smoke curling through the bars. What could be burning outside?

Dragging the cot under the window, she stepped up on the cot and peeked out the barred window.

Mary gasped, but she drew in too much smoky air and started to cough. Her eyes burned and watered. She rubbed them and looked again. White smoke and huge red flames were being blown straight toward the jail by the wind. It looked like the building next to them was engulfed in fire. Hot winds blew in through the window bringing more smoke.

She was trapped!

Mary yelled out the window, "Help me!" But every time she opened her mouth to scream, she gulped smoke and that set her to coughing. So she climbed down and sat on the cot. What could she do to help herself?

Damn Carter Monroe for leaving her like this!

She grasped the bars on the cell and looked over at the keys. Her eyes were still watering and burning, and she had to wipe away the tears. There were the keys, hanging on a peg, promising her freedom, but too far away to do her any good.

As she coughed and wiped her eyes again, the door of the jailhouse flew open. At first she thought it might be Carter, but a man she didn't recognize ran in.

"Who are you?"

"I was sent to get you out of here before the place burnt down," the stranger said as he retrieved the keys from the peg.

Mary thought the jingle of keys had never sounded so good.

The man unlocked the door. "You're to come with me."

Mary put her hand over her mouth against the smoke and nodded. Her eyes were watering so badly that she could barely see. But she followed the man to two horses, figuring he had to be one of the men from town.

The horse was skittish from the smoke, and it took Mary several tries before she mounted the animal. She did notice this wasn't the horse that she had ridden to town, but she figured with the fire the man had grabbed the first animal he came to.

There was still shooting going on, so it didn't surprise Mary when they rode around the back of the buildings and out of town.

"Where are we going?" Mary asked.

"Someplace safe," the man answered.

Mary breathed in the fresh air. She was too thankful to get the smoke out of her lungs to question him, and her eyes were finally clearing, too. She figured they would go to where some of the other townsfolk were gathered and they'd sort themselves out later.

But they didn't. Instead they kept going.

Apprehension began to creep over her. True, the man had saved her life when no one else had bothered to look in on her, but why were they going so far out of town? Mary pulled back on the reins. "Wait a minute. I don't want to leave town. My brother is back there, and Carter. I need to see if they're all right. Who are you anyway, and where are we going?" she demanded. "I'll go no farther until you tell me!"

The man swung around and rode back to her. Now that she could see clearly, Mary realized there was something vaguely familiar about him. She stared at him, waiting for him to say something.

What was it about that face?

But he said nothing. Instead of answering her, he reached up and tugged at his ear. What was he—?

Mary knew nothing else.

McCoy felt cold contempt for the girl as he stared at her for a moment. "What were you saying?"

"I don't remember," Mary replied, confused.

"That is what I thought." The man smiled. "Now you are going to ride behind me and say nothing."

"I will ride behind you," Mary said, her voice dull and automatic.

McCoy nudged his horse. They rode through a

couple of canyons until they reached Box Canyon and the hidden road. He stopped, moved the brush, then led their horses through. After McCoy replaced the brush, he grabbed his horse's reins and Mary's, then led the two horses into the camp that he and the Carlsons had set up.

After tying his horse, he held Mary's mount's halter. "Get down." He watched her obediently follow his command, then he left her to tie her horse beside his.

He returned to find her standing in the same spot, just staring off into the distance. Boy, he had her trained good, he thought with pleasure. "Mary, go and sit by that rock and do not move until I give you further instructions."

She went quietly and did as he instructed.

It wasn't long before Sammy Carlson and two of his men galloped into the ravine where the campsite had been set up. The two men were wearing tasseled sombreros and short jackets.

"I see you got her," Sammy said, nodding toward the girl. He dismounted. "Boys, get some grub going."

"I told you I would," McCoy told him. "Where is your brother?"

Sammy yanked his saddlebags from his horse, then tossed the reins to Fred, one of his men, before answering McCoy. "Dead."

McCoy frowned. "Dead? I thought you were just going to hold them off until I could get the fire started."

"You took your damn time about getting that fire lit," Fred said, dusting off his hat on his chaps. "We damned near all got shot."

"I was working by myself," McCoy informed them.

"You should have been on our end," Tom, the other hired gun, said.

"Why is that?"

Sammy handed a sack of beans to Fred so he could put them in the pot. "Because they had somebody new who was damn good with a gun. Don't know where he came from. The marshal has always been fast, but this guy—he looked like a 'breed. Poor Randy never saw it coming. That 'breed took him out before Randy could blink twice."

Sammy dug down in his saddlebag and fished out some strips of material, then sat down in front of Mary. "Make yourself useful and bandage my arm."

Mary didn't move.

"What's wrong with her? Is she deaf?"

"She's in a trance," McCoy said. He bent over and looked at the girl. "Mary, look at me." Slowly she lifted her head. "Bandage the man's arm, but be careful you don't hurt him."

Mary got up on her knees, then reached for Sammy's arm and tore the sleeve up over the wound. Next she wrapped the strips of cloth around his arm. When she'd finished, she sat back down.

"Well, I'll be damned," Sammy said. "Why isn't she saying nothing?"

"Because I've not told her to."

"So exactly what have you done to her? It's the craziest thing I've ever seen. Sure wish I could get all women to do what I say without a bunch of arguin'."

McCoy sat down beside Mary. "I have put her into a hypnotic sleep."

"What does that mean?"

"Even though she looks awake, she is actually asleep and under the influence of my suggestion."

Sammy looked very skeptical. "I don't believe you. How do you know she'll carry out our plan?"

"I'll show you while Fred and Tom cook the beans. Are you sure we don't need to ride farther out?"

"Nope. We're all set for them to come after us, but first they have a mighty big fire to put out." He laughed.

McCoy frowned. He just hoped the cowboy was right. He touched Mary's shoulder. "Mary, all your fingers on your right hand will ball up into a fist and you will not be able to unclench your hand no matter how hard you try. The hand will cause you great pain until I release you. Do you understand?"

She nodded.

"On the count of three you'll wake up. But when I ask you about your hand, you will feel the pain. One . . . two . . . three."

Mary slowly blinked. What was happening? She felt such pressure in her head. "Where am I? And who are you? Where is Carter?" She didn't have any idea how she'd gotten here. She did recognize the man who led her out of town . . . and there was something else about him.

"What's in your hand?"

She looked at her fist and tried to open it, but she couldn't no matter how hard she tried. And the pain was excruciating. "My fingers! They're not working. I can't open my hand," she said in a panicked voice. "I don't know who you people are, but I'm going back to town even if I have to walk."

"Mary!" McCoy snapped to gain her attention. As soon as she looked at him, he tugged on his ear, causing her to go back into a trance. "Sit back down."

When she was seated again, McCoy said to Sammy, "Try and open her hand."

Sammy took her fist and tried to pry Mary's fingers out, but he couldn't do it. She cried out in pain, and he tried harder. Finally, he gave up and slapped her hand away from him. "The bitch is strong," he grumbled.

Mary stood there, silent tears running down her cheeks.

McCoy laughed. "Not the person, but the mind. Mary, would you like to get rid of the pain you're in?"

"Yes," she said with a whimper.

"All you have to do is kiss me and your pain will simply go away."

Mary leaned over to McCoy, put her arms around his neck, and kissed him intimately. At the same time, he unbuttoned her blouse and caressed her breasts. Then he let her go.

When Mary sat back, her hand was open just as if nothing had ever happened.

"Button your blouse," McCoy instructed.

"You know, I think I'm going to like this arrangement," Sammy said. "Maybe after she's done the murders, we could have her rob a few banks and provide some pleasure for me and the men."

"Whoa." McCoy held up his hand. There was really no need for trouble now, so he would have to tread carefully. After all they were a hard, dangerous-looking bunch. "That wasn't our agreement. After she kills the marshal, I'm taking her back to Gregory Gulch—that is, if she's still alive. There is a matter of a gold mine I need to see to. If you boys want to go straight, you can come and work the claim. It will make you rich, according to my dear, departed brother."

Sammy frowned. "Sounds like a lot of work to me."

"Beans are ready," Tom said as he spooned out a helping onto his plate. "I'd rather other folks make the money and we take it from them."

Amusement flickered in Sammy's eyes as he said in his slow drawl, "That's why I like you boys."

# Chapter 17

The inky black fingers of dust were slithering across the sky, stilling the light as Carter and Thunder rode through the gorge. The fir and aspen trees guarded the sides of the slopes like soldiers.

It didn't take them long to reach Box Canyon, where they had been instructed to go. The sound of the three-hundred-foot waterfall greeted them. They found what they thought looked like the safest place, next to a stream. With the stream protecting their backs they could see whoever approached them. After agreeing, they started preparing to settle in for the night.

Thunder built a campfire next to the stream. Since they wanted the outlaws to know exactly where they were, they didn't worry about keeping the fire small. Carter tossed out their bedrolls, though he doubted either one of them would get any sleep. He worried as he waited and hoped that the Carlsons were kinder to Mary than they had been to his sister.

"I don't know about you, but all I can smell and

taste is smoke," Carter said as he straightened and stretched his aching back. "You watch out while I wash up, and then I'll do the same for you."

Thunder nodded, and a wry smile touched his lips. "That sounds good."

"What's so funny?"

"Do you realize that is the first time we've agreed on anything?" Thunder asked.

Carter smiled. "I knew you'd come around to my way of thinking sooner or later." He went to his saddlebags and dug out clean clothes. He was glad now that he always kept a change of duds in his bag.

The water felt wonderful and fresh as he dove under. When he came up, he listened to the peaceful sound of the waterfall as he relaxed. After several minutes of floating, Carter finally began to lather his arms with the small chuck of lye soap that Thunder had in his gear.

Carter thought about Mary. Was she being treated well? Was she frightened?

Somehow he couldn't picture her as a scared little mouse. His mouth twitched. His Mary was more like a mountain lion. Yep, that would describe Mary, all right. In spite of his concern, he couldn't help smiling.

But if the outlaws made the mistake of hurting her, he would personally make their deaths slow and painful.

Had he just thought of her as *his* Mary? Where had that come from? Carter shook his head. His focus must be a little fuzzy at the moment. He understood that once he had Mary back, he was still going to have to take her back to Gregory Gulch to stand trial. Somehow that didn't set right with him as it once had.

Yet, there was no concrete proof that Mary was innocent—and too much circumstantial evidence to suggest that she was guilty. Carter blew out a long, disgusted sigh. Now that he knew Mary, he found it hard to believe that she was a cold-blooded murderer. Oh, he had no doubt she'd shoot a man—most likely himself, if she were angry enough—but she wouldn't carve someone up with a knife.

He had some real issues where Mary was concerned. One big, looming question was whether he could let her walk out of his life. Hoping to get the cobwebs out of his mind, he ducked under the cold water.

When he emerged, he had his answer and it wasn't fuzzy anymore.

He couldn't let Mary go.

If they found her guilty, then he'd help her fight, and if that didn't work, he'd break Mary out of jail and they would go someplace where no one would find them.

"Are you going to stay in there all damned night?" Thunder's voice rang out loud and clear.

"Hold your horses. I'm coming," Carter snapped, then he added, smiling to himself as he called back to Thunder, "Did you fix supper?"

"Try some beef jerky."

When Carter walked back to the campfire, they glared at each other, but he couldn't resist saying, "Maybe that water will cool off your hot head."

"Don't count on it," Thunder grumbled.

It didn't take Thunder as long to bathe as it had Carter, and soon they were both settling down on their blankets, their backs propped against their saddles, facing each other, separated by the blazing campfire. Both placed their guns within reaching distance.

"Want some jerky?" Thunder asked.

Carter nodded, so Thunder tossed him a couple of strips. Carter also made himself a pot of coffee. Good thing Thunder had been traveling and had had all his provisions with him or they would have nothing but each other.

*What an awful thought.*

As Carter leaned back with a cup of hot coffee in hand, he said, "I've heard bits and pieces about your family from Mary. It sounds like quite a group."

Thunder laughed. "They are most unusual and very special in their own way."

"Mary said you didn't want any part of them at first."

Thunder folded his arms across his chest. "That is probably putting it mildly. I told Brandy very bluntly to go find somebody else."

"What made you change your mind?"

"A marshal just like you," Thunder said with a slow smile. "I was in a gunfight and killed a man. It was clearly self-defense, but because they thought I was a half-breed, the marshal didn't want to hear my side. He intended to lock me up."

"So that's why you don't like the law." Carter chuckled.

"I practice law," Thunder pointed out. "However, the law can be blind and deaf if left in the wrong hands."

"Believe it or not, I can agree with you there. But what made you change your mind?"

"Brandy." Thunder smiled.

The thought of his pretty wife waiting at home could turn even that ill-tempered son of a bitch into putty, Carter thought.

"She told the marshal that I was their guide and

that she'd be responsible for me. So it was hang or go with them."

Grinning, Carter replied, "I would have liked to have been there just to see the expression on your face."

"I bet you would," Thunder said sarcastically.

"All joking aside, tell me what Mary was like when she was younger."

"About like she is now, only stubborn and much harder to get along with. She hated everybody."

Carter's brow rose. "That does describe her, though I can't see her being much more stubborn than she is now."

"But she was worse when she was younger," Thunder said with a smile. "You'd tell her to go left, she'd go right. Get the picture?"

Carter nodded.

"And she hated Brandy," Thunder added.

"What made Mary change?"

"We had to take the wagon across the Missouri River. Mary and Brandy were riding on the raft when Mary tumbled overboard. Her heavy skirts pulled her under and she damned near drowned because she couldn't swim, so Brandy jumped in and saved her. After that, Mary mellowed out some and was a little easier to live with."

Carter stared at the embers burning low as he thought about what Thunder had just told him. Carter could picture the defiant young woman in his mind's eye. He had a feeling that Mary had been trying to prove something all her life. "Thanks for sharing your story with me."

"Now I have a question," Thunder said.

"Ask."

"Why are you so interested in Mary? Or do you take an interest in all your prisoners?"

Carter nodded. "That's a fair question. The truth is, I'm not sure what Mary is to me. I care a great deal about her and I don't want her to get hurt."

Thunder gave him a knowing look as he said, "I figured as much."

Carter's gazed snapped up. "Figured what?"

"Mary has you hooked." Thunder grinned.

"Well, I don't know about that," Carter shot back quickly. Perhaps too quickly. Maybe it was better to talk about something else. "When do you think the Carlsons will show?"

"I figure around dawn when they think our guard is down," Thunder explained. He pushed his hat down over his eyes. "I'm going to get some shut-eye while I can."

After a few moments of silence, Carter asked, "Have you ever wanted something so badly that you could taste it, yet you were afraid to reach out for it?"

Thunder shoved the brim of his hat up off his face and looked at Carter before answering him. "Yes."

"What did you do?"

"I married her," Thunder said with a smile, then pushed his hat back down to signal the end of the conversation.

Carter stared at the fire, pondering Thunder's words and thinking of Mary. What was it about the woman that both attracted him and made him feel like he was losing his mind at the same time? And what was he going to do about it? He recalled the unselfish passion they'd shared when he'd held her in his arms. He seemed to be blind where she was concerned, but he'd also taken an oath to uphold the law, and he was a man of his word.

With his mind in turmoil, he didn't remember falling asleep.

What he woke up to was the click of someone pulling the hammer back on a pistol.

"Mary," McCoy said, "I want you to take this six-shooter." He placed the gun in her hand. Her hand quickly fell to her side with the weight of the gun, but she didn't drop it. "Do you know how it works?"

"Yes," she said with that same blank stare in her eyes and dullness of voice that pleased him.

"Bring me the horse, Sammy," McCoy shouted, then turned back to Mary. "As I was saying, Mary, you are to ride this horse until you come to the next camp. You must stop before you get there because bad men are in the camp. Do you understand?"

"Bad men," Mary repeated just like a performing puppet.

"You are to take the gun in your hand and shoot Carter Monroe, then turn and shoot the other man. You're to kill both men—no matter what it takes. Understand?"

"Kill both men."

McCoy took the gun. He held the horse for Mary to mount, then he handed her back the gun. "You are to keep the gun hidden in the folds of your skirt."

Since she was looking straight ahead, he drew her attention back to him. "Look at me," McCoy said. "You're still in a deep sleep and you'll feel nothing, but when you hear the gunfire, you'll wake up and you will remember nothing. You will not remember how you got here, and you'll not remember who I am. Now bend down and give me a good luck kiss."

Mary did as she was instructed, then she straightened and obediently rode off. "You know, I could get used to that girl," McCoy said, wiping his mouth. "Damn fine kisser."

"You realize that they'll probably kill her," Sammy said as he moved up beside McCoy. "When she shoots Carter, the other one will surely shoot her."

McCoy glanced at Sammy and grinned. "I know. And that's why I'm leaving you boys now." He grabbed up his gear. "By taking care of your problem, I took care of mine," he said after he mounted his horse. "Now I have a mine that needs claiming." He wheeled his horse around. "See you boys around. Nice doing business with you."

Sammy sauntered back to the campfire. "Now the only thing we have to do is wait."

Carter heard the gun a second before he rolled to the side. His eyes flew open. He reached for his gun, but Thunder had already thrown his arms around Mary.

"Mary!" Carter got to his feet, a little dumbfounded. Thunder was trying to control her. She still held tight to the pistol. She was struggling like they were her enemies.

"Bad men," Carter heard her say.

She was going to kill him! And to think a moment earlier he'd thought he loved her.

"Are you going to stand there or help me?" Thunder bit out.

Carter moved in and wrestled the gun from Mary's fingers, then tossed it to the ground before grabbing her arms.

Thunder stepped back. He was a little dazed that his sister had stolen into their camp without either him or Carter hearing her. Not to mention the fact that she was trying to kill both of them.

Carter shook Mary. "Why did you do that? What the Sam Hill is the matter with you?"

"Kill Carter," Mary repeated.

"But why, Mary? Why?"

Thunder finally felt his wits return. He could see that his sister did not look like herself or act like herself. She looked more like some evil spirit had entered her body and taken her wits. "Look at her, Carter."

"I am looking at her, for Christ's sake," Carter snapped. "She's damn lucky I haven't slugged her. Explain yourself, Mary!"

"Kill Carter."

"Yeah, yeah, I got that part. The question is why?"

"Kill Carter."

Thunder put an end to the shaking of his sister. It wasn't getting them anywhere. He grabbed Carter's arm. "Look at her eyes. She is looking at you, but it's as if she is in a daze and doesn't see you at all."

"Mary!" Thunder called her name loudly. She didn't respond.

Carter lightly slapped her cheek. "Snap out of it." Still, she had that dazed stare that he could really see now.

"Kill Carter."

"I'd better retrieve the gun before she does just that," Thunder said. He reached for the gun and it went off with a loud bang.

"Shit," Carter swore, and grabbed Mary to protect her even though she was still mumbling, "Kill Carter."

"Can't you be more careful?" Carter yelled at Thunder.

"The hammer was pulled back," Thunder said tersely. "You better be damn glad that I woke up when I did or you wouldn't be here."

"Carter," Mary murmured.

Carter sighed. It was going to be a long night. "Yeah, I know, kill Carter." He repeated the words he'd already heard from her a dozen times before.

"How did I get here?" Mary asked as she shrugged out of his grasp.

"Mary?" Carter and Thunder said at the same time.

She blinked several times and looked around. "Where are we?"

Carter noticed the dazed look was missing from her eyes. "We're just outside of town."

"How did we get here?" Mary asked. She had the oddest feeling, like a part of the day was missing and both Thunder and Carter were looking at her as if she were loco. The feeling she had now reminded Mary of how she'd felt right after she found Big Jim murdered.

"Don't you know?" Carter asked, a little dumbfounded.

"If I did, I wouldn't be asking you," she said begrudgingly, then added, "My head hurts. And why are you both looking at me that way?"

"Because, my dear sister"—Thunder paused—"you just tried to kill Carter."

"I did not," she said firmly. However, neither one of them was smiling. "Did I?"

They nodded their heads in agreement.

"What is the last thing you remember?" Carter asked.

"The fire. The smoke. I thought I was going to die," she recalled. Then Mary looked at Carter accusingly. "Because *you* left me locked up."

"And," Carter prompted.

"A man came to let me out. He said that you had sent him, so I figured it was because of the fire. I rode out of town with him, but he kept riding farther and farther away, so I stopped and demanded to know where we were going." She paused, taking a deep breath. "I don't remember anything after that."

"What did he look like?" Thunder asked.

"He . . . I don't remember."

"How can you not remember?" Carter's frustration was coming out in his tone of voice.

"That's enough," Thunder said, putting an end to what was going to be another argument. "There has to be a reason Mary can't remember. We're just missing that piece of the puzzle."

Carter rubbed his jaw. "I don't think Mary rode very far. I bet the culprits are near."

"I might not remember the man's face, but I do remember where I rode from," Mary said with a smile and pointed. "It's that way."

"Let's ride," Thunder said, already grabbing up his saddle.


It didn't take them long before they reached where the outlaws' camp was supposed to be. They stopped before getting there and left Mary behind with the horses.

Thunder and Carter split up so they would come at the outlaws from different directions, and crept toward the camp.

Carter peered through a scraggly bush, careful

not to make any noise. He counted three men. One of them was Sammy Carlson, but how had Carlson been able to take Mary when he had been in the middle of that gunfight? Something didn't add up. Again it was as if the missing piece of the puzzle was still plaguing him.

Looking across the way, Carter saw Thunder's signal. They both jumped from behind their cover and stormed toward the campfire.

"You boys are under arrest!" Carter yelled.

The outlaws didn't surrender, but went for their guns instead.

Thunder went after the two Mexicans, and Carter went after Carlson, who was fumbling to get his gun out of its holster.

Sammy roared and swung, catching Carter in the belly. It stunned Carter long enough for Sammy to get the edge, and he landed two more punches.

Carter rolled and fought for his breath. Then he managed to scramble to his feet, slightly unsteady. When Sammy came at him again, Carter ducked and caught Sammy on the side of the head with his fist.

Sammy retreated two steps and grabbed a large, clublike stick and swung at Carter. Carter backed up, tripping on a log. He went down on one knee, but he could see the club coming down, so he threw up his arm in a vain attempt to protect himself. He took the blow on his arm and pain shot all the way up to his shoulder, but something inside Carter snapped. All he could feel was rage.

He saw Sammy going back for his gun, and at the same time caught a glimpse out of the corner of his eye of one of the other men pointing his gun at Thunder's back. Carter swung around and fired his Colt, sending the man stumbling backwards so fast that he looked as though he'd been jerked by a rope.

A bullet whisked by Carter's head, making him turn, thank God, in the right direction. He fired and caught Sammy in the right shoulder, forcing him to drop the club. But Sammy didn't stop. He bent down and grabbed his .45 and shot at Carter.

Carter fired back. His second shot took Sammy down. Looking down at the man, lying half sprawled on the ground, Carter was of two minds. He knew he should take the man in alive even after all this time, but he wanted nothing more than to see the man dead.

He glanced behind him to see that Thunder had killed one of the remaining men and had the other tied up. Carter turned his attention back to Sammy, who was reaching for his gun.

Carter kicked the six-shooter away from Sammy's outstretched hand. "So, Sammy, now we finally meet face-to-face."

Sammy just looked up at him, his eyes shaded by shock. "Looks like you win, Marshal."

"The law always wins," Carter pointed out. "But tell me one thing. How did you get Mary to try and kill us? It almost worked."

Sammy grinned. "Wasn't me. It was McCoy."

"Who?" Carter asked again.

Thunder's head snapped around at the mention of McCoy. He strode over and stood beside Carter. Then Thunder noticed Mary at the edge of the clearing and motioned for her to come stand with them.

"What was McCoy's first name?" Thunder asked.

"John."

Mary gasped. "That is Big Jim's brother."

Carter could see that Sammy was fading fast. His voice had grown faint, so Carter knelt down. "How did McCoy do it?"

"Something he called hypnotism," Sammy said faintly. "It works pretty good, too. I saw it firsthand. She don't remember a thing. Never will."

"We need to get this man to a doctor," Thunder said. "He could be a witness in Mary's trial."

They tried to pick up Sammy, but when they moved him, too much blood gushed out, staining the ground.

"You boys are wasting your time." Sammy gave a halfhearted laugh. "Don't want to rot in no prison anyway."

"Where is McCoy now?" Carter persisted, trying to get as much information out of the dying man as possible.

"Gone . . ." Sammy's voice was trailing off.

Carter leaned closer. "Gone where?"

"Back to Gregory Gulch," Sammy said with his last dying breath.

Thunder looked down at the lifeless body. "There goes our witness."

Mary had a puzzled look on her face when she asked, "What does he mean, hypnotism?"

"I've heard of it," Carter said, but he'd never seen anyone who had been hypnotized.

"I had a friend I went to school with back in Boston. He is actually an expert on the subject," Thunder said. "Let's get these men buried and then go back to town. I need to send a telegram." He looked at Mary and squeezed her arm. "There still might be some hope. You see, when you are hypnotized it's possible that you don't remember anything. Which explains why you answered that you couldn't remember when asked."

Mary thought for a moment. "It also means that I could have killed Big Jim because I was told to."

Thunder looked at Carter and then back to Mary. He saw the stricken look on her face. "Yes, kid. It could mean exactly that."

Mary burst into tears, and Carter pulled her into his arms, holding her close. "Don't cry. We'll figure something out."

Just who was the monster in all of this? Carter thought with a frown. It seemed like all the answers were just whispers on the wind, and catching and understanding them could mean life or death for Mary.

# Chapter 18

The first hint of daybreak threatened to seep through the blackness as Carter, Mary, and Thunder rode back to Windy Bend with the prisoner in tow.

Since there wasn't a jail, or much of a town left, they rode to the livery. Carter sent a boy to go find Rick, then told Mary to get down and stretch her legs while he took care of the prisoner.

Carter shoved the prisoner into a stall and tied him to a post. Next he instructed the stable boy to water and feed the horses. They would be leaving by midmorning, and the prisoner would be Rick's problem.

By the time Carter returned to the tack room, Thunder was leaning against the wall talking to Mary. He glanced up as Carter approached. "It's been a long night. I probably forgot to thank you back there for watching my back."

"No problem. You would have expected me to do the same. I'm going to get some canteens and a few supplies and then we're heading back out."

Thunder nodded.

But before Carter could say more, Rick strode into the stable, still tucking in his shirttail. "What happened?"

Carter swung his head toward the stall. "That's what's left of the Carlson gang."

Rick sauntered over and jerked the prisoner to his feet by the scruff of his neck. "Now to find someplace to lock him up."

"Why don't you stay and help Hank?" Carter suggested to Rick. "He's going to need a hand, and I won't be here. I'm going to take Mary back to Gregory Gulch."

"I'll handle everything," Rick said. He turned to Mary. "It has been a pleasure to meet you, ma'am. I hope everything works out for you."

"Thank you," Mary said.

Rick shoved his prisoner out the door, mumbling, "Come on, you no-good trash. We need to find someplace to keep you. Then I need some grub. If you're lucky, I might toss you a crumb."

Once Rick had left, Thunder said, "I'll see you both back at Gregory Gulch. I'm going to contact my friend, Delaney Shoff. He's always wanted to travel out west, so maybe he'll look forward to coming out here."

"How can he help?" Mary asked.

"Delaney can explain how someone is hypnotized, and maybe he can help us solve the problem of what actually happened the night of the murder," Thunder explained. He gave Mary a hug. "I'll see you later, kid."

When they were alone, Carter finished tying the supplies on his horse, then turned to Mary. "Are you up to the ride?"

She nodded. "Yes. Better get it over with."

"If we ride all night, we should be there some-time tomorrow afternoon."

Mary mounted her horse. It looked like Carter was anxious to get rid of her. He could have suggested that they get some rest before continuing, but it seemed Carter had a job to do. She realized that once he turned her over to the sheriff, his duty would be done and she'd never see him again. Maybe that was the way he wanted it, she thought as they rode out of town. Maybe the other night meant nothing to him.

Mary sighed wistfully. How she'd love to see Judith. She'd bet Judith would take her in her arms and tell her everything would be all right. Because right about now, nothing in Mary's life was all right. She had started out to make a lot of money, figuring that money would make her happy and solve all her problems.

Now Mary was a wealthy woman in her own right, but the money hadn't solved anything. It had just brought her more problems.

She watched Carter riding ahead of her, and she admired the way he sat his horse, his trim hips and broad shoulders. The sun was just coming up over the horizon, and the bright orange ball seemed to peek out from behind the mountain, promising them a new day. That was what she would like, not only a new day but also a new life. One with none of the problems she had now.

Mary realized the only time she'd truly been happy was when she had been at Carter's home. Mary loved the ranch. It had truly felt like home. But it wasn't her home, it was Carter's, and she didn't belong there.

That was the problem. She didn't belong any-where.

Mary felt very much alone as they rode. Maybe she wasn't the type to settle down and have children. She actually couldn't picture herself with children, so she probably didn't need a husband anyway. And she knew she didn't want a man telling her what to do. Mary smiled at that thought, but it was a sad smile.

The rest of the day, they rode in silence. Mary wondered why Carter wasn't saying anything. Then after awhile she didn't care. She was numb after not sleeping the night before, and she rode in a daze, wondering why she couldn't be a normal woman. Her eyelids felt so heavy. They would start to drift closed and then she'd jerk herself upright. The process had gone on for the last hour. Maybe if she shut her eyelids for just a moment she'd feel better.

Carter had a damned headache.

He'd been battling with himself half the day, and still he didn't have the answers he sought. Why didn't he take Mary and run? They could start a new life someplace where no one knew them. He knew the answer even before he asked the question. Mary's guilt or innocence would always hang over her head.

Was he plumb loco? He sounded like he was planning a future with the girl, which would mean giving up the law. He'd never considered giving up the law for anyone.

Not even a wife.

A thump sounded behind him followed by a moan. Carter turned and glanced behind him. "What the hell?" He jerked his horse around and trotted back to where Mary was sitting on the ground, rubbing her eyes. She evidently had fallen off her horse. When he reached her, she was blinking in confusion, her long, golden hair hanging in her face.

Carter slid off his mount to help Mary up. "What happened?"

She yawned before answering, "So you do know that I'm alive." When she realized he wasn't going to reply to her barb, she continued, "I must have fallen asleep and slipped off."

Carter felt lower than a wagon rut as he realized he'd been driving Mary pretty hard. He was used to such travel, but Mary wasn't. "I should have let you rest."

Mary brushed off her skirts, but her head snapped up at his remark. "It has been evident from the start that you're in a big hurry to get rid of me, so let's not stop now. Let's get this over with."

"That's what you think?" Carter asked, but he didn't wait for her to answer. He brought the horses around and held hers. "We are almost there. I can see that you're still sleepy. Do you want to ride with me so that you can sleep?"

Yes, she wanted to ride with him. She wanted Carter to hold her, to tell her everything would be all right, but her pride kicked in. "I'll ride my own horse, thank you." After all, he was going to leave her once they got there. She might as well get used to it.

Again, they started riding, but this time Mary rode beside Carter and he kept his eye on her. He really didn't know what to say to her. He knew that she was angry with him for bringing her in. He really couldn't blame her, but dammit, it was his job—it didn't mean he didn't care about her. How in the world were they going to close this gap between them? He had no idea.

Sure enough, a half hour later, Mary began to nod. This time Carter didn't ask, but instead pulled her in front of him and told her to be quiet when she started to argue. She gave up the struggle and rested her head on his chest.

It took another hour before they rode into town, but when they arrived, it was time to wake Mary. "Wake up. We're here." Carter nudged her.

She blinked several times. "This isn't Gregory Gulch."

"No, it isn't," Carter said with a smile. "I thought you might like a bath and a good night's sleep. We're in Appleton."

Carter liked the surprise he saw in Mary's eyes as she looked at him and whispered, "Thank you."

It didn't take long before they were settled in the Stratford Hotel. Carter had ordered a hot bath for Mary at the front desk, and she had to admit she was looking forward to easing her aching body into the tub. The past two days had been draining both physically and emotionally.

"This is a nice hotel," Mary commented as she looked around the room. There was a big feather bed and two overstuffed chairs that faced a fireplace. It stood cold and empty at the moment, but she knew in the winter there would be a blazing fire.

"We've stayed here once before," Carter said.

"We?"

Before he could say anything else, the maids brought in the last buckets of hot water for the bath. They filled the tub, then left as quickly as they had come.

Carter started to leave with the maids, but paused,

his hand on the door. "You relax and take your bath. I'll be back in an hour."

"All right," Mary said as he strode out the door without looking back. She was a little disappointed that Carter was leaving, but she didn't know why. Maybe she was getting used to having him around, and that wasn't good.

However, the water was so inviting, she quickly forgot her disappointment and settled into the tin hip tub. She did nothing for a long while but soak. The water did its job, soothing her aching muscles. She'd been through a lot in the last twenty-four hours, and the part of it she didn't remember scared her. What if the men had taken advantage of her? She shivered at the thought. Then again, maybe it was better she didn't know what had happened.

Mary scrubbed her body until it had a nice pink glow, then she washed her hair. Feeling much better, she stepped out of the tub and dried off in the bath sheets the maids had left. She wrapped her hair up, then slipped on her chemise. For a moment, she thought about getting completely dressed and then decided against it as she climbed into the middle of the bed. As she rubbed her hair with the towel, she decided she was tired of fighting herself over Carter. She wanted him, if only for a day, an hour, whatever she could get.

As if she had conjured Carter up, the door opened. He stopped short when he saw her sitting in the middle of the bed. He must have taken a bath, too, because his hair was still damp, clinging to his forehead, and he was dressed in black, looking very mysterious. When Carter didn't move, Mary said, "Come in. The bath was wonderful. Thank your for arranging it for me."

Carter saw the heartrending tenderness of her gaze and felt more like a fool than ever. Her half-clothed body short-circuited his brain. There was so much to say, so much that needed to be said, but not knowing where to start, he stated the obvious. "You're beautiful."

Mary blushed.

Carter attempted to regain his composure. "Here, slip on my shirt. I've ordered dinner in our room. It should be here in a minute."

"How did you get dinner brought to our room? Hotels are not usually that accommodating."

Carter gave her a slow smile. "They are with enough money handed to them."

Mary felt alive with excitement as she slipped on Carter's shirt, which was three times too big for her. Why was he going out of his way to make this a special evening?

Even a condemned man got one last meal, she thought wryly.

A knock on the door got their attention. When Carter answered it, the staff brought in several trays and placed them on the round table by the window.

After everyone had left, Carter asked, "Would you care to join me for dinner?"

Mary smiled as she walked over and took her seat at the table. She had to adjust the shirtsleeves of Carter's shirt so she could see her hands.

He lifted the lids, which consisted of big pots turned upside down over the plates, off the food. The aroma of fried chicken and creamed potatoes made Mary's mouth water.

"I don't know about you, but I'm starved," she admitted as she took a crispy chicken leg and bit down into the juicy meat.

Carter laughed. "I'm kind of hungry myself. Jerky isn't very filling."

At first, they were too interested in eating to talk, but once she had her stomach halfway pleased, Mary reminded him, "Earlier, you said we had been here before."

"That's right. After we found you in the snow, the storm was so bad that we stopped here to spend the night and have a doctor look at you." Carter wiped his mouth with the linen napkin and sat back with a cup of hot coffee in his hands. "As a matter of fact, we stayed in this same room."

Mary's brow raised slightly. "We? As in me and you?"

"Yep. I slept there right beside you." He pointed to the bed.

Mary gave him a sexy smile. "At least you were a gentleman."

"Always a gentleman. However, in your condition you looked more like a drowned cat," Carter said. He glanced at her. "Tell me what happened for you to be out in the snow."

Mary grew serious. "First, do you think that I killed Big Jim?"

Carter studied her for a long while before he finally said, "No, I don't." The smile Mary gave him warmed his heart.

"In that case, I'll tell you. Most of it I'm sure you heard when I told Thunder. I was so scared that I didn't know what to do. I wanted to go for the sheriff, but I looked guilty, even to myself, so the only thing I knew to do was run. I gathered the only dress I had and a couple of bags of gold. I figured that I would go someplace until I could remember what had happened. But"—she smiled—"as you know, there was a terrible snowstorm, I lost my grip on the reins, the horse stumbled, and I went flying."

"Well, that certainly explains why you were head-first in the snowbank." Carter laughed. "It's a wonder you didn't break your fool neck."

Mary placed her napkin on the table and got to her feet. "I guess I should thank you for rescuing me. Although I must admit that a marshal was the last person I wanted to see." She leaned over and placed a kiss on his cheek, then said, "Thank you."

"I think you can do better than that," Carter said as he stood up.

She held out her hand as he reached toward her. "I promised myself that you wouldn't kiss me so easily the next time, unless I knew how you felt about me."

He paused and looked at her. He was waging a war with himself. Finally, he took a deep breath as if he'd come to a decision, and said, "Don't you know?"

"No, I don't," Mary said.

"I care a great deal," Carter murmured, his eyes brimming with tenderness and passion. "If you say the word, we will leave this hotel and go anywhere but Gregory Gulch."

Mary's heart slammed hard against her ribs. "You would break the law for me?"

"Yes."

She could feel the tears pooling in her eyes.

"What's wrong?"

"I—I never thought you would do that for me," she admitted as she lowered her hand to wipe a stray tear from her cheek. "I think I'd feel much better if you'd hold me."

She didn't have to ask twice. Carter wrapped her in his arms.

"If we ran," Mary finally said, "then I'd always look guilty, and you would always have some small doubt that I might have committed the murder." She pulled back to see his face. "You see, I still don't remember what happened, so even I'm not sure if I killed Jim. I want to stand trial."

He looked down at her. "Are you sure?"

She nodded. "But I'm scared."

Carter took a deep breath, folding her back in his arms. "I know, sweetheart. The unknown is always frightening, but I'll be here for you."

She felt so small and helpless in his arms, he thought—until he remembered it was Mary that he held.

He placed kisses on his little spitfire's face, and she responded by molding her body into his. His anticipation was almost unbearable, and the blood pounding in his head told him it was impossible to go slower much longer. He wanted to remember every moment with her, but it wasn't enough to satisfy the fire within him.

As he pressed his mouth a bit harder, she parted her lips and Carter found heaven. Mary was so warm and loving, and he was drowning in pleasure like he'd never known existed. He slipped his arm behind her knees and lifted her into his arms. She kissed the side of his neck as he carried her over and placed her on the bed. Quickly, Carter dispensed with his clothes to join her.

Carefully, he slipped off her shirt then untied the ribbons of her chemise and slipped the garment slowly down her body. His lips followed where the flimsy material had been, across her breasts, lower over her stomach, until he reached her thighs. She tightened her legs. "Don't," he rasped.

Mary wasn't sure what he was doing, but she decided to trust him. She relaxed. Then Carter showed her a kind of pleasure that she hadn't known existed. She whimpered and groaned and then he was back. Their kisses were frenzied now as if they both knew they might never be together again. His hands began a lust-arousing exploration of her soft skin.

Carter's kisses were promises of things that might never be, but Mary knew, in this moment, that the rest of the world could go away and leave them both alone because she never wanted to lose Carter.

But she also realized that she would lose him if she ended up dangling at the end of a rope. So she held nothing back. She gave as much pleasure as she received.

In one swift move, she rolled on top of Carter, placing feathery kisses on his neck, on his chest, and then she moved lower until she heard his gasp at her touch.

Mary knew she was in control, and she liked seeing the dazed look in Carter's eyes when she tasted him.

When Carter could stand no more, he yanked her back up so he could devour her mouth. He couldn't seem to get enough of her. He kissed her urgently as the flames of passion burned within her.

Enough. He wanted her now. All of her.

Carter lifted Mary's hips and guided her up and onto his rigid erection. She gasped as he filled her. His hands caressed her breasts as she moved up and down.

Mary felt his heat deep inside her, throbbing and moving with her until red hot desire built to bursting and they found the tempo that bound their bodies together.

Exploding in a downpour of fiery sensation, Mary's world spun out of control and she called Carter's name.

Carter felt her release and then he sought his, holding her firmly as he thrust up and spilled his seed into her warmth. He reached for Mary and pulled her down to lie within his arms.

The room was quiet except for the heavy breathing of the couple who had found happiness, if only for tonight.

# Chapter 19

The next morning Carter and Mary started riding up the mountain to Gregory Gulch. The view was lovely and the ride much more pleasant than the last time she had ridden down this road. There were wildflowers scattered all over the ground and growing out of small cracks in the rocky walls of the mountains.

Even though Mary knew where she was heading and why, she felt at peace this morning.

She knew Carter cared for her, and that was more than she'd ever thought possible.

Mentally, she gave herself a hard shake as Gregory Gulch came into view. Main Street loomed ahead, if it could be called that. Mary knew she had to get her mind off what lay ahead. She had to take it one day at a time. If she could survive the whorehouse and the orphanage, she could survive anything—she hoped.

The mining town hadn't changed much. The rough wooden sign said they were in Gregory Gulch. However, it dangled by one chain so Mary had to turn her head sideways to read it. Everything in Gregory Gulch appeared peaceful—or maybe a better word was dead.

Log cabins lined both sides of the street that was muddy from rain. Everything was barren and lifeless brown. Each cabin looked like the next, though some didn't have windows.

No one was outside as they started up the street. Most everyone would be in the mines this time of day. Mary had almost forgotten what a normal mining day was like: up at the crack of dawn and working until late in the afternoon. Her throat clogged with emotion as a vision of Big Jim smiling at her brought his memory fresh into her mind. He was a good man, and he hadn't deserved to die.

Slowly, they approached the small jailhouse. The door stood open and the windows had been thrown open since it was a warm spring day. They stopped in front and tied their horses to the hitching post. Mary drew a deep breath of fresh air and started up the steps.

Carter touched Mary's arm outside the door. "Everything will turn out all right," he said, trying to assure her.

She gave him a small smile, then ducked quickly into the office. It was better to just get it over and done with.

Marshal Forester, who had been sleeping at his desk, reared back in his chair and jerked awake. He licked his dry lips then lowered his chair to the floor with a hard thud. "Sorry, folks. You caught me checking my eyelids for holes," he said with a smile. "Can I help you?"

"I'm Marshal Carter Monroe," Carter said, extending his hand. He shook the man's hand. "I've brought in Mary Costner."

Mary noticed that Carter hadn't referred to her as a prisoner, but considering the charges that was little consolation.

Surprise registered on Forester's face, then his gaze settled on Mary. "I guess there is no need for an introduction, although you sure had me fooled."

Mary wasn't sure what the marshal meant by that. He wasn't smiling. "I beg your pardon?"

"I never figured you for a girl. You sure looked like a boy to me," Forester said with a chuckle. Then he shoved slowly out of his chair and retrieved the keys. "Guess you know I have to lock you up."

"I thought being mistaken for a man was safer," Mary said with a smile. She had always liked Marshal Forester, and she hoped he hadn't judged her beforehand. Dreading the thought of being behind bars again, she watched as he unlocked the door.

"And you were right." He opened the door and stood back.

Mary stopped before entering the cell. "I didn't kill Big Jim," she said simply. She wasn't sure why she wanted the marshal to know that, but she did.

Forester closed the door without comment. Then he asked, "Can you tell me what happened?"

Mary shook her head. "I wish I could, but the fact is I don't remember anything about what happened that night."

"You know that doesn't sound good," he pointed out needlessly.

Mary stood on the other side of the bars, her hands closed around the cold iron. She looked squarely at Forester. "I know how it sounds. Why do you think I ran?"

The marshal nodded. "I see what you are saying. I can tell you, I've met your family. They're real nice people. As a matter of fact, Thunder has been looking for you."

Mary smiled. "He found me. He'll be along shortly."

"You know M-Mary—" Forester chuckled. "Can't get used to calling you Mary instead of Mark, even though you don't look one bit like Mark anymore. Anyway, I tend to believe you, but I should tell you, the men in town are still looking to blame somebody. And so far that somebody is you."

"In that case, I had better stay around to keep an eye on her," Carter said. "Just in case there's trouble before Thunder gets here. He should be here anytime, but we're not sure when. After he arrives, I'll leave."

Mary gaped at Carter, but he didn't seem to notice. As usual, he wasn't paying her any attention. She couldn't believe that he had already anticipated leaving her, and that hurt. Did he realize that having him near her would be a comfort? Then again, maybe he didn't care.

Forester strode back to his desk and tossed the keys down. "Good. I heard the judge is in Appleton, so that's where her trial will be held."

"Figures," Carter said with a frown. "Wish we had known that before we came here."

"Well, it's too late to head back today," Forester told him as he picked up his tan-colored Stetson and settled it on his head. "You can spend the night and go back to Appleton tomorrow. Let's go get some grub. We can bring Mary back a plate when we're done."

Carter glanced at Mary, then the marshal. "Will she be safe?"

Forester nodded. "It's too soon for word to have

gotten out that Mary is back in town, so I think
she'll be all right for now. I want you to fill me in
on what you know."

Mary watched them leave, then settled wearily
down on the hard cot. Carter hadn't even bothered
to tell her good-bye. That certainly showed how
much he cared about her. And she didn't like the
way he had referred to her as "she"—like he really
didn't know her at all.

Mary wrapped her arms around herself, gazing
at the closed door. She remembered the tenderness in Carter's deep voice and the way he'd held
her last night. It was strange how the air seemed to
vibrate whenever Carter was near, and when he
was gone the world seemed so colorless. Without
him, nothing was the same. She felt empty. Sighing,
she sank down on the bunk to wait, but she was so
tired from the little sleep she'd gotten the night
before, she soon fell asleep.

Much later, Mary was awakened by men shouting. Slowly, she pushed herself up off the bunk,
rubbing her eyes as she tried to remember where
she was. It didn't take long to see the bars and remember she was once more in jail. However, this
time the front door was open, and she saw the
flicker of torchlights in the street and heard what
sounded like an angry group of men. She strained
to hear what was going on.

"Let's lynch her!" someone in the mob shouted.

Mary gasped and her heart seemed to stop beating. Out of pure reflex, she jerked back from the
bars. It was a lynch mob. And they wanted her!

Screwing up as much courage as she could, she
looked again. Thank God! Marshal Forester and
Carter stood on the porch between her and the
seething crowd.

"Yeah!" everyone shouted. "Get out of the way, Forester. She done and killed Big Jim. We have our own justice up here. She needs to hang! And if you ain't gonna do it, we can take care of it ourselves."

Mary recognized that voice and the small hairs on the back of her head seemed to stand on their own. It was John Wiley, somebody she'd thought was a friend.

Carter spoke next. "I suggest all of you return to your homes," he said calmly. "Mary will stand trial for the crime. If she is found guilty, she will be punished."

"Who the hell are you?" another man shouted from the back of the crowd.

"I'm a U.S. Marshal. And I should warn you that I can arrest most of you for forming a mob," Carter told them, his voice showing all the authority he had with his badge.

"We want justice now!"

"So you think she's guilty?" Carter asked.

"Sure, who else could have killed Big Jim?" Wiley asked.

"I think any of you could have killed him," Carter pointed out reasonably, "just to gain his half of the claim. Mary already had the money."

Tears filled Mary's eyes as she listened. Carter was actually taking up for her. Defending her.

Wiley turned to the crowd. "There's only two of them. We can take them real easy."

"I'd think twice about that," Forester warned. "All of you could end up in jail."

Mary gripped the bars so tightly that her knuckles were white. The mob was right—they were big and there were only two lawmen standing between her and that mob. She shivered in dread. It sounded as if everybody in town hated her. These were men she'd seen every day, men who she'd thought liked her. Now they sounded like a pack of angry dogs over a carcass, waiting for the first one to make his move.

What if they overran Forester and Carter?

"Or dead," Carter added to Forester's remark. He pointed his gun towards Wiley. "You first. There may be more of you, but I assure you, I'm going to take a half dozen of you with me before I go down."

"And if Carter doesn't take you down, Marshal Forester and I will take care of the rest of you," Thunder said from the back of the group. "As for myself, I can take you down the easy way with a gun, or I can take your scalp with my knife."

There was a lot of mumbling among the men.

"So what's it going to be, boys?" Forester asked.

Mary could hear the crowd mumbling, but they seemed to be backing up because the torchlights were dimming. She eased her grip on the bars and forced herself to breathe.

It must be over.

A few minutes later, three men sauntered in through the door. Thunder came over to her. "How you feeling, kid?"

"Scared."

"I can see why. Mobs are always scary. And very unpredictable."

"Do you think they will come back?" Mary asked.

Thunder looked at Forester for the answer.

"I don't think so," Forester assured Mary, then he asked Thunder, "Did you hear that they will have the trial in Appleton?"

"Yes, I did," Thunder said. "I stopped today and spoke with the judge." He looked at Mary. "Your trial is in two days. The only problem is I'm not sure Delaney will be here in time for the trial."

"Who's Delaney?" Forester asked.

"He's a doctor from back east who has studied hypnotism. I think that he can help with our case."

Forester drew his brows together in confusion. "What does that have to do with anything?"

"We believe that could be the reason why Mary can't remember anything," Thunder explained.

"I've heard about such before. Just never seen it," Forester explained, then looked at Carter. "Have you?"

"Nope. Sounds weird to me," Carter said.

Thunder folded his arms across his chest. "I know this is a long shot and I might not be able to find Delaney, but I'm going to try."

Carter nodded. "I'm all for trying anything, but I think we should head out in the morning."

Thunder nodded. "I agree, but first I'd like Mary to take a look around the cabin again to see if being there brings back any memories. We can go there in the morning before we head to Appleton."

Mary felt faint and slumped down on the cot. She wasn't sure if she wanted to go back to the cabin when she was trying so hard to forget the gruesome, bloody sight. As she curled up on the small cot, she prayed sleep would come soon.

The next morning, Carter and Thunder were preparing to leave when the front door swung open. Mary was out back using the outhouse, so they figured it was Marshal Forester returning from the post office.

Sure enough, Marshal Forester and another gentleman strolled inside. The other man was tall and beady eyed.

Carter disliked the man immediately.

"Before you leave this morning," Forester said, "I thought you'd be interested in what this gentleman, John McCoy, just told me."

"John McCoy, as in Big Jim's brother?" Thunder asked.

Forester nodded.

Carter noticed that McCoy's face had gone completely white.

"So what's up, McCoy?" Carter asked.

"I'd heard the girl was dead, so I've come to collect my brother's mine," McCoy said defensively.

"What makes you think that she's dead?" Carter asked. He wanted so much to lock this man up that it hurt, but the only witness that could swear to McCoy taking Mary from jail in Windy Bend was now dead, so unfortunately Carter didn't have anything on the man.

"I was passing through Windy Bend when I heard it."

"Sounds convenient to me," Thunder said.

"Who are you?" McCoy asked.

"Thunder."

McCoy involuntary took a step back. "What are you trying to say, mister? I'm the next of kin."

"I'm ready," Mary said, walking back into the room. She stopped upon seeing McCoy and frowned like she was trying to remember the man.

"As you can see"—Carter held out his hand—"Mary is still very much alive."

"So I see."

"Mary, do you recognize this man?" Thunder asked.

"I . . ." She hesitated and finally said, "Something . . ."

McCoy reached up, but Thunder caught his arm, pinning it behind his back. "No sudden moves. Maybe you'd better get out of here while you can. I'll see you in court in Appleton."

As soon as McCoy left, Carter looked at Thunder. "We have to get that man."

Thunder frowned. "I know. But it's going to be difficult. I need hard evidence."

"Who was that man?" Mary asked. It seemed that both men had forgotten she was still standing there.

"That was John McCoy," Thunder grated out.

Mary gasped, but quickly got control of herself. "He doesn't look anything like his brother."

"Let's get going," Carter said. "Forester, we'll see you in a couple of days in Appleton."

"I'll be there."


Goosebumps rose on Mary's arms when she saw the log cabin. She reached for the doorknob, but before she turned it, she glanced at Thunder. "I don't want to do this," she said, her voice trembling.

"I know, kid," Thunder said. Then he touched her arm. "But I need you to show me what you remember, so I can picture it when I defend you."

Mary nodded, then pushed through the door. The cabin she'd once called home was dark and musty when she stepped inside. They lit a couple of lamps, and then Mary felt panic sliding over her like a cold, dead hand, touching her face. Faint images of that night flashed before her, but nothing clear. "I—I remember Big Jim going to the door and opening it . . . then nothing." She walked around the room with tears trickling down her cheeks. Could she possibly have done this?

She paused in front of the fireplace where a large bloodstain was on the floor. She stood staring at the spot.

Carter and Thunder walked around the room looking for any kind of clue as to what had happened. In a few minutes, Carter stepped out, holding something in his hand. "Wasn't this Big Jim's room?"

Mary nodded.

"I found something," Carter said. He held up a green plaid coat.

"Oh my God," Mary whispered. "That's the coat I saw at the opera house, but I couldn't have seen it there if it was here." Her voice rose as she remembered something else. "However, I don't remember ever seeing Jim in this coat or anything like it."

"Remember that piece of material you showed me?" Thunder asked.

Mary nodded. "Yes, I thought maybe I had torn it from the intruder's coat. But I couldn't have if the coat was in Big Jim's room all along. Unless . . . unless it was Big Jim's coat."

Carter looked the garment over. Slowly he turned it around.

Mary's eyes grew big.

The room started to spin out of control as she mumbled, "I must have killed him."

# Chapter 20

Once again, Mary was in another cell, only the town was different. She was back in Appleton. However, she wasn't alone, there were two prisoners in the next cell. When they asked what she was in for and she told them murder, their faces had gotten real white and they hadn't bothered her since.

Though the other prisoners didn't bother her, she was beginning to feel like a criminal. And waiting for the trial was killing her. She needed to get everything over with. She'd been living in an indeterminate state long enough. Too long. Mary just prayed that Thunder could pull off a miracle.

This morning, Thunder had told her he was going over to the courthouse to pick the jurors. Having been much too nervous to go with him, she stayed behind. Besides, Mary trusted his judgment. And lately she was so nervous that she stayed queasy.

It was late afternoon when Thunder finally sat down behind the long table that had been assigned to him as defense attorney. The courtroom was quiet now, and he stopped to consider what was to come. Lacing his fingers behind his head, he stretched his long legs out under the table, then crossed his feet as he leaned back and thought about the long morning.

They had interviewed fifty-six potential jurors before filling the jury box with twelve men. A man by the name of David Degar was chosen foreman.

Thunder was satisfied with the jury. The members looked like honest citizens. However, he knew he didn't have much of a defense. Though largely circumstantial, the evidence against Mary was convincing. He realized that his only hope lay with his friend Delaney, and Thunder prayed that he was on the way.

Carter had arranged for a special Overland Stage to take him to Independence to meet Delaney, and together they would come back to Appleton. It was a long trip but with a nonstop stage only stopping to change horses, they could make it. On the way back, Carter was to fill Delaney in on everything that had happened.

Thunder left the courthouse in a foul mood as he headed back to the hotel. There was nothing left to do, and he hated waiting. Nothing had gone right in the last two days, and with each day that passed, Mary's depression about her plight deepened. Oh, Mary had said everything was all right, but he'd seen the dark circles under her eyes. She'd even thrown up her breakfast a couple of mornings, which he figured was a direct result of her being so nervous. He felt Mary needed a woman with her, and he damned sure needed his wife.

So just maybe . . .

\*  \*  \*

The time of reckoning had finally come.

Midmorning, Thunder came to get Mary.

He walked with her and the sheriff over to the courthouse. No one said anything. What was there to say? Besides, she felt if she opened her mouth she'd start to cry.

As they neared the building, Mary glanced up at the sign hanging over the courthouse and smiled. In big, old letters, its message was, "Justice for one and all." She prayed the sign was correct as she entered the building.

The courtroom was simple yet functional. Four windows stretched across the back, and it would have looked like an ordinary room, if not for the platform that held a huge desk where the judge would sit. For now, it was empty.

Mary could tell that the spectators' seats were full, but she didn't dare look while Thunder escorted her to the front. She did not want to know the people who were going to be staring at her and wondering if she really had murdered Big Jim McCoy, the closest thing to a father she'd ever had.

For the hundredth time, she wondered where Carter was. The only thing she knew was that she hadn't seen him since he had deposited her in jail. She had no idea where he was, and she was too proud to ask Thunder. There was no way she'd let on to anyone how much Carter mattered to her. Not even Thunder.

Maybe Carter had only said he cared for her, so she'd come along peacefully. Her stomach knotted as she sat down behind the long, brown table. No wonder she stayed sick to her stomach. Anyone would be sick, considering what she was going through.

The jurors came in single file. Each one seemed to glare at her before seating himself.

Mary raised her chin and looked each one in the eye. She was tired of being made to feel guilty, and she'd be damned if she would hang her head.

"All rise," the bailiff called.

Judge Parker entered from a side door. He proceeded to the platform, pulled out a straight back chair, its legs scraping the floor, then took his seat behind the desk.

The court crier said in a booming voice, "Hear one and all, the Honorable District Court of the United States for the Western District of Colorado, having criminal jurisdiction of the Indian Territory, is now in session."

After everyone had quieted down, Judge Parker turned to the jurors and said, "Do equal and exact justice; permit no innocent man to be punished, but let no guilty man escape; and let no politics enter here. Do this and you will have done your duty as jurors of this court."

Mary clutched her hands together. She realized she could be in deep trouble if things turned out wrong. All this time, she'd been hoping that something would happen to prove her innocence. Now, time was running out. She was scared. More than scared. She was terrified.

Judge Parker turned to the clerk. "Clerk, please refresh my memory."

The clerk shuffled some papers until he found the precise one he was looking for. "United States versus J.K. Jones. Charge, violating revenue law. Guilty. Charge, introducing liquor into Indian Territory. Guilty. He's been committed to jail here where he's awaiting sentencing, Your Honor."

Judge Parker nodded. "I remember now. Very

well. Bailiff Winston, please bring him up for sentencing first thing on tomorrow's session. Now, today I see we have a murder trial. Let's begin, as I'm sure this will be a long one."

The prosecution called several witnesses, most of them men Mary had worked with at the mine. To her surprise, the men didn't say anything bad about her, other than that she'd deceived them, which seemed to have irritated all of them.

Then the prosecution called Mary. She felt guilty the moment she stood up. The prosecutor, Charles Bryan, was a young man with a stocky build who looked like he hadn't smiled in ten years.

He glared at Mary for a long time, then he said, "Can you tell us what happened the night Big Jim was killed?"

Mary shook her head. "I don't remember anything," she admitted as she looked out over the sea of people who had gathered for her trial in Appleton. She heard several of them gasp, but she knew no one. She'd never felt so alone.

The prosecutor gave Mary a skeptical look before he said with a sneer, "If I'd murdered someone, I'd forget, too."

"Objection," Thunder shouted as he came to his feet. "We don't care about Mr. Bryan's opinion."

"Sustained," Judge Parker said, then looked at Bryan. "Should I remind you that your job is to prove Miss Costner guilty without your comments?"

"I'm trying to do that, Your Honor."

The judge looked at Bryan over his glasses. "Do you have any more questions for this witness?"

"Yes, I do." Charles turned back to Mary. "Tell us your relationship with the deceased."

"Big Jim and I were partners in the Lazy Dollar

Mine. We had been partners for two years. During that time, I came to think of Jim as a father who I loved very much."

"Well, Miss Costner, you have a strange way of showing love," Charles said on his way back to his table. "No more questions for now, but I would like the right to recall."

If Thunder, who was going by his white name Thomas Bradley, could have beat the shit out of the prosecutor, it would have given him a great deal of satisfaction at the moment. But it would only land him in jail, and then he'd be of no help to Mary.

However, things were not looking good for Mary, Thunder thought. He had hoped that Carter would have been here by now. Thunder sure hoped Carter wouldn't let them down. It could mean Mary's life.

Thunder slid his chair back, rose from the pine table, then strode over to the witness stand. This was the second time he'd had to defend a member of his family, he thought. He cleared his throat. "Mary, did you and Big Jim get along, or did you constantly disagree?"

"After the first day when we met, we rarely argued."

Thunder began to pace to calm his agitation. "Can you tell me what your deed says?"

"We both had the same clause written into the deed. It states that if something happens to either of us, the other partner inherits the mine."

Thunder stopped and looked at her. "And why did you do that?"

"We both worked very hard in the mine. We didn't want an outsider moving in on the other partner."

Thunder shrugged. "Some would think that might be a motive for murder."

"There was plenty of money for both of us," Mary said.

The door rattled at the rear of the courtroom and drew Thunder's attention.

Carter and a man Thunder recognized as Delaney entered through the doorway. Thunder didn't smile. He didn't want to give away anything to the prosecution, but he sure was relieved. Delaney was their best hope. He might be their only hope.

The interruption started the crowd talking as the two strangers moved toward the row behind the defendant's table. Judge Parker slammed his gavel on his desk. "Order in the courtroom."

Thunder stepped over to the judge. "I'd like to request a recess. Information that I've been waiting for has just arrived."

The judge slammed his gavel and said, "Court is adjourned for fifteen minutes." Then he retired to the side room.

Mary was so stunned that Carter was here that she didn't bother to move or question who the man was with him. He was probably just another lawman. Mary watched him as he spoke to Thunder. She'd figured that she would never see Carter again. After all, he'd done his duty by bringing her in, so why was he here now? Why had he come back?

The three men put their heads together while they discussed something. One would nod and then the other would nod. Mary shifted in her hard chair. It would be real nice if someone would let her in on what was going on, since it was her trial. She was all but forgotten.

Mary sighed. She felt so helpless not being able to help herself. For once in her life had to depend on others.

Again, the back doors of the courtroom opened and a crowd of people surged through. They found seats in the back.

Mary couldn't see until the doors were shut. Then her eyes widened. Brandy, Helen, Scott, Ellen, and Willie had marched into the room and were seating themselves in the back row. Scott and Willie both waved.

Mary smiled. They had come. The people who truly loved her had come to support her. It made her choke up; she'd never felt so loved as she did now.

How long had it been since Mary had seen Helen, Thunder's mother? She had been back east visiting her parents when Mary first went to the mine. Helen must have come back in the last few months or Brandy would have written to her about it. It would be good having her back on the ranch. They all thought of Helen as the mother most of them had never had.

Carter broke away from the crowd and started toward the witness stand. He stared at Mary for a long while, as if he were trying to memorize her face before they hung her. She should have taken him up on his offer to flee; then she wouldn't be going through this agony. But they would never have been able to return to the ranch and Carter's mother, and she would never have been able to forgive herself.

The way Carter looked at her gave Mary a very uneasy feeling. He looked tired and worried. Could he be worried about her? Did he truly care?

"How are you holding up?" Carter asked, and reached for her hand. The warmth of his skin felt good on her cold fingers. Even though it was hot outside, Mary felt cold all over.

"What are you doing here?" she asked. "I thought you were gone for good." Carter had hurt her, and at the moment she had a thin grip on her emotions.

"I'm here because of you," Carter told her.

Mary gave him a sarcastic laugh. "You've already arrested me and brought me to justice. Must you see them hang me, too, before you realize that your job is finished?"

The hurt that flashed in Carter's eyes surprised her. And for a moment, she felt bad that she'd lashed out at him. But it was the truth. He'd left her when she needed him the most.

There was pain in Carter's eyes when he replied. "I guess I deserved that."

The judge came back in the courtroom, drawing their attention. "We'll talk more later. Come on, according to Thunder you need to sit over at the table for now."

Carter walked with Mary back to the table, then sat down besides her, taking her hand in his. She didn't jerk her hand away, but it was because she selfishly needed Carter's comfort. However, she also remembered how easy he could dismiss her, so she looked at him questioningly. "What do you want, Carter?"

A slow smile slipped across his face as he whispered to her, "You."

Mary's traitorous heart soared. But she was cautious, so she didn't say anything. She knew at the moment her life was dangling by a thread and there might not be a future with Carter. Or anyone.

The court was called back into session, and the judge asked for the next witness.

Charles Bryan stood. "I'd like to call John McCoy to the stand."

Mary squeezed Carter's hand tightly. Her stomach ached at the mention of that man's name. She didn't know why, but she had a gut feeling he had something to do with the murder . . . if she could only remember what.

The stranger who'd come in with Carter tapped him on the shoulder, then whispered something in his ear.

Carter leaned over to Mary and whispered, "No matter what you do, do not look directly at John McCoy."

"Why?"

"Because we believe he's controlling your mind by giving you some kind of a signal. Every once in a while, glance at him, but only for a moment, so we can pick up on the signal."

"Who is that man that came in with you?" Mary asked.

"He's Thunder's friend, Delaney. Remember, Thunder told us about him?"

Mary shook her head. "There has been too much going on. I had forgotten all about him."

Bryan started first. "Can you tell me how you were related to the deceased?"

"He was my half brother."

"I see," Bryan said. "And when is the last time you saw Jim?"

"The night he was killed."

Carter nudged Mary. She glanced up at McCoy, and found he was staring directly at her, his eyes accusing. His hand started toward the side of his face, and Mary glanced away.

Charles Bryan cleared his throat before asking the next question. "Can you tell us what happened?"

"Jim invited me to dinner. When I arrived, I met

young boy named Mark, or so I thought," McCoy said with a disgusted grunt.

"Can you explain?"

McCoy leaned against the back of the chair, confidence stamped all over his face. Carter tightened his jaw. Oh, how he'd love to mop the floor up with that man.

"The boy was really a woman who dressed as a man. Everyone in camp thought of her as Mark," McCoy explained.

Bryan walked toward Mary as he asked, "Can you identify this woman?"

"She is right over there." McCoy pointed.

Mary looked up at her accuser, and again McCoy's hand started toward his face, so she looked away.

"I see," the prosecutor said as he, too, glanced intently at Mary. "Can you tell me what happened that night?" he asked McCoy without looking at him.

"We had a pleasant dinner until Mark—I mean, Mary—and Jim started to argue. They were arguing over the mine. Mary wanted a bigger cut of the rich gold vein they had just struck. She claimed she was the one that found it."

Mary leaned over to Thunder. "He's lying."

Thunder glanced at her. "I know." Then he turned and leaned over to speak with Delaney in a low voice. "Did you get it?"

Delaney nodded.

"No more questions," the prosecutor said.

Slowly, Thunder rose from his chair. "Mr. McCoy, can you tell me how Mark was dressed that night?"

"He had on Levi's and a faded flannel shirt."

"And his hair?"

"He had on a cap. I couldn't see it."

"Well, the lady who you just pointed to has long blond hair. How can you be sure it's the same person you saw? She doesn't look anything like a boy to me."

Several murmurs ran thorough the crowd.

"It's her, all right." McCoy shifted and leaned forward. He didn't look as sure of himself as he once did. "I remember those eyes."

"Could it be that you remember so well because you never did leave the cabin, but stayed and found out that Mark was really Mary?"

"I done told you, I left and slept in my wagon. I have an alibi."

"Oh, that's right. Marshal Forester told me you stayed the night with the town whore—someone who can be bought, given enough money."

"Objection," the prosecutor shouted.

"Overruled," the judge answered.

"Tell me, Mr. McCoy, what kind of work do you do?"

"I travel around in my wagon, selling elixirs."

"Is that all you do?" Thunder asked casually. He had a feeling that McCoy was the kind of man who liked to boast and Thunder was getting ready to give him a chance. "I heard that you can make people do funny things. Can you explain?" Thunder watched as McCoy's eyes lit up with a possibility to talk about himself. Good, Thunder thought. He was hoping for such a reaction.

"I hypnotize people to act like dogs and chickens. The crowd gets a big kick out of it."

"Really." Thunder leaned on the rail. "What is hypnotism, and how can you do such a thing?"

"It's like when we drift off and enter the sleep state, we pass through the state of awareness known as hypnosis."

"Let me understand this, you can make people do what you want them to do, such as acting funny, once you put them under?"

"Yep."

"I see," Thunder said, rubbing his chin. Suddenly he stopped and looked McCoy dead in the eye. "So how do we know that you didn't hypnotize Mary? It would explain why she can't remember anything. And it would be very convenient for you to do the murdering."

McCoy's face turned an angry red. "You ain't got no proof."

"Oh, but I think that I do," Thunder said. "Your Honor, may I approach the bench?"

"Both of you and Mr. Bryan approach the bench," the judge snapped. "McCoy, you can step down for the moment, but remember you are still sworn in."

The judge peered at Thunder. "I want to know where you're going with this line of questioning, Bradley."

Thunder explained his theory, but in order to prove it, he asked the judge to clear the courtroom.

"This is highly unusual but an interesting theory, to say the least," Judge Parker admitted. "However, you had better prove your point fast. If you don't, it won't look too good for the defendant."

# Chapter 21

The courtroom was cleared of everyone except the jury, the lawyers, Carter, and Delaney. Thunder stood, waiting for the judge to signal him to continue. Thunder had a lot riding on what would happen next. If this failed, he wasn't sure how he could prove Mary innocent.

Finally, as the doors were closed and locked, the judge nodded to Thunder for him to proceed.

"Your Honor, this is Delaney Shoff," Thunder said, indicating Delaney, who had moved up beside Thunder. Delaney was as tall as Thunder with blond hair and a kind face, Mary thought.

Thunder continued. "Delaney has studied hypnosis. I feel that something is blocking Mary's memory. We believe that Delaney can hypnotize Mary and make her remember what happened the night Big Jim was killed."

The judge held up his hand. "First, I have a few questions. I need for you to explain hypnosis to me." He turned to Delaney. "And exactly what are your qualifications, Mr. Shoff?"

Delaney stepped forward. "I'll answer your second question first. I am a doctor, and I have had the opportunity to study hypnosis for many years, Your Honor, at the universities back east. Hypnosis is a normal and natural state of awareness, which most, if not all, people experience on a daily basis."

The judge leaned forward and propped his chin on his hand, peering at Delaney. "I find that hard to believe."

"Yes, I know. I thought the same thing when I first learned of hypnosis, but let me finish. Our conscious mind"—he pointed to his head—"or awareness, sometimes known as our waking mind, is the portion of our brain that we access to analyze things. This is generally referred to as critical thought. Every action we have begins with thought. Think about it, Your Honor, do you ever do anything without first thinking about it?"

Judge Parker thought for a moment then said, "I guess not."

"So, you see, the brain does not send messages to other parts of the body until it is told what to do by a thought. When we remove the analytical process from our thinking, as we do when we are in a state of hypnosis, our subconscious mind is opened to redirect information so that it may empower us in our actions and behaviors. We can actually direct someone not to remember anything."

"That is an interesting theory, but do you have some proof of what you say?" the judge asked, his look still very doubtful.

"Yes," Delaney nodded. "And I will demonstrate in a moment on Mary. But first I want to tell you about a documented case that happened in the 1820s in Germany. A woman by the name of Cindy Berg was controlled for seven years and made to do things against her will. And the sad part was she knew nothing of what she had done for those years. It was a big black hole to her."

"Seven years!" Judge Parker bellowed.

"That's right, Your Honor," Delaney said with a nod. "A hypnotist named Wolfgang for seven years extorted thousands of dollars from Cindy, used her sexually, and sold her services as a prostitute. That was bad enough, but then he compelled her to attempt murder on her husband six times." Delaney glanced around the room as he walked over to get a drink of water. He definitely had everyone's attention and that was good.

Mary sat glued to Delaney's every word. Could terrible things have happened to her, too?

Delaney took a sip of water before he continued. "Wolfgang met Cindy on a train. She was alone, as her parents didn't have enough money for another ticket. Wolfgang just happened to sit down next to Cindy. She was seventeen and traveling to find a doctor to help her with the terrible headaches she'd been having. Cindy knew she shouldn't speak to strangers, but she was lonesome so she started talking to Wolfgang. Cindy told him her purpose for traveling to the city, whereupon he replied that she was in luck because he was a doctor and could help her.

"When the train stopped to get coal, Wolfgang clasped Cindy's hand and stared into her eyes. He channeled so much mental command through that gaze that, after a moment, Cindy felt as if she no longer had a will of her own. And she didn't. As I said, Wolfgang controlled her for the next seven years, putting the poor woman though a hell that none of us would want to go through. When Cindy was away from Wolfgang she lived a pretty normal life. She even married. But those post hypnotic suggestions kept Cindy returning to Wolfgang.

"Wolfgang began to resent her husband, so Wolfgang suggested that she try to kill him.

"After she tried to kill her husband, he grew suspicious and knew something was wrong, because Cindy wasn't of a nature to kill people. However, every time she went to the doctor, she came home and did weird things. But Cindy couldn't tell him the name of the doctor she was seeing. Of course, he thought that was strange, so he went to the police.

"After hearing what her husband had to say, they called in Dr. Ludwig Mayer, the most respected medical hypnotist in all of Europe. Dr. Mayer did not believe that unethical hypnosis was possible. That is, until he hypnotized Cindy. Then he found out the ugly truth. She'd had pain induced by the evil doctor which could only be relieved by bringing him money. Wolfgang used her as a whore and then gave her to his friends. He suggested that she not only poison her husband, but when that didn't work, he suggested shooting the man. And she remembered nothing until Dr. Mayer dove into her subconscious."

Delaney approached the bench. "And that is what I want to do today, Your Honor. I want to put Mary in a hypnotic state and hear from her own lips what happened. I think I've found the signal that was used to put her under."

Judge Parker shook his head. "This is most unusual, but you do have my interest, so please proceed."

Delaney glanced over at Mary. "If you will take the stand, Mary."

Mary was shaking so hard that she could barely

walk as she made her way to the witness stand. She felt as though she were going to her own execution. What Delaney had just revealed scared her. What if she'd done terrible things like Cindy Berg had? The thought made her skin crawl.

Finally, she made it to the chair. Once she was seated, she glanced at Carter and saw the sympathy in his eyes. That warmed her heart. But what if Delaney could do as he claimed and then she divulged she'd done horrible things? How would Carter react?

Delaney touched her hand, drawing her attention. "I want you to relax, Mary."

Mary gaped at the man as if he'd lost his mind. He wanted her to relax when she was being tried for murder. Yet, those very words sounded familiar, as if she'd heard them before. However, Delaney had a calming effect on her. She noticed that he was staring into her eyes, holding her so she couldn't glance away, and then he reached for his ear and . . .

Mary's head fell to the side. Delaney looked at the judge. "You see, Your Honor, by tugging on my ear, which was the previous cue she'd been given, Mary has gone under, quickly. You see, if a hypnotist is attempting a re-hypnotization and he uses the same induction or deepening routine as the former hypnotist, progress will be substantial. Mary is in a trance, but at the moment, it's light.

"Look at me, Mary," Delaney said, and when she did, he tugged on his ear again. She nodded, but she didn't close her eyes as she watched him. "Can you tell me what you remember?"

"No."

"Your Honor, what good is this doing?" Bryan

protested. "She's saying the same thing—she can't remember."

The judge looked at Delaney and waited for his answer.

"If you'll just give me a few moments. You see, the mind is very complicated. The person who hypnotized her, who we believe is McCoy, has probably threatened her unconscious with terrible things if she breaks the amnesia rule. If she remembers forbidden information and betrays his secret, someone could fall dead. First, I have to undo that command."

The judge nodded.

"Mary, do you remember anything?" Delaney asked in a very calm voice.

"No."

"Watch me, Mary," Delaney instructed. "When I pull on my ear, nothing bad will happen to you if you remember back to the night of the murder."

"I will hang if I talk."

"No, Mary. You will feel good for remembering the burden that you've carried around. You will feel peaceful for telling us what happened, and when you wake up you will remember everything that has happened to you." He waited for a moment, then said, "On the count of three. One, two, three." Delaney paused, making sure he had her full attention, then he tugged on his ear again.

"I want you to close your eyes and remember back to the day when you struck the vein of gold. How did you feel?"

"I felt wonderful," Mary said with a smile, even though her eyes were still closed. "I couldn't wait to tell Jim."

"And did you tell him?"

"Yes. Jim was happy. He said we'd have all the money we could spend in a lifetime. We worked all day, side by side, until quitting time."

"Then?"

Mary sighed. "We were tired, so we headed home. I told Jim I was going to cook a big supper, and he said, 'Good.' Then he told me there was a possibility that his brother might come and have dinner. Jim said his brother had just arrived at the camp."

"What was his brother's name?"

"John McCoy."

"You are doing fine, Mary," Delaney praised. "And with each thing that you remember your burden will become lighter." He paused. "Now, did he say anything else about his brother?"

Mary nodded. "He said John was his half brother and they had never been close. He said John was more or less a vagabond and didn't stay long in one place. He wanted to come and help us in the mine, but Big Jim said once John saw how hard the work was he'd change his mind."

"And did John come for supper?"

"Yes." Mary nodded, her eyes still closed. "I had just placed the last dish on the table. Big Jim told me to stay dressed as a boy because his brother tended to have a big mouth, and we didn't want the other miners to know that I was a woman."

"What happened next?"

"John came into the cabin and shook my hand. There was something about him that I didn't like right away. It was his beady eyes or something, but I had a hard time looking away from him. We all sat down to dinner. Big Jim excused himself to go out back to the outhouse. So I sat at the table with John while we waited for Big Jim to return. John wanted to know if I wanted to play a game that he knew. I thought he was a little crazy, but he was a guest, so I humored him. He said that he could make me fall asleep just by pulling his ear."

She paused, her forehead scrunching up as if she were trying to remember every little detail.

"And," Delaney prompted.

All of a sudden, Mary became agitated. "I can't remember. If I tell, I will have pain so intense that I will want to kill myself."

"Mary, I am going to take away your pain—all of it—but you must trust me," Delaney urged. "I want you to pretend that you are floating in the air and seeing everything around you. You'll be able to see everything, but you'll feel no pain as long as you listen to the sound of my voice.

"Now you are back at the supper table waiting for Big Jim to return. What did John say?"

Mary took a deep breath. "John told me to look deep into his eyes and not look away. He told me I was sleepy, and I told him I was not, but then he repeated the words and told me I would be asleep when he tugged on his ear."

"And?"

Mary began to shake her head, as if to say, "No, no." Delaney knew she was finally in a deep trance, reliving something that had happened to her, and it wasn't pleasant. She made pushing-away movements with her hands and then she began to cry softly.

"For Christ's sake, do something," Carter said, seeing how upset Mary was becoming.

Delaney looked at Thunder. "I'm going to have to bring her out for now."

Thunder nodded.

"On the count of three, you will wake and remember," Delaney said. "One, two, three."

Mary's eyes snapped open from the trance and she looked around the room until her gaze met Thunder's. "Now I know. I know everything," she sobbed.

Carter rushed to her as the judge banged the gavel.

For a long time, Mary cried in Carter's arms. For so long she'd wanted her memory back and now she had it.

Mary remembered everything.

# Chapter 22

When Mary had finally calmed down, Carter returned to his chair. The judge banged his gavel
against the desk and looked very flustered. "Order,"
he demanded. He hit the desktop again. "This is a
most unusual case," the judge stated, rubbing the
back of his neck, "the likes of which I've never seen,
but we must continue." He turned sideways and
asked Mary, "Are you ready to proceed?"

She nodded.

"Since this is such a sensitive issue, I'm going to
leave everyone outside so you'll not be so nervous."
Judge Parker glanced at Thunder. "Mr. Bradley, do
you want to take over the questioning?"

Thunder nodded and came to stand in front of
Mary. "Tell us in your own words what you *now* remember. Take your time."

Mary glanced over at the jury. It appeared as if
each one of them had stopped breathing, and all
eyes were glued on her, waiting in anticipation for
her to tell them the truth.

Her memory had seemed like a puzzle where

she'd only had a few pieces, until now. However with the help of Dr. Delaney, she finally had the rest of the puzzle. "Oh God," she whispered to herself as she gripped the sides of the chair. They were not going to like the story.

Mary swallowed hard. She couldn't look at Carter nor Thunder while she revealed the ugly truth. So, knowing that the next few moments would be some of the hardest she'd ever faced, she focused on a light in the back of the room.

"John McCoy placed his hand on my forehead," she said softly.

"Speak up," the prosecutor shouted.

Mary jumped from the tone of his voice, but her next words were indeed louder. "I had no control of what I wanted to do. It was as if I were in a fog, waiting for someone to guide me. My eyes were open, but I couldn't see.

"John told me, 'Now, with no will of your own, you will do anything I ask you to do. And you will remember nothing of what happens here today. Do you understand?' He then told me to pick up Big Jim's bowie knife and slip it into the back of my breeches at the waist.

"When Jim returned from outside, I was to let him begin eating, then get up to fetch something from the cabinet so that I would be behind Jim," Mary said, then took a deep breath.

"I did as I was told. Jim and John were talking when I pulled the knife from my breeches and came at Jim from behind. Slowly, I raised my arm, knife poised, ready to come down in the middle of Big Jim's back." A small sob escaped Mary's lips. She swallowed hard so she could continue. The bile trying to rise in the back of her throat tasted terrible, but she had to get everything out. Hopefully, the jury would understand and the truth would set her free.

"But something happened." Mary felt the blood drain from her face as she remembered.

"I stood there poised to kill Jim, but I couldn't move my arm. John hollered for me to do it now! I tried to obey, but Big Jim swung around and, seeing the weapon, caught my wrist. I remember screaming and struggling as Jim swore. And then I saw Jim's eyes . . . the surprise in their depths . . . the hurt. I'll never forget the hurt."

Mary choked on her words. Several moments passed before she could contain her crying, and she had to swallow a couple of times to calm her breathing. Finally, she continued. "John yanked out his own knife and started stabbing Jim over and over again. I remember screaming. 'Don't! Don't do this!'

"Blood was everywhere! And I could do nothing but stand there and watch. It was as if I were stone," Mary sobbed. "Tears streamed down my cheeks. I wanted to help Jim, but my arms wouldn't move. Even though I couldn't stab Jim, his brother was still very much in control of me.

"When Big Jim fell to the floor at my feet, John grabbed my arm. He snarled, 'You little bitch, you'll follow my commands one way or the other.' He touched my head and I quit crying.

"I still had the knife clutched in my hand. He forced me to kneel down, then he jerked my arm over my head and forced it with a mighty thrust into Big Jim's body. I remember the warm b-blood spattering my face. Over and over again, guided by John, I stabbed Big Jim." Mary was crying harder now. "I—I couldn't stop. John wouldn't let me. I had blood all over me, too.

"John told me I was the one who killed Big Jim, and I would always remember his murder, and the blood. But if I was asked what happened, my mind would go blank and I wouldn't be able to remember anything.

"I grabbed for his coat and tore a small piece of the green material as I begged him to let go of my arm, but he kept pushing my arm with the knife into Jim. Then he made me help him drag Jim in front of the fireplace. I could hear gurgling coming from Jim's throat, and I knew he wasn't dead yet. And I couldn't do anything for him. Nothing!"

Mary paused to gather her composure. She took a few deep breaths, then continued, "John grabbed my wrist and led me to my bedroom, where he pushed me, still clutching the knife, onto my bed. His last words were to hang onto that knife all night. I—I don't remember anything else. When I woke up in the morning, I didn't know what had happened.

"I was scared. I knew I looked guilty. I didn't know what to do, so I ran," Mary finished with a sob.

"I have no more questions, Your Honor," Thunder said softly, patting Mary's hand.

The judge looked at the prosecutor. "Do you have any further questions?"

Bryan slowly rose. "How do we know she isn't a very good actress"—he waved his hands in a big circle—"and making up this entire story to protect her own skin?"

"That's a very good question," Judge Parker said. "However, if she is telling the truth, then we have an entirely different case." He paused, rubbed his forehead, and looked up at the bailiff. "Bring in McCoy."

A few moments later, the bailiff escorted McCoy into the courtroom.

"What's going on?" McCoy asked.

Mary watched the slimy worm walk into the court with all the confidence in the world, and he looked so innocent. If she hadn't been in the cabin the night of the murder, she might be inclined to believe him rather than her preposterous story. But she knew what he had done. And if she'd had a gun right now, would have done everything she could to even up the score.

The judge turned to McCoy. "Mr. McCoy, you realize that you are still under oath?"

McCoy nodded. He wasn't sure what had gone on while he had been outside with the others, but he knew he had control over the girl and she'd never remember anything. They didn't have anything on him.

"While you were out, we had Miss Costner hypnotized and she revealed some very interesting facts."

"By who?" McCoy snapped the words out. He'd never thought about them finding another hypnotist. But would the new man be able to undo his suggestions?

"By Dr. Delaney."

McCoy appeared confident as he asked, "And what were those interesting facts?"

"The small fact that you killed your own brother."

"What nonsense!" He gave a half laugh. These people were bluffing. "You have no proof."

Carter tapped Thunder on the arm and whispered, "Mary doesn't look like she's feeling well. Let's ask for a recess."

"Your Honor, I would like to request a recess so that I can obtain some additional information."

"I could use a breather myself," Judge Parker admitted. "However, in light of this very unusual case, Bailiff, I'd like to take Mr. McCoy into temporary custody. You can hold him in a hotel room."

"That ain't right, Judge. I ain't done nothing," McCoy protested.

"Time will tell," the judge said. He stood and banged the gavel. "Court is adjourned. It will reconvene tomorrow at noon."

All rose as the judge made his way to the side chamber. Then Mary was taken back to jail.

Carter, Thunder, and Delaney left the courtroom. After the revealing information, all three of them needed the fresh air and time to plan what they were going to do next.

They hadn't gotten very far down the sidewalk when a woman came running up to them, throwing herself into Thunder's arms.

Carter arched a brow. The woman was beautiful. "An admirer?"

Thunder chuckled. "I sure hope so." He eased the woman's arms from around his neck. "This is my wife, Brandy. Brandy, this is Carter Monroe, the marshal Mary has been staying with."

Brandy gaped at Thunder. "Why was she staying with him?"

"It's a long story. I'll tell you later."

Brandy glanced at Carter, then extended her hand. "Sorry for being so rude, but Mary and I have had problems with the law in the past. It's nice to meet you."

"Your reaction was very similar to Mary's when she first learned I was a lawman. I've heard a lot about you and your family," Carter said with a smile. "I think you and Mary are probably more alike than you think."

Brandy laughed. "Well, don't tell Mary. If she was talking about me, just remember it was probably a lie. I'm not that bad. Now, tell me what was going on in there and why we have been barred from the courtroom. I didn't like that one bit."

"I'm sure," Thunder said. He smiled, and then looked around. "This is Delaney, a friend of mine." After Brandy shook his hand, Thunder asked, "Where is everyone else? I'm sure they want to hear this, too."

"Come on, they are in the lobby of the hotel," Brandy said, and tugged on Thunder's hand.

Everyone went to the hotel, where Thunder told his family what was happening. They seemed a likable group, Carter thought as he watched each one.

"So, what are you going to do?" Scott asked Thunder.

Thunder glanced at Scott and smiled. "That is what we are getting ready to discuss."

"Delaney, what will happen when we return to court? Will you have to hypnotize Mary again?" Thunder asked.

"I don't think so. I'm sure she's told us everything she knows. What you need is some hard evidence or a witness. The only witnesses are Mary and McCoy, so that's a dead end."

"What about the coat?" Carter asked. "She mentioned the coat as she remembered. The coat has to be the key."

"The coat is a key," Thunder agreed. "We need to find McCoy's wagon."

Brandy turned. "Who is McCoy?"

"A snake oil salesman and Big Jim's half brother," both Carter and Thunder answered.

Helen walked over to where they were standing.

"When we came into Appleton, I saw a wagon outside of town," she told them. "There was some funny writing on the canvas, like 'World Famous Medicine.' It was red and yellow and very hard to miss."

"Sounds like what we're looking for," Carter said, then glanced at Thunder. "Kind of glad your family came to see you."

Thunder chuckled. "Delaney, I know you've had a long trip. Why don't you go ahead and get your room. Carter and I are going to check out the wagon."

"Yeah, I'm kind of tired. But I'll be ready when it's time to go back to court."

Scott and Willie walked up to them. "Can we ride out with you?"

"Sure," Thunder said, ruffling Willie's hair.

As they rode out of town, Carter said to Thunder, "I brought the green coat we found at Big Jim's cabin with me. Mary said in there that John McCoy was wearing the coat. I hope she isn't confused in her facts. Maybe Big Jim was wearing the jacket and she got the cloth from him. I sure hope that isn't the case. But I do think the jacket is the key."

"But how could she see the coat when it has hanging in Big Jim's closet?" Thunder thought out loud.

"Unless there were two coats," Carter said with a smile.

"Good point." Thunder nodded. "Hope you're right."

When they reached the wagon, the four of them all but turned the wagon upside down as they searched, but the only things of interest they found were a couple of books on hypnotism.

The tension finally got to Carter. He threw a

bottle of elixir out the back of the wagon. "I could have sworn that there would be two jackets. Now we're back where we started."

Willie marched up beside them. "Does this mean they are going to hang Mary?"

"Not if we can help it," Thunder said

"I can guarantee you she'll not hang," Carter assured Willie. "If it comes down to it, I might have to break the law to free her, but I will get her out of jail one way or the other."

Thunder glanced at Carter. "You love her, don't you?"

Carter nodded. The idea was still too fresh to put into words.

Scott walked up to where they were. "This coat we're looking for," Scott said, "if Mary said she saw a man in the green coat, then I believe her. But I heard Carter say she was in a group of people, so wouldn't somebody else have seen the man?"

"Rick, my deputy." Carter paused. "That's it. It isn't much, but Rick said something about the man in the green coat. So he'd have to have seen somebody."

"How long will it take for him to get here?" Thunder asked.

"If he rides all night, he'll be here by noon tomorrow."

"Well, what are we waiting for? Send him a telegram. It isn't much, but it's something."


Mary heard a noise in the front office. When she looked up, three women were being escorted in by the sheriff. He opened the door so they could enter the cell. She grinned as she recognized Brandy, Helen, and Ellen.

Mary hugged Helen first and was comforted by her warm, motherly bosom. "It's so good to see you," Mary said.

"It's good to see you, too, but not like this."

Mary hugged Brandy and Ellen. "Thank you so much for coming. I was surprised when I saw you enter the courtroom."

"Thunder told us about the trial," Brandy said. "They wouldn't let us in. I still don't understand why the family could not be present, and I'd tell that judge exactly what I think if I could find him," she said indignantly. Then she paused. "However, I find it hard to believe that someone was controlling your mind. Lord knows, I never could control you."

Mary chuckled. "Thank you. I can't remember when I've last laughed. I'm finding everything hard to believe. I feel like I'm in the middle of a nightmare, and I want someone to wake me up and tell me it has all been a very bad dream." She sobered. "I don't think things are looking very good for me right now."

Brandy gave Mary an encouraging smile. "Remember, my trial didn't look too good either. And I know I killed the man. Thunder will think of something."

"I do remember. I'll just be glad when everything is back to normal."

"What will you do then?" Ellen asked as she sat down on the small cot with Helen.

"Hire someone to run the mine," Mary said. "My mining days are over."

"And about time," Helen said.

"But what are you going to do?" Ellen asked again. "Come back to the ranch?"

"No. I'm going to take some of that hard-earned money and buy a house."

"And settle down with that Marshal Monroe?" Brandy asked with a sly smile.

Mary looked at her sister, wondering how she would even know that they had some kind of a relationship, however strange it might be. "What made you say that?"

"We met him after the trial. He said you'd been staying with him. And he seemed very worried about you."

"He is so good looking," Ellen said.

Mary smiled. "Yes, he is something to look at, but he's the marshal that brought me in." She motioned toward the cot for Brandy. "Sit down and let me tell you the rest of the story."

Nearly an hour passed before Mary had filled them in with all the details.

"Oh my," Brandy said when Mary finished with her story.

"So you see, Carter was only doing his job by bringing me in," Mary said with a sad frown.

"But he is still here," Helen pointed out. "If his job is over, there is nothing to hold him here—unless it's you."

Mary looked at Helen and said, "I never thought about that."

They all got up to leave. "It's time for us to go, but we'll see you in the morning. I understand we will be allowed back in the courtroom," Brandy told her.

"Wish me luck," Mary said, then she hugged each one. And when she got to Helen, she said, "Thank you for those words."

It was almost noon and Rick still hadn't arrived, which was making Carter's disposition a little more surly than usual. He volunteered to go get Mary from the jail and bring her to the courthouse.

She was sitting on the edge of the cot when he came back with the keys. She stood as if on cue and moved forward right past him.

Since they were alone, he grabbed her arm and turned her toward him. "How are you holding up?"

She shrugged and then she glanced up at him. The pain Carter saw in Mary's eyes made him want to slug someone.

"I'm surprised that you want to have anything to do with me after hearing my testimony yesterday," Mary finally said.

Carter groaned and pulled her into his arms. "Do you think that anything they have said could change the way I feel about you?"

"And how do you feel?"

Carter looked at her a long moment. He had found something he cherished more than anything, and loving her made him more vulnerable than he'd ever been in his life. That wasn't something he was used to. Carter was used to not feeling anything. But he knew the threat of losing Mary had begun to haunt him night and day.

"You don't know the answer to the question, do you?"

Carter chuckled and pulled her into his arms. "Yes, I know the answer. I love you," he said simply, and before Mary could say anything in response, he smothered her words with a hungry kiss. Carter had his answer with his kiss, because Mary kissed him back with all the love he knew she felt for him.

He loved her. He really loved her. His words were like whispers on the wind.

A part of Mary wanted to jump for joy, but—and

it was a big 'but'—she didn't know what was going to happen today. She pulled away from him and said, "There are so many things that I want to say. However, I'm afraid. I don't know what will happen today, so I can't talk about a future until the verdict is passed. Until I know what my future will be."

Carter gave her a heart-wrenching smile. "I understand," he said, crushing her to him. "Let's go."

As they neared the courthouse, Carter could see Thunder, Delaney, Brandy, and a stranger Carter didn't recognize, but evidently Mary did. She broke away from his grasp and ran to the man, throwing herself into his arms.

And the stranger wasn't backing off, Carter noticed. As a matter of fact, he didn't like the way he held Mary at all.

"It's so good to see you," Mary told the man.

"It has been a long time," the stranger admitted as he kissed her on the nose. "You've gotten yourself into a real pickle this time."

"Who the hell are you?" Carter challenged.

"I'm not sure that's any of your business."

Mary moved away from the man, looking very embarrassed, and Carter thought she should look more than embarrassed because it was very evident that she cared a great deal for this sidewinder.

"Carter, this is my brother, Billy."

Carter was still irritated. "Just how many brothers do you have?"

Mary laughed. "Three. No, make that four if you count Thunder."

Billy held out his hand and said, "Marshal."

Carter shook his hand, but he'd be damned if he'd apologize.

Thunder stepped up and placed a hand on Billy's arm. "He has it bad."

"So I see," Billy said with a laugh. "Mary, they have filled me in on what has happened. I didn't realize that Big Jim had a brother."

"Half brother," Mary said.

A rider came galloping up at breakneck speed, and Carter breathed a sigh of relief. He grabbed the halter of Rick's horse so he could dismount.

"You could have given me a bit more notice," Rick grumbled as he slid to the ground. "But I see that I've made it in time. What do you want me to do?" he asked as he tethered his horse.

"We want you to tell the jury what you saw the night at the opera house," Carter said as they stepped up on the boardwalk. "Remember the green coat?"

Rick nodded.

Before Thunder could instruct Rick, the Appleton sheriff and Marshal Forester strode into court with McCoy. McCoy glared at the group as he came through the doors.

"Who was that?" Billy asked.

"Big Jim's brother," Carter answered.

"Sure doesn't look anything like his brother," Billy commented.

"Did you know Big Jim?" Carter asked.

Marshal Forester came back out and took Mary into the courtroom.

"I'll be there in a moment," Thunder told her. Then he looked at Billy. "I'd forgotten that you took Mary to Gregory Gulch and stayed with them for a little while."

"That's right. I liked Big Jim."

Carter took the green coat out of a tow sack that Delaney held and shook it out. "Did you ever see Jim wear this jacket?"

Billy shook his head. "Nope. He was more into

overalls." He took the coat and held it up, then laughed.

"What's so funny?" Carter asked.

"This can't belong to Big Jim."

"Why?" Thunder asked.

"Because Big Jim was a huge man." He gestured with his hands. "He was this wide through the shoulders. There isn't any way he could have worn this coat."

Carter and Thunder exchanged smiles, and then Thunder said, "Gentlemen, we have our defense. Let's go present our case."

# Chapter 23

For two hours, the trial had gone back and forth. Neither side seemed to be gaining an edge.

When Rick was called to the witness stand, he explained to the jury about people thinking that they had seen someone, but they couldn't describe him. Rick acknowledged that he had seen a man in a green coat, as well.

Cross-examination was brief. Bryan cleared his throat as he stood. "You just said that you had seen a man in a green coat, is that correct?"

"It is," Rick said.

"Can you identify that man?"

"No." Rick shook his head. "I wasn't close enough."

Bryan smiled at the jury. "No more questions."

Thunder had been afraid that would happen, but he had to set the groundwork for his next witness. Now he realized it was now or never. "I'd like to recall John McCoy."

Looking like he didn't have a care in the world, McCoy took his seat in the witness stand. It was that confidence that Thunder hoped would destroy the man. "Mr. McCoy, you have heard us speak of the green coat."

McCoy nodded. "Several times."

"Do you own such a coat?"

"No. My brother had a green coat."

Thunder spun around. "It is my understanding that you'd not seen your brother in a long time."

McCoy nodded. "That's right."

"Then how do you know what kind of coat he had?"

McCoy smiled slowly. "He had it on the night we had dinner together."

Mary jumped out of her chair. "He's lying!"

The judge banged his gavel. "Order!"

Carter placed a hand on her shoulder and she sat back down in her chair, glancing at Carter, "But he is."

"I know," Carter whispered.

Thunder felt as though he'd hit a brick wall. McCoy was thinking fast. He might be a little smarter than he and Carter had given him credit for.

"I agree that someone had on the coat the night of the murder," Thunder said. "We know that Mary tore a piece of material from the coat," he added.

"I told you I don't have a green coat. It was Big Jim's."

Thunder placed his forearm on the rail and leaned against it, trying not to appear worried as he asked, "Are you blood related to the deceased?"

"Yes. He was my half brother," McCoy replied.

"So you don't look alike?" Thunder persisted.

"Not much."

Thunder turned to the judge. "Your Honor, I would like to submit for evidence the green coat in question." Thunder walked over to Delaney and retrieved the tow sack. He opened the sack and pulled out the green coat. He held it up for the judge and jury to see. "I believe the killer wore this green jacket. As you can see," Thunder said, turning the jacket around to the jury, "there is a piece of material missing at the bottom."

The judge nodded, then asked, "Where did you find this coat?"

"In Big Jim's cabin," Thunder said casually.

The judge nodded.

Thunder held the coat up in front of McCoy. "Is this your brother's coat?"

"Looks like it," McCoy answered.

Thunder smiled. "I would like for you to try this coat on."

"I told you it was my brother's," McCoy snapped, his face reddening. A light sheen of sweat coated his forehead.

"I remember," Thunder said. "But I still would like for you to try it on."

McCoy glanced at the prosecutor, who then stood and said, "Objection. What does Mr. McCoy trying on a coat have to do with this trial?"

The judge turned to Thunder.

"You asked for some evidence, Your Honor," Thunder told the judge. "The coat is evidence. We know that someone wore it the night of the murder." Thunder turned back to McCoy. "I hope to prove that this coat belongs to John instead of Jim."

"Overruled," the judge ruled. He glanced at McCoy and instructed, "Try on the coat."

McCoy stood up and slipped on the garment. "I told you that it belongs to my brother."

Mary gasped. Now she knew for certain everything that had happened that night. That damned green coat had plagued her dreams.

"Now face the jury," Thunder demanded.

Slowly, John did as he was told.

"As you can see, this coat is a perfect fit." When he heard the murmurs coming from the jury, Thunder announced, "No more questions."

The prosecutor approached McCoy. "I only have one question. Is this your coat?"

"No," McCoy stubbornly insisted. He jerked off the coat, glared at Thunder, then went back to where he had been seated with Marshal Forester.

"I would like to call Billy West," Thunder said.

As soon as Billy was seated, Thunder asked, "Is it true that you escorted Mary to Gregory Gulch and you met Big Jim?"

Billy nodded. "That's correct. I was there when they drew up the deeds, and then I stayed until Mary could get settled."

"Is this Big Jim's coat?" Thunder asked.

"No," Billy said with a shake of his head. "It can't possibly be."

Thunder folded his arms as he stood before Billy. "How can you be certain?"

"Because Big Jim was a giant of a man. That is where he got his name. He was bigger than most men. He wouldn't have been able to get his arm into that coat. It definitely belongs to someone else."

Horace, one of the miners, stood up in the back and yelled, "I remember seeing John McCoy when he came into town. He asked where his brother lived. John had on that very coat. I remember now."

All hell broke out in the courtroom as everyone started talking excitedly among themselves. The judge banged his gavel. "Order! I want order in this courtroom!"

Taking advantage of the confusion, McCoy grabbed Forester's gun and yanked him up. He used the man as a shield as he backed out of the room.

"If you come after me, I'll blow his head off," McCoy shouted.

Carter and Rick both jumped to their feet, but they didn't draw. They didn't want to hit Forester, but Carter saw something that McCoy couldn't. Mary's brother Scott had slid out of his seat and crouched down on all fours.

McCoy tripped over the kid as he backed out of the courtroom. His gun went off, but before McCoy could get off a second shot, Carter was all over him, beating the man half senseless before Rick was able to pull Carter off.

Thunder turned to Mary and draped his arm around her shoulder. "It's all over. You're free."

Mary smiled, then hugged him. "I'm so glad to have a lawyer in the family."

Thunder laughed. "I am, too, since my family can't seem to stay out of trouble. That's two of you down and three more members of our family to go."

"Maybe they will be good." Mary laughed, then accepted her family's hugs. When Billy hugged her, she asked, "How is Claire? Did she have the baby?"

"Claire is just fine. We have a baby girl," he said with the beaming smile of a new father.

"So what did you name her?" Brandy asked.

Billy turned to Mary and said, "We named her Mary."

Tears sprang to Mary's eyes and she whispered, "You named her after me?"

"Had to name her after my best girl," Billy told her with a smile.

"She's my girl now," Carter said, moving up beside Mary.

Billy grinned wickedly. "Are you sure about that?"

Carter lifted Mary's chin so he could see into her eyes. "Mary, will you marry me?" Carter thought the silence that followed was the longest he'd ever experienced as he waited for her.

"No." She flinched at the hurt in his eyes.

"Why not?"

"Because you're a lawman, and every time you left on an assignment, I'd wonder if you were coming home. I want a home and family and somebody who is home with me every night. I don't want to wonder if you're going to leave me and never return. I—I— I'm going to be sick," Mary said. She dashed through the crowd out the front door and to a side street. She threw up what little she'd been able to eat that morning.

In a few minutes, Helen was by Mary's side. When Mary had finished being sick, Helen asked, "Do you feel better?"

"Yes and no. I was hoping after the trial that I'd quit having this nervous stomach, but I'm still sick as ever. And I feel so bad about Carter. I love him, but he'll never give up being a lawman," Mary said miserably.

"Mary," Helen said, gaining her attention. "You're going to have Carter's baby. That's why you've been sick. I think that you should tell him."

"Baby?" Mary said, looking completely surprised. "Me?"

Helen nodded. "You are a woman, after all."

"But I can't imagine me with a baby. A mother?" Mary shook her head. "There isn't anything mothering about me."

"Unfortunately, there aren't any rules to being a mother, dear. But I think you'll make a fine mother."

"Really?" Mary said.

Helen nodded. "Now, go and tell Carter. If you don't want to marry him, that's fine. You can always live with our family, but the child's father has a right to know."

"Where is he?"

"After you ran out, he went to the jailhouse."

Mary made her way to the jailhouse. The door was standing ajar, and she paused outside before she entered. When she heard Marshal Forester say, "Are you sure about this?" Mary didn't go any further.

"I'm sure," Carter said. "When I became a marshal, I had a mission to accomplish. I've done that. Now it is time for me to start living my life. I'm going home to the ranch."

"We're losing a hell of a lawman," Forester said.

"And a damned good partner," Rick added.

Carter chuckled, but it was a sad laugh, Mary thought. "You can always come by the ranch and visit me."

"Can I visit you?" Mary asked as she slipped into the room.

Carter swung around. "I was kind of hoping that you would. But a visit isn't what I had on my mind."

Mary took a step closer to him. "And exactly what did you have on your mind?"

"I was figuring on a more permanent relationship. But since you refused to be my wife, I'm not sure what we can come up with."

Mary draped her arms around Carter's neck and looked up at him with all the love she had as she said in a teary voice, "How about the mother of your child?"

The look of shock that crossed Carter's face was

worth a bag of gold to Mary. She'd bet no one had ever surprised Carter.

"Do you mean . . . ?" Carter's voice was rough with emotion.

Mary nodded.

"Well, I'll be damned," Rick said from behind them. "I'll be glad to arrest him for tampering with a lady's affections," he teased.

"I don't think that will be necessary," Mary said, and then she looked up at Carter. "Will it?"

"A baby," Carter repeated, still sounding stunned.

"You gave up the law for me?" Mary asked, but she knew the answer. "Ask me again."

Carter's arms tightened around her. "Will you marry me?"

"Yes," Mary said with a soft smile. "But marriage to me probably won't be easy."

Carter laughed. "After meeting your very unusual family, I somehow don't doubt that, but I'm willing to take the risk because life without you, my love, isn't worth living."

Thunder and Brandy appeared in the doorway. "Don't just stand there," Thunder called from the door. "Kiss her before she changes her mind and I have to shoot you."

Mary glanced at both of them with a sly smile. "You heard about the baby?"

They nodded.

"Well, Carter, you heard them. It's either kiss me or get shot."

His mouth hovered just above hers as he said in a very sexy voice, "In that case, I'd better kiss you. I want my child to have a father."

And Carter did just that. He kissed the tip of her nose, then her eyes, and finally he kissed her soft mouth.

A kiss that would last a lifetime.

As a summer breeze swept in through the door of the office surrounding them, Mary thought that their love would always be whispers on the wind.

Whispered until eternity . . . Carter loved her.

# Author's Note

First I want to thank my critique partners, Bonnie Gardner and Cindy Proctor-King, who figure out my dyslexic writing so that you can read the books. They are both very good authors so be sure and check out their books.

I hope that you have enjoyed the Misfit Series. WHISPERS ON THE WIND is the third book. As of this writing, I'm not sure which book I will do next, but I hope it will bring you as much pleasure as my other books. It seems everybody has their favorite book.

Please check my web page for contest information. As always, the first fan who writes a letter about this book will receive a special gift from me, and the first five will receive an autographed cover.

Keep those cards and letters coming. I do answer all fan letters—some a little later than others because of deadlines. A SASE is appreciated.

May all your dreams come true.

Brenda K. Jernigan
80 Pine St. W.
Lillington, N.C. 27546
*Bkj1608@juno.com*
*http://www.bkjbooks.com*

# Complete Your Collection Today
# Janelle Taylor

# Experience the Romance of
# Rosanne Bittner